LP
Fic
Hea

Healy, Erin
The baker's wife

(31.00)

LP   Healy, Erin
Fic   The baker's wife
Hea

THE BAKER'S WIFE

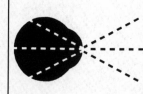

This Large Print Book carries the
Seal of Approval of N.A.V.H.

THE BAKER'S WIFE

ERIN HEALY

THORNDIKE PRESS
A part of Gale, Cengage Learning

GALE
CENGAGE Learning®

Detroit • New York • San Francisco • New Haven, Conn • Waterville, Maine • London

GALE
CENGAGE Learning®

LIBRARY OF CONGRESS CATALOGING-IN-PUBLICATION DATA

Healy, Erin M.
    The baker's wife / by Erin Healy.
      p. cm. — (Thorndike Press large print Christian fiction)
      ISBN-13: 978-1-4104-4439-4 (hardcover)
      ISBN-10: 1-4104-4439-2 (hardcover)
      1. Large type books. I. Title.
    PS3608.E245B35 2012
    813'.54—dc23   2011045446

Published in 2012 by arrangement with Thomas Nelson, Inc.

Printed in Mexico
1 2 3 4 5 6 7 16 15 14 13 12

For Tim
Hope born of suffering
will not disappoint.
— a paraphrase of
Romans 5:5

VEIL

In this low place between mountains
fog settles with the dark of evening.
Every year it takes some of those
we love — a car full of teenagers
on the way home from a dance, or
a father on his way to the paper mill,
nightshift the only opening.
Each morning, up on the ridge,
the sun lifts this veil, sees what night
has accomplished. The water on our window-
screens disappears slowly, gradually,
like grief. The heat of the day carries water
from the river back up into the sky,
and where the fog is heaviest and stays
longest, you'll see the lines it leaves
on trees, the flowers that grow
the fullest.

— TODD DAVIS

CHAPTER 1

March

The day Audrey took a loaf of homemade rosemary-potato bread to Cora Jean Hall was the day the fog broke and made way for spring. Audrey threw open the curtains closest to the dying woman's bedside, glad for the sunshine after months of gray light.

Audrey moved quietly down the hall into the one-man kitchen, where she sliced the bread into toast, brewed tea, then leaned out of the cramped space to offer some to Cora Jean's husband, Harlan. He refused her without thanks and without looking up from his forceful tinkering with an old two-way radio. Over the past month, his collection of CBs and receivers had overtaken the small living room. His grieving had started long ago and was presently in the angry stage. Clearly, he loved his wife. The retired pharmacist dispensed her medications with faithful precision but didn't seem to know what else to do. If not for the radios, Audrey believed, he might have wandered the house helplessly and transformed from smoldering to explosive.

As Audrey arranged the snack on a tray, one of her earrings slipped out of her lobe and clattered onto a saucer, just missing the hot tea. She rarely wore this pair because one or the other was always falling out, but Cora Jean liked the dangling hearts with a rose in the middle of each. The inexpensive jewelry had been a gift to the women of the church on Mother's Day last year.

She put the earring back in her ear, then carried the tray to Cora Jean's room, settled onto an old dining room chair by the bed, and steered their conversation toward happy topics.

Cora Jean was dying of pancreatic cancer, the cancer best known for being unsurvivable. Audrey sat with the woman in the late stages of her illness for many reasons: because she believed that people who suffered shouldn't be left alone; because she was a pastor's wife and embraced this privilege that came with the role; because Cora Jean reminded Audrey of her own beloved mother.

She also went to the woman's home because she couldn't *not* go. In the most physical, literal sense, Audrey was regularly guided there, directed by an unseen arm, weighty and warm, that encircled her shoulders and turned her body toward the Halls' house every week or so. A voice audible only to her own ears would whisper, *Please don't leave me alone today.* It was no pitiful sound, and Audrey never resented it, though from time to time it surprised her. In these moments she thought, though she had never dared to try it, that if she applied her foot to the gas pedal and took her hands off the wheel, her car would take her wherever God wanted her to be.

This five-years familiar experience had not always involved Cora Jean, but others like her, so Audrey had long since stopped questioning how it happened. The why of it was clear enough: Audrey was called by God to be a comforter, and she was glad for the job.

Audrey had a knack for helping people in any circumstance to look toward the bright-ness of life — not the silver lining of their own dark cloud, which often didn't exist — but to the Light of the World, which could be seen by anyone willing to look for it. In Cora Jean's case this meant not dwelling too long on the details of her prognosis, but in reading aloud beautiful, hopeful, complex

11

poetry, especially the Psalms and the Brownings and Franz Wright. It meant watering the plants (which Harlan ignored) and offering to warm a meal for him before she left. It meant giving candid answers to Cora Jean's many-layered questions about Audrey's personal faith — in particular, about sin and forgiveness and justice.

And about the problem of so much suffering in a world governed by a "good" God. Cora Jean seemed preoccupied with this particular question, and her focus seemed to be connected to the yellowed family portrait hanging on the wall opposite the bed.

There were two brunette girls in the thirty-year-old picture. Audrey judged the age by Cora Jean's bug-eyed plastic-framed glasses, Harlan's rust-colored corduroy blazer, and the children's Dorothy Hamill hairstyles. Audrey had a similarly aged childhood portrait of herself with her parents. She guessed the daughters to be nine, maybe ten, and they appeared to be twins, though one of them was considerably chubbier than the other.

A pendant on a large-link silver chain hung from the upper left corner of the cheap wood frame. The pendant was also silver, crudely hammered into a flat circle, like a washer, that framed a small translucent rock. Audrey suspected it to be an uncut diamond.

It would be rude to ask whether she was right about the stone, but on the day the fog broke and the sun brought a wispy smile to Cora Jean's pale face, Audrey decided to ask about the portrait she often stared at.

Audrey lifted her teacup to her lips and blew off the steam. "Tell me about your family," she said gently, indicating the picture with her eyes.

Cora Jean's smile crumpled, and the soft wrinkles of her skin became a riverbed for tears.

Audrey wished she hadn't said anything. Meaning to apologize for having heaped some kind of emotional ache on top of the cancer's pain, she returned her sloshing teacup to the tray, then reached out and placed her hands on top of Cora Jean's, which were clutching the sheets.

That was the second unfortunate choice Audrey made that day, with a third yet to occur before the sun set. The woman's sorrow — if it could be thought of as something chemical — entered Audrey's fingertips, burning the pads of her fingers, the joints of her knuckles, her wrists. The flaming liquid pain seeped up her arms, searing as it went:

elbows, shoulders, collarbone. And then the poison found her spine, an aqueduct that delivered breathtaking hurt to every nerve in Audrey's body. She yelped involuntarily. Here was a sensation that she had never experienced.

She wished that she could save the dying woman from the terror. She also wished that she had never dipped her toe into these hellish waters.

The pain bowed her over Cora Jean's fragile body, a posture at once protective and impotent, and paralyzed Audrey. The women cried together until every last drop of the agony had let itself out of Audrey's eyes.

In time Cora Jean said, "Thank you for understanding," and fell asleep, exhausted.

Audrey, who understood not a bit of what had transpired, said nothing. She tuned the radio to Cora Jean's favorite classical station, then waited, agitated and restless, for the hospice nurse to arrive.

Audrey stumbled out of the house, forgetting to give Harlan a polite good-bye. She stood on the square front stoop, stunned and spent and a little bit frightened, and leaned against the closed screen door for a long minute. She fiddled absentmindedly

14

with one of her rose-in-a-heart earrings.

She began to wonder if she wasn't as well-suited for her divine calling as she had once thought. Surely sitting with a person through suffering didn't mean sharing the pain like *that,* experiencing it firsthand. How had it happened? She wasn't sure. She wasn't sure of anything except that she would prefer to avoid that kind of intensity in the future. She would do what she was able to do, and there was no point in feeling guilty about her shortcomings, if guilt was the right name for this emotion.

Audrey sighed and finally walked off the Halls' stoop and across the lawn. Cora Jean's windows weren't the only ones opened that day. Because the fog was gone, others in the working-class neighborhood had raised sashes to lure cleansing breezes into their homes. This is what Audrey would later blame for her third poor choice of the day.

Wide oaks offered shade on both sides of the street. The separation from the sun would be a gift from God come summertime, when the air was too tired to stir even a single leaf in any of the towering eucalyptus trees.

The fleeting question of whether Cora Jean would be alive then passed through

Audrey's mind. She kicked it out of her consciousness, still feeling raw and drained. She moved toward her car, wanting to go home and find answers in her sleep.

When she stepped off the curb to round her parked car and climb into the driver's seat, she felt the atmosphere move. Invisible but solid, thick air stepped in front of her like a large man who intended to hijack her car or snatch her purse. Her keys, hanging from her fingertips, jangled as if she'd struck something. She steadied herself with one hand on the hood of the car, bracing her surprise. She had never experienced this "leading," as she called it, so close to another event. The effects would either pass shortly or lead her onward.

Heat like a strong arm snaked across the back of her shoulders. Audrey stepped forward to get out from under the weight. The move was reflexive, a whole-body flinch that sent her right into the invisible obstacle again. This time she was met with pressure, square and flaming over her sternum, and a crushing pain went straight to her heart. The grip on her shoulders squeezed, keeping her upright where she couldn't escape the wounding.

The hurt was blunt and weighty, a pestle grinding in a mortar. Audrey's lips parted

16

and flattened, stretching out like a cry, but no sound came out of her mouth. The skin around her nose and eyes bunched up until she couldn't see, but there were no tears. She folded at the waist, her body bending over the car just as she had drooped over Cora Jean. This connection was unwelcome, and Audrey resisted it.

The arm let her sag, all but dropped her, and she lowered her forehead onto the hood. The drill into her heart kept turning, creating a whining noise that grew louder in her own ears until it drowned out everything else on the street. No birds, no cars, no children playing on lawns or in driveways.

And then the violence stopped. The body of heat released her, and Audrey found herself breathing heavily and wondering if anyone had witnessed her bizarre behavior. Her head pounded, every blood vessel in it taxed as if she'd been wailing for hours. Audrey rested her cheek on the smooth shell of the hood and waited for her heart and lungs to find their rhythms again.

The sound of real sobbing reached her then.

Cora Jean? Audrey jerked away from the car, looking, her breathing still deep and quick. The earth tipped, then leveled out again. The muscles at the base of her neck were painful knots.

After three or four seconds she stepped back onto the curb and crossed the grassy easement to the sidewalk. The noise wasn't coming from the Halls' house but from somewhere down the street. She started walking, hesitant to follow the heartache, unable to do anything else.

The terrible sound pulled her toward one of the neighborhood's nicer homes, a single-story brick house with an attached garage. The cries came from an open window at the front of the house. Audrey stepped off the sidewalk and cut directly across the lawn, getting as close to the window as the bordering juniper hedge allowed. The dirt underfoot was still soft from the rain that had escorted in winter's final batch of fog. A sheer curtain in the window blocked her view of anyone on the other side.

"Hello?" She raised her voice. "Hello? Are you okay?"

Abrupt silence answered her.

"I'm sorry to intrude, but do you need help?"

The house in front of her was as still as her own when her husband and son were out. Audrey waited.

"Are you injured?"

She understood that she might be facing a

delicate situation in which her confident desire to help someone could cause more problems than allowing that someone some privacy. But in her view, it was worse to be lonely than to be embarrassed by a good Samaritan — and even worse for her to disobey God's clear direction — so she decided to persist at least until the person told her to stop.

"Maybe there's someone I can call for you?" she offered.

"I know how to use a phone." It was likely that the female speaker was the same one who had been crying. Her *N* sounds were nasal and stuffy. But the tone was far more irritated than grieved. As a pastor's wife, Audrey understood the fine line between the two emotions.

"Of course you do," Audrey said gently. "But sometimes it helps to assign tasks to other people. Take a load off your own shoulders."

At the edge of the elevated windowpane, the curtain flickered.

"You're trespassing."

Audrey's defenses went up. Her compassion had been rejected on many occasions, but never beaten back with accusations.

"That's true, I am. I'm sorry, but I . . ."
She had yet to land on an easy explanation

for the experiences that led her to other people. Geoff's position as a church leader required that Audrey's choice of words — and confidants — be discreet. Anyone who thought she was outside of God's will, or heretical or occult or misguided or just plain loony, would frown on her husband too. Even so, Audrey believed people deserved simple, no-frills truth. The world was so full of deceptive spin that most days she worried it might gyrate right out of orbit.

"I just sensed you could use a friend right now. My name's Audrey and I go to Grace Springs Church. My husband's the pastor there. Maybe you've heard of it? Doesn't matter, I'm not trying to recruit anyone. Anyway, do you like fresh bread? Geoff and I bake bread as a hobby, to give it away. I'd like to give you a loaf. I have some with me in my car because I was visiting one of your neighbors before I heard you crying. I'm parked right down —"

A door slammed inside the house and the curtain rose, then sank.

Audrey waited for a minute while the juniper leaves tickled the legs of her jeans. Sometimes people came back. Sometimes they wanted relief so badly that they didn't care if it was offered by a total stranger.

But not this time.

Audrey left the yard, returned to the sidewalk, and started walking back toward her car, thinking about the woman inside the house. She passed the mailbox on her left, and her thoughts were interrupted. Her feet took her backward two steps, and she took another look at the side of the black metal receptacle. The name *MANSFIELD* was applied to the box with rectangular stickers, black block letters on a gold background.

Mansfield. *As in Jack Mansfield, the church elder?* She glanced at the house number. She'd have to check the church directory. Mrs. Mansfield, Jack's wife, was a math teacher at her son's high school. Ed had her for geometry his sophomore year.

Audrey resumed walking, trying to bring up the woman's face. They'd met once, at a school event. Mrs. Mansfield refused to attend church with Jack, and Audrey had understood this reality to be a tender bruise on the elder's heart, maybe even on his ego.

Julie. Her name was Julie. And their daughter's name was Miralee, which was easier for Audrey to remember because until last week, the start of spring break, her son had dated the girl for a brief time.

If that had been Miralee crying, her refusal to come out was completely understandable. And Audrey was a fool not to have realized where she was. She still wasn't sure if the kids' breakup had been Ed's call or Miralee's. Audrey's nineteen-year-old had been so strangely tight-lipped that she assumed Miralee had broken things off. Secretly, Audrey wasn't sad to see that relationship end, though she hated that Ed was in pain. Now, after being subjected to the sounds of the broken heart in that house, she wondered if her assumptions had been wrong.

The thought passed through her mind that she should go back, knock on the front door like a respectable friend, apologize, and get to the bottom of things. Fix what Ed had broken, if necessary, though Ed wasn't prone to breaking very many things in life. He was a good boy. A careful boy. Man now.

Audrey looked back at the redbrick house.

A flash of light, a phantom sensation of liquid fire tearing through her body, prevented her from returning to the Mansfields' property. She had no desire to press Miralee for details of the heartbreak. Especially not after the girl had refused.

She had done what God asked of her. This excuse propelled her back toward her car, the sunny air rich with the scent of

22

rosemary-potato bread pushing against her face.

Audrey didn't second-guess this decision for three months. In June the Grace Springs Church board, spurred to fury by none other than Jack Mansfield, fired her husband and barred him from seeking another post as pastor.

CHAPTER 2

November

For some sins, there was no atonement. Diane Hall had believed this all of her adult life, and twenty-five years of prison chapel services hadn't altered her perspective. Penance, however, was a different matter. For all sins, punishment was required even when pardon was out of the question. By her own logic, if not by God himself.

This was the truth that had hounded Diane through her years at the women's penitentiary in Central California, where she'd lived as though half dead since she was seventeen, tried and convicted as an adult. It was the truth that prevented her from sleeping through the nights at the halfway house after her release, where she lay awake at age forty-two while her housemates snored and dreamed.

It was the truth that finally kicked her out of bed after midnight one November morning, two months after her prison sentence was completed. She loaded a backpack in the dark and then slinked out the doors onto the streets of freedom, where she would have been lost if not for the guiding compass of penance.

Diane headed home.

On the southbound side of the highway, she stuck out her thumb wondering how hard it would be for an overweight middle-aged woman to get a ride on a road that passed through jail country. Her answer arrived within ten minutes in the shape of a hairy bass player whose various guitars were stacked high in cases on the backseat.

"How far south you going?" she asked through the open passenger window of his sedan. She estimated him to be half her age.

"All the way to Sin City."

"I'm not going that far this time," she said, and when he didn't ask her for specifics, she didn't offer.

She threw her few belongings onto the floor under the dash, and driver and passenger didn't say anything more for quite some time. Apparently he didn't care that she was from the penitentiary any more than she cared that he might have a harmful bent. Perhaps her past wasn't outwardly obvious. She didn't have enough experience yet to know how to assess outsiders' judgments of her, "outsiders" being anyone who'd never served a sentence. Diane had survived the pitfalls of prison life by learning how to be invisible, a strategy that involved (among other things) feeding her already ample body into largeness. She was smart, wily if necessary. She could outwit a kid musician if she could outwit anybody.

The fog rolled in, a familiar visitor that would stay for most of the cold season. Diane left the window cracked open at the top and closed her eyes, let the fog blow in and caress her cheeks. The sensation reminded her of her mother's touch, a gesture so long forgotten that tears pooled like memories behind her lids.

Eventually her driver tried to make small talk, and she tried to be polite.

"Where you headed?" he asked.

"Home."

"And that'd be?"

"About an hour more."

"Cornucopia, is it? That's a nice town."

"A small town."

"Not the smallest in these parts."

"Too small for me."

He glanced at her pack, which contained a clean pair of jeans, a flannel shirt, underwear, socks, a new bar of soap, toothpaste,

Arundhati Roy's novel *The God of Small Things,* and four hundred dollars cash, her meager savings from two months' work plus what was left over from her release fund. "You travel light," he observed.

"It was a short trip." Metaphorically speaking. She had been willing to stay behind bars for another twenty-five years. For life. But she had not been so lucky. "You play guitar?"

"Since before I could walk. My older brother taught me."

"The two of you are close?"

He shrugged. "I got better at it than him. You know how that goes."

Diane guessed she did, but not in the way he meant. "I never had a brother," she said. They traveled another mile before she added, "It's probably a good idea to steer clear of jealous siblings."

The kid — Diane could hardly think of him as a man in spite of all the hair on his arms and face — laughed as if they shared some inside joke. "You sound like my mom. But my brother's got his own thing going, you know? He'll find what makes him happy, and then we'll be okay."

Diane stared at him, disbelieving that *her* mother's very words from decades ago were pouring almost verbatim from this boy's mouth. Her mother had been so terribly wrong.

But he rambled on, and Diane didn't have to say anything else. Eventually she collected the backpack.

"Just drop me at the next off-ramp," she said.

"Take you into town?"

"No need. No one's up waiting for me. I mean, at this hour."

It was a little before three when she thanked him and wished him good luck with the guitar gig and slammed the car door, then set out eastward for the city limits. She walked just off the road's shoulder through darkness, remembering the terrain by scent rather than sight. She passed harvested fields that smelled like dry grass. The inseam of her jeans made a sound like a zipper as she walked, her heavy thighs brushing together.

Diane lifted her chin and imagined she could see the distant ridges of the Sierra Nevada, which rose gently from the horizon like the rim of a shallow bowl. The Great Central Valley was a bowl, in fact, and the fog its favorite winter stew. She wished for sunrise to come early over the mountaintops. She wanted to see them, needed proof that they were unchanging and reliable.

Because everything else, including what was planted in these fields and who lived in her childhood home today, was probably different now.

The nighttime chill passed through her cotton sweater and the thin T-shirt underneath it. It was time to purchase a real jacket. On the other hand, she thought, people like her didn't deserve warmth. And she was fat enough now that she practically carried her own insulation. She shouldn't need more.

Six miles passed under her feet like a dream. Fog followed her, a ghost of the past, nudging her onward and gathering density.

By the time she arrived in town, the damp had penetrated her hair and her clothing. A streetlight allowed her to catch her reflection in the plate-glass window of the old battery shop. Her appearance was limp and discouraged. Just what had she expected to do when she got here?

You're crazy, and you look like it too.

Diane turned away from her reflection and stepped out of the spotlight.

Crazy's nothing. Crazy is all that's keeping me going right now.

You can always go back. The other women won't even know you were gone.

The six-mile walk back to the highway was

too great a distance to face. She hesitated. The sound of a puttering engine caught her attention, and she turned her head as a slow-moving motor scooter passed her, cautiously heading east like Diane, its light-colored frame a skeleton animating the fog.

The bike passed through the intersection, and the shallow runoff drain that carried water from the blacktop into the street sewers under the sidewalk caused the scooter to bounce once. An object flew into the air like a flea off a dog, then hit the street inaudibly under the noise of the engine and separated into two pieces.

"Hey," Diane said, barely able to hear herself. Then, embarrassed by her own reticence, she said more loudly, "Hey!"

The driver kept going, oblivious or uncaring.

Diane went into the street to see what the object was. She saw it glinting in the gutter inches from a storm drain. A cell phone.

Several of the women in the halfway house had these phones, had spent a fair chunk of their release funds on the technology, which Diane thought was an impressive but unnecessary invention. Why would anyone want to be at the constant beck and call of the telephone? Of course, that was a dumb question for someone like her to ask, someone who had no one to call.

Diane picked up the two pieces and turned the parts around in her hands, guessing how they might fit together. They snapped into place.

She would have to figure out how to use the thing, with its shiny black face and minimalist buttons and icons that everyone else seemed to understand. No — she was smart. She could figure this out if the owner didn't come back looking for it. If he did, she'd give it up. The thing looked expensive, and there was no point in going back to jail over something as silly as a ball and chain.

That accidental joke cheered her up a little. She decided not to hike back to the highway. She let her backpack fall forward across her stocky body and put the phone into the small zippered pocket on the front.

She kept walking in the same direction, retracing the steps she had taken nearly every day of her life as a child, with Donna by her side. Donna, skipping instead of walking home from school or church or the grocery store. Home was a straight shot down Main Street from nearly anywhere in town. In her mind Diane heard the *skiff scuff, skiff scuff, skiff scuff* of Donna's feet next to her gliding over the sidewalk. Her momentary cheer vanished. She covered her

31

cold ears with her hands.

Almost two hours after leaving the bass player's car, she found herself on the corner of Main and Sunflower, standing in front of the old drugstore her parents once owned, stunned. She'd expected anything but lights on within. The exterior had been painted red, and the tiny scalloped awning looked blue in this light, with a white stripe on the curving edges. Simple curtains had been drawn back to the edges of the French-paned bay windows, one on each side of the inset door. Like a child, Diane placed both hands on the glass and gawked.

It was a bakery now, with sloping racks half filled with fresh bread where the shelved cigarette boxes used to be, and glass display cases and café tables rather than rows of shampoo and aspirin and prepackaged snack foods. Blackboards with colorful chalk lists of breads instead of advertisements for cosmetics covered the walls. Only the wood floors were the same.

A man about Diane's age emerged from the storeroom — probably a kitchen now. He carried a large baking sheet loaded with oversized muffins and slid this into one of the glass cases next to a tray of bagels. His lips were pursed to whistle a tune she couldn't hear.

He straightened and wiped his hands on the white cloth tucked into his jeans. He lifted his head, noticed her.

Diane jerked back. She'd left handprints on the window. The man glanced at the large digital clock hanging over the kitchen doorway — 4:59 — and came around the display cases toward the door. She turned away and walked as fast as she could, squaring her load on her back. Behind her she heard the tumbling sound of a lock being turned, then the jingle of a tiny bell on an opening door.

"You want to come in?"

The invitation startled her so much that she stopped and turned around. She wanted nothing more than to go in, except perhaps *never* to go in. Why would he allow it? He leaned out over the sidewalk, bracing the door.

"Y-You're open?" she asked.

"Open due to fog," the man said, eyeing her lightweight clothing. "Weather's nicer inside." He had the gentle look of a harmless man who smiled a lot and liked to eat a little more than he ought to. "Hungry? The muffins are still hot."

Do I look hungry? Are you one of those people who thinks fat girls are always hungry?

She was ravenous. She hadn't eaten since

33

breakfast the day before.

Diane shifted her weight to one foot and glanced back into the bright room that was golden and warm.

"I can bring one out to you if you'd rather," he offered.

It could be no more dangerous inside than it was out here. And going in would put her that much closer to where she wanted to be anyway. She nodded her thanks without looking at him and walked back to the bakery, then entered, slipping her backpack off her shoulder.

The sweet scent of expanding yeast and crisping crusts caused her to sigh. Goose bumps rippled down her arms and legs, receiving the dry warmth of the room. He let the door fall closed without locking it again and pulled out a chair for her.

No one had ever pulled out a chair for Diane Hall.

She sat slowly, wondering, keeping her eyes averted so he wouldn't see her blush.

"Coffee's not on yet," he said, going back around the case. "But my wife should be here any minute. She'll have my hide if I try to work that thing." He nodded to an espresso machine at the other end of the counter while placing one of the muffins in a wicker basket lined with waxed paper. He brought it back to Diane's table and set it in front of her. "You want an orange juice or something?"

His kindness made Diane wary.

"Would water be okay?" she said.

His eyes crinkled at the corners. "Can't think of why not."

Which made her feel a little stupid, though she doubted he meant to. While he went to get a glass, she leaned over the smell of pumpkin pie spices and candied pecans that floated up from her unexpected breakfast. The soft cake warmed her fingers when she picked it up. She bit into the muffin's crisp-soft mushroom top. There was no food like this in prison. Maybe not in the entire world.

He set the glass of water next to her basket and extended his hand. "Geoff Bofinger."

His fingers were dusty with flour. She let it transfer to her palms.

"Diane," she said around the wolfish bite she'd just taken. There were crumbs gathering in one corner of her lips. She hated her own idea of herself.

"Stay as long as you like then, Diane. I've got loaves to get out of the oven."

After he walked back into the rear of the shop she thought to say, "What do I owe you?"

"Nothing," he said as he vanished into the kitchen. "First-timers are on the house."

She'd never heard of such a thing, but times had changed while she was inside.

At the end of the L-shaped counter and cases, in the rear right corner of the dining area, a universal sign on a push-through door indicated there were bathrooms on the other side. She'd have known this without the sign. Unless there had been remodeling since she'd last used those toilets, yet another door beyond the ones marked for men and women would lead to a rear stairway and a small apartment above the bakery.

That door would probably be locked. Her parents had always locked it.

She wondered.

Diane stood and peered through the round glass window in the top half of the swinging door. The hallway beyond was dim. She shouldered her backpack and picked her muffin out of the basket. She took another bite and crossed the room, pushed through that door, and walked right past the bathrooms to the end of the hall, which still smelled like the bakery but wasn't as warm.

The red stenciled letters that spelled out the word *private* were scratched up but legible. Diane reached for the round stainless-steel knob with the keyhole in the middle.

She gripped it, and it turned. The fact required her to reevaluate: how far was she willing to go with this? She had come to this long-anticipated moment so swiftly, so unexpectedly, that she hadn't properly prepared.

But that was only an excuse, wasn't it? What kind of preparations could a person really make when the time came to stare a demon in the face?

Diane went through. She entered the landing at the bottom of a dark stairwell lit only by emergency lighting on every other step. Her sweaty fingers let go of the knob before she meant to, and the heavy door slammed, bouncing the cannon boom around the small space like her heart within her ribs. She took a calming breath and waited for her pulse to fall.

When it did — or at least when it wasn't so high up in her throat — Diane wiped her free hand on her jeans and gripped the skinny wood handrail. The stair treads were lined with warped nonskid mats that gave in to her weight as she ascended. *Pop-pop, pop-pop.*

At the seventh popping the door below her opened, startling her into dropping the remainder of her muffin. The ball of bread took the descent two steps at a time, raining crumbs, and came to rest at Geoff Bofinger's feet.

"Help you find something?" he asked kindly, as if she were truly lost and not invading his privacy.

She hesitated. Such a man deserved no lies, but the truth might be unnecessarily cruel. "The sign out there, uh, said there were bathrooms?"

He looked back down the hall as he stooped to pick up her food. "Right there. I sometimes walk right by them myself this early in the morning."

Diane doubted it. "Duh on me," she said, faking a laugh.

"No worries. I heard the door slam and remembered I didn't lock up after I restocked the paper goods this morning."

He must think she was a sinister person. She descended, afraid now because she needed to get in touch with her distant past, but it seemed her recent past was going to be forever in the way.

"I'm an ex-con," she blurted. She would either affirm his worst fears or allay them — a truthful ex-con was better than a dishonest one, right? "I just got out two months ago."

He nodded as if she had said this was a great town to live in. "Well, I'm an ex-pastor," he said. "And I just got out four months ago. Maybe we've got some things in common." He laughed at that, but she didn't. Geoff cleared his throat. "Besides my knack for flat jokes. I never did master that part." He pointed with the broken muffin to the ladies' room. "Here you go. If you want, come into the kitchen when you're done. I'll get you something else to eat."

Diane watched him push his way back into the dining room, disbelieving his unaffected reaction. In two months the number of outsiders who continued speaking to her after they learned she had a criminal record was one. This one, this former pastor. She wondered if he regretted having pulled out that chair for her. Maybe she should have just said, *I'm a killer, you shouldn't invite me in like this! What if I kill you too?* Maybe that would shake him up.

She opened her mouth, daring herself.

There was no time for words. From the street that passed the bakery outside, the ear-drilling sound of colliding metal and breaking glass came straight through the thin walls as if it were coming for her.

CHAPTER 3

In the Great Central Valley of California, fog settled like dead bread dough in a bowl: dense, heavy, unwilling to rise. Audrey sat erect in the driver's seat and hugged the steering wheel, fingers gripping twelve o'clock and elbows squeezing the sides, as if pulling her body forward would help her to see the road better. Her car schlepped along at fifteen miles an hour, which was too fast for these conditions but a risk she was willing to take. It was five in the morning, she was late to the bakery, and traffic was light. She'd seen only one vehicle on this rural road in the last ten minutes — a pickup transporting field-workers toward the pecan and orange groves for harvesting.

In the passenger seat her son yawned, his maw wide enough to drink the scented air that poured through his open window. Plowed earth. Barley seeds. Winter on its way after the most brutal summer their family had ever endured.

Ed rested his head on the doorframe. When he regained control of his mouth he said, "You and Dad've gotta hire another person."

"We hired you," Audrey murmured, straining her eyes to keep track of the street's white fog line on the right and dashed yellow lane divider on the left. Her own headlights worked against her efforts, bouncing off the waterlogged air and glaring into her windshield. But it was that or drive in blackness.

"I mean someone who *likes* getting up when the rest of the world is going to sleep."

She chuckled. "Again, that'd be you."

"If you were running a nightclub maybe." He crushed his eyes with the heels of his hands and rubbed.

"It's good of you to help like this. Your dad and I appreciate it. We really do."

Ed sniffed and said something under his breath. Audrey shot a glance at him, then tried to refocus on the barely visible road. *Hypocrites,* she believed she'd heard.

"I didn't mean you," he said, more alert.

"I know. I understand."

The road's white fog line broke on the right for a wide dirt driveway that belonged to an orchard. It was Audrey's "fogmark," as she called it, the indication that she could expect a street signal a hundred yards ahead, though she wouldn't see it until she was right on top of it. She slowed the car to ten and craned her neck toward the dashboard, looking.

Her son said, "As if none of them ever made a mistake in their pathetic lives."

"Ed." Her warning was gentle. It was a tender scab he kept picking at, the family's mutual wound, and she had no more emotional salve to apply to it.

She almost changed the subject by asking if his friends had decided about going to Mammoth to ski for Thanksgiving, or whether he would fill out the application to the community college, or how he was thinking about spending the next six months of his "time off" besides earning a few bucks at the bakery she and Geoff had opened after being thrown out of the church. It was important that she learn the answers to all of these questions, but the moment she opened her mouth she understood that she'd fail to change the subject at all. In Ed's mind, the various threads of his destiny were hopelessly tangled. This young man had watched his carefully knit plans for life unravel into a heap at his feet, and he'd been staring at the knots, disbelieving, for months.

She released the steering wheel with one hand and squeezed his knee.

The green light appeared, ghostly and floating over the road, where Audrey would have to enter the intersection and take the left turn. It was impossible to detect oncoming traffic, but nearly as dangerous was any vehicle that might be following her. Its driver might see the green overhead before registering her turn signal.

She turned the wheel and stepped on the gas.

When she had moved to California's inland valley and was told to expect foggy winters, she had hoped for something poetically beautiful. Shimmering water droplets. Wispy ballerinas, slender and light-footed, dancing among trees and grasses. The occasional moody mystery. She had not expected this: a gray tomb that not even sunlight could fully penetrate, weather that muffled sounds and swallowed cars and killed by the dozens every year.

Tule fog, it was called, after the thick tule grasses that grew throughout the valley.

A blaring horn startled her. She punched the gas pedal and her little sedan was catapulted to safety. In her rearview mirror she saw the smudge of yellow and red that were the lights of another car passing through the intersection she'd just cleared.

"There's got to be a better way to do this," she said and blew her spiky blond bangs off her forehead.

"Ditch this commute, move into town." Ed put his sneakered foot on the dash. "You should give up that sorry excuse for a rental house and move into the rooms over the bakery."

"Living there would be quaint."

"European."

"Old subject, Ed. You'd go stir crazy. It's microscopic, hardly a home. You need your space. We don't want you to feel . . . tied to us, to this venture. Besides, I was talking about driving, not housing."

The first dim streetlights of town came into view.

"If I moved out, would you do it? I'm not supposed to be here anyway. I'm supposed to be pulling all-nighters, playing college basketball, struggling to make the transition to independent living, that kind of thing."

"Don't start with that. You're here, and we're glad to have you."

"You won't be saying that when I'm thirty."

"You won't be so morose when you're thirty, I promise. Stay, go, duck when life throws stuff at you, and come home to see us now and then. Your dad and I won't live anywhere that doesn't have a decent place for you to crash. Deal with it."

"Aw, Mom, where's your tough love?"

"You don't need tough love. You need to give yourself a little grace is all. For that matter, just accept the grace everyone wants to give you."

"This little town is just full of grace, isn't it?"

Audrey pursed her lips and had no comeback. She understood in a new way that her only child probably wouldn't stick around for many more months, even if it meant leaving before their hearts had healed. *Stay, go.* Her maternal heart was already torn.

They crawled past a mechanic's graveyard and several east-facing, weather-bleached storefronts, then turned right into a clear pocket of air. The tule fog, in its predictably unpredictable manner, had receded here and formed walls like a stadium's, turning Main Street into a socked-in arena. Whereas a second ago Audrey couldn't see ten feet in front of her, now she could see all the way to the Honey Bee restaurant three blocks away. The yellow awnings the owners had installed last spring had already paled a little in the blistering summer sun. Even so, under the streetlamps they seemed to give off their own light. The bakery was a block beyond on the northwest corner, still shrouded in fog.

Audrey accelerated to a much more productive pace. Twenty, twenty-five, thirty. Storefronts clicked by her window under the light-shadow-light-shadow rhythm of the streetlights.

It might have been that the shifting patterns deceived her, but as she approached the end of the good visibility, a movement on the left side of the street drew her eyes. A gliding form passed through a cone of light quickly, a leaf bag caught by the wind. There was no wind, though, and Audrey supposed on second thought that the shadow had been larger than a bag. Larger than a bag and more weighty than breeze-tossed plastic, moving like a living creature: a leaping dog, a stooped person dashing through a rainstorm, a cloaked villain.

Ed said, "I still think we could have taken over a failing bakery in some town where the Mansfields don't live."

Audrey's head swiveled away from the street and toward her son-of-the-stubborn-perspective. She was going to say *We don't run from problems* or *We made this decision as a family* or something similar to remind

46

him that several good people had chosen to stand by him in the universe of his particular heartache, at no small cost to themselves, but she ran out of time.

In the space of a second her car plunged back into fog like a bullet passing through flesh. Her foot found the brake in half a second more, but she entered the intersection of Main and Sunflower blind. The tires squealed, but her good reflexes were not enough to overcome the laws of physics. The sedan bulldozed something solid and heavy where nothing solid and heavy should have been.

Audrey gasped and threw her arm across Ed. He reached out for the dash, body folding over his elevated leg, but his seatbelt held him back. The object they struck stayed in front of the car, metals cracking and screeching. Ed shouted and Audrey felt the front end of the car rise and then fall again as it was lifted by whatever part of the obstacle had slid under the wheels. The thing came apart and clattered, separated, scattered beneath the blanket of fog. The street stilled.

Mother and son glanced at each other in shadows, stunned. Ed's steady but heavy breathing was the only human sound to reach Audrey's ears, and that's what frightened her the most.

She began to fumble with her seat belt, praying aloud — "Jesus, Jesus, Jesus" — and mixing this with jumbled instructions: "Where's your phone? Call 9-1-1. Did we hit someone? Stay in the car. Please, Jesus. Sweet Jesus." It took longer than it should have to find the seat belt button and release the latch. She clawed at the handle and pushed the door open. Ed had his phone to his ear.

The fog hid what she needed to see, what she hoped not to see. She swung her feet out of the car and gripped the top of the doorframe with her right hand, then hauled herself up — an old habit that, this time, probably saved her from breaking her neck. Her legs went out from under her before she was upright, her shoes sliding across the paved road as if it were covered in ice. She lost her grip on the door as she went down and felt the strain in her shoulder as the jolt tipped her sideways. She landed on the heel of her left hand, tiny shards of deteriorating asphalt puncturing the skin at her wrist, then cracked her elbow on the threshold of the car's frame.

"Mom!" Ed was not about to stay put in the passenger seat, and Audrey heard him talking to an emergency operator while he climbed out of the car on his side and ran around the back.

Shooting pain from her wrist doubled up at her elbow and immobilized her entire arm for a few seconds. Something damp seeped in through the denim of her jeans as she sat there on the ground, and when she could move her fingers again she noticed they were covered in a dense, sticky goo.

Ed's tall form bent over her. "She's conscious," he said into the phone. And then to her: "Did you hit your head?"

"No. Watch where you step."

He took first note of the spill.

"It must have busted an oil line or a gas line or something," she said, wondering at the same time if that was even possible. She knew nothing of auto mechanics. Audrey rolled cautiously to her knees, holding her injured wrist to her stomach. There at eye level, she saw where some of the fluid had splashed onto the body of the champagne-colored car. It dripped slowly down the sides, dropping truth into Audrey's mind with a revolting splash.

"That's a lot of oil," Ed said. He moved toward the front of the car, eyes on the slippery hazard, phone still to one ear.

"Ed, no. Go get your dad." The bakery was right there on the corner, mere feet

49

away from the intersection, a saving distance from the possibility of a broken human body. Her son did not need images of the dead dancing on the graves already dug in his mind. Audrey lifted her throbbing hand to her nose. She sniffed and then recoiled, having no idea what to do with the coating on her skin and clothes. This was no oil.

"Help's coming, okay?" Ed said. "But they wanna know if anyone's hurt."

"Yes, but I'll go see."

He stepped in the wrong direction around the periphery of the disaster, then disappeared.

"Ed!"

Audrey moved as quickly as the blood — *So much blood! Dear Jesus!* — would allow. "Ed!" She was on her feet, tiptoeing to dry ground as if she might have more balance that way. The reach of the streetlights, diminished by the moisture in the air, cut across the sedan. She saw the steaming radiator and the disfigured bumper and the crushed metal under the tire. "Ed, wait!"

He was only steps away, and she nearly collided with him where he stood still, staring down at the mangled form of a small motorcycle. It was a motor scooter, actually, light blue or yellow or white, with a platform for feet directly in front of the

50

stumpy seat. The shredded cushion was also spattered with the terrible liquid. The front end of the scooter had been swallowed by her car. Something that looked like a storage compartment had separated from the bike and tumbled down the road.

Audrey looked around. "Where's the rider?"

"I don't know." Ed was staring at the wreckage. The hand holding his cell phone dropped to his side.

"He must have been thrown," Audrey said, thinking she would have to find and follow a trail of blood leading from this lake. She was shaking, nauseated by the shock of what she'd done.

"That's what the dispatcher said."

"What?"

"That the rider would have been thrown."

Audrey turned away. "We'll look until emergency workers get here. I've got a flashlight in the trunk."

Fog caressed Ed's shoulders. He was fixated on the bike.

"Go get your father. Ed, we need to find the rider." The clammy moisture on her forehead and upper lip wasn't from the weather. *"Ed."*

He gestured at the wreckage. "That's Julie Mansfield's scooter."

CHAPTER 4

Sergeant Jack Mansfield was a city detective, not a patrol officer, and so under ordinary circumstances he wouldn't have been the one to respond to dispatch's announcement of an 11-83, even though both Cornucopia and its force were small. Vehicle accident, no details available, except that the caller described it as car versus motorcycle, which meant that injuries were likely. An ambulance had caught up with them half a mile back and now tailed the cruiser at a safe distance, only its flashing lights visible in the rearview mirror.

An 11-83 was as common as an orange tree in these parts, in this season, at these hours. For the next four or five months people would spend most of their time on the road driving blind. The locals were pretty good at that, having had their entire lives to practice, but enough people were idiots, especially the young ones, and ignorant of how their tragedies happened until some emergency responder explained it to them.

He didn't have a lot of sympathy for idiots.

Technically, Jack wasn't responding on this early Wednesday morning; he only happened to be in the car of the officers who were, because the last thirty-six hours had been anything but ordinary. He'd been on duty since five Monday afternoon, collecting and chasing evidence in a rare murder, only the third in the county this year. Even more rare, however, was a break with an eyewitness who had the information Jack needed to connect crime and criminal faster than a TV drama.

It was the paperwork, not the sleuthing, that ate up the hours in this particular case. Both killer and evidence had to be properly processed, and for this reason the paperwork on both had to be pristine. If any case as straightforward as this fell apart, it wouldn't be because Jack had lost his grip on it. Details, details. Jack never overlooked details.

Not even strange details, like the ones Jack's wife and the victim held in common: both were five six, 135, early forties. Both had their nails done at Studio Six Salon and bought locally roasted coffee at The Midnight Oil. The victim was a first-grade teacher at Hartford Elementary School; his wife taught math at Mazy High.

The parallels brought to mind the unpleasant scenario of how his life might change if Julie were no longer a part of it, and this brought grim memories of how their daughter, Miralee, had exited their lives in a flurry of expletives.

These details were curious but not relevant, so he moved on to other thoughts.

Specifically, to procedures. There was a reason for the many regulations and guidelines that governed scenes and labs and interrogation rooms. Follow the rules and reap the reward: another lowlife behind bars. Do it once, do it right. Renegade bad-boy cops who followed their own rules were the stuff of Hollywood myth — and perhaps New York City — and Jack would as soon shoot one on the street as allow him to walk through the doors of his precinct.

The principle worked in life as it did at the office. The theology of grace had been abused, in his opinion. Old Testament law made more sense to him than the ambiguous "everything is lawful" fluff. How could a man build logical systems of behavior out of that?

It was such a mind-set that allowed him,

in less than two days' time, to cuff the victim's husband, secure the chain of evidence, dot the i's and cross the t's of his report, and finally go home.

This goal was hampered only by his mechanic, who didn't follow procedures with Jack's level of integrity and didn't have the Jeep ready when promised Tuesday afternoon. So Jack decided to take his vehicle somewhere else next time, and at 5:07 Wednesday morning, while Julie slept soundly at home, he caught a ride from Officers Carlisle and Rutgers, who would pass through his neighborhood on their routine patrol.

When Carlisle arrived at the scene of the 11-83 and parked the car in the middle of Sunflower, Jack considered walking home, just two miles away, or rousing Julie by phone in spite of the hour. Carlisle left the blues and reds going as a hazard indicator for inbound traffic, then called dispatch to ask for blockades on the other streets until the wreck could be cleared.

From the backseat of the cruiser, Jack saw the cone-shaped beams of streetlights cutting through the gray air on his right. On his left he saw the lights on inside a corner store and the silhouettes of three people standing outside in front of the bright

55

window. Maybe eyewitnesses. Maybe passengers from the sedan in the middle of the intersection. One of the three approached the cruiser on Carlisle's side.

Through the distorting filter of fog, the no-details accident in the center of the intersection took on just enough clarity to capture Jack's eye: that was a hard-shell cargo compartment lying on the ground. It was light blue, like Julie's scooter, which had just such a chrome-plated top case mounted behind the matching blue seat. And that was a bumper sticker above the keyhole, and Jack thought he knew what it said even though he couldn't make out the words from his position.

I TEACH KIDS MATH. WHAT'S YOUR SUPERPOWER?

He was out of the cruiser before the officers had unbuckled their seat belts. He measured his breathing and his steps and approached the wreckage as he would approach any crime scene. He noted the dismantled blue-and-white Vespa, the champagne-colored Corolla, maybe fifteen years old, the car fluids spilling out from under the car's carriage.

Where was his wife?

The ambulance had circled the block to approach from a different direction and came to a stop behind the wreck in the middle of Main, shining its low beams on the site. Those were not engine fluids on the ground.

Behind him, the voices of Carlisle and the bystander took calm turns. Rutgers approached with a flashlight. The officer whistled as the beam passed over the blood.

"That's a couple quarts, you think?" Rutgers said. "Two? Three? Where's the body?"

Jack motioned for Rutgers to hand over the flashlight. "Julie!" he called out.

The murmuring at the patrol car ceased. Rutgers glanced at Jack. "Your Julie?" he asked.

"That's her bike," Jack said, refocusing. Of course, Julie wouldn't be here. "Where's the rider?" he called out in Carlisle's direction.

"No rider," Carlisle shouted back.

"What do you mean, no rider?"

"Can't find anyone."

"Well, who's looked?" Jack muttered. He circled the sedan, scanning it with the beam, and Rutgers followed. The EMTs were already on the other side of the wreck with their lights, sweeping.

"Sarge, let me take the lead on this."

"Let's take it slow. Julie's fine. My guess is someone stole her ride."

There was no good reason why Julie would have been out at this time of the morning. She had classes in just a few hours. She hated rising early after staying up late grading papers and prepping lessons. She'd been sleeping more than usual of late, recovering from a routine surgery. And if she *had* gone out in spite of all that, in these conditions she would have taken her car.

"Is the driver of the sedan on the scene?" Jack called out to Carlisle.

"Right here."

"How fast was he going?" He homed in on the blood, looking for a source.

The answer came after a few seconds. "It's *she*. And about thirty."

"Fast enough to throw a rider," Jack said to Rutgers. "Grab another light. Clock's ticking if anyone's hurt." Then to the medical techs: "Spread out. Could be anywhere, but most likely that direction." He pointed.

A thief would have fled the scene. A victim who had been thrown wouldn't have left this much blood behind on impact. And a victim who had been thrown from a scooter shouldn't be too far from the scooter itself. *And* a victim who had lost this much blood wouldn't be going anywhere under her — his — own steam.

Jack turned these thoughts around in his mind but couldn't get any new perspective on them.

The blood seemed to have risen from the ground like a natural spring under the Corolla. It puddled under the driver's side door, which was still open, and a swirled mess like black finger paints smudged the ground beneath it. From there, sticky shoe prints led to the broken scooter and then away from the scene, back down Sunflower where Carlisle had parked. *Driver,* Jack registered.

Tracks behind the front tires were smeared as if the car had skidded through the stuff. There was blood on the scooter's carriage too, and on the seat, spilled in a pattern Jack had never seen in twenty years on the force.

He stared at the spatter, committing it to memory even though there would be photos taken. Holding the flashlight in his left hand, he pulled his cell phone out of the case on his belt and pressed the speed-dial button for home. It rang four times before the recording picked up. Julie was a heavy sleeper. He left a long, loud message instructing her to wake up. He called again, and a third time.

When she didn't answer, he called her cell

phone, which might be on her nightstand or might be buried in the depths of her purse, depending on her frame of mind at the end of the previous day. She would make things easier for both of them if she would get in the habit of always placing it in the same spot.

No answer there either.

It was possible she was in the shower. Slim, but not out of the question.

The lights of Rutgers and the EMTs bobbed on the other side of the fog. Sun would be up in an hour or so. Jack would have dispatch send a team with a crime scene kit. He'd left his at the office. He'd also ask them to send a car to his house. Check on Julie. Take a report about the stolen scooter.

Jack turned around and followed the bloody shoe prints down Sunflower toward the cruiser. They led to the curb in front of the bright corner store, which actually was a bakery, which explained why it was lit up at this dim hour. It would open soon if it hadn't already. He glanced at the gold foil lettering that arched across one of the windows.

RISE AND SHINE

The Bofingers' new place.

On Sunflower and Main. That was right.

He'd heard something about this from . . .
from . . . from Mrs. Olsen, who wasn't sure
whether she could in good conscience
patronize the place.

Jack weighed this revelation and balanced
it on his mental scale with the likelihood
that the Bofinger kid had something to do
with his wife's mangled bike. Swipe the ride,
park it, get someone to run over it. Teenagers. The Toyota —

Of course. The Corolla belonged to Pastor
Geoff, who was just Plain Geoff now.
Sunday after Sunday for five years, that
nondescript car had parked in the same slot
under the oak tree as far from the church's
front doors as it could get. There was no
shortage of these cookie-cutter economy
cars, but was it such a leap to think —

Yes, it was a great leap, and a good detective would not have taken it. Jack huffed
and returned to the moment. Carlisle had
separated the three adults, probably to take
their statements. From several yards away
Jack could hear the officer asking questions
and another male voice responding. In the
window of the shop, light shone around
another figure, about six two, about 160,
and by Jack's judgment also male.

And in front of Jack, sitting on the curb
where the sticky footprints led away from

61

the scene, was none other than Audrey Bofinger.

No leap at all, this: the other two men must be Geoff and Ed.

Audrey flinched when the glare of Jack's light hit her eyes. She raised her left arm as a shield, and Jack saw the cuts on her palm and the smears down the sleeve of her shirt. The left side of her pants was coated with the blood.

"You three know how to find trouble," he said.

"Jack," she said, not all that surprised. Maybe she'd recognized the bike. Maybe she'd premeditated the whole event.

"Best keep this formal. Call me Sergeant Mansfield."

"I don't see what difference that'll make."

"Were you driving the car that hit the scooter?"

"Jack —"

"Ma'am."

Audrey sighed. "Yes."

"What happened?"

"I already told the other officer."

"Tell me again."

"Please, I —"

"You really need to consider what it will look like if you're uncooperative with me."

The woman's eyes challenged his threat.

Some people were so hard to keep in-line. Their sense of entitlement was ruining the world.

"When are you going to let go of this thing?" she said in a voice that Carlisle wouldn't be able to hear. Jack matched her tone.

"Your own sins were your downfall. Nothing to do with me."

"It's time to put all of it behind you."

"Why don't we head on down to the station?" he said, and Audrey relented. She gave an unhelpful statement that failed to shed any more light on who was driving the scooter or where that person might have gone.

"Are you injured?" he asked when she was done. All the blood he could see on her was consistent with her story and the smeared blood at the site. He flicked his light in Ed's direction. The kid scowled at him, but he was clean. At least outwardly.

"Not really," Audrey said. "My wrist —"

"I'll get you a first-aid kit." He turned to the car.

"Has anyone found your wife?" Audrey asked. "We looked for —"

"Julie wasn't riding," Jack said.

"I'm glad to hear it." The relief in her voice might have been motivated by guilt.

"Don't get too happy. That blood belongs to someone, and you're covered in it."

Jack went to find the Band-Aids. He felt a prick of irritation that his wife was ignoring his calls.

CHAPTER 5

Audrey sat on the bakery stoop between its twin bay windows, worrying about leaning against the door and transferring blood to the fresh white paint that Geoff had applied a week ago. Then she worried about why she would worry about such a petty thing at a time like this. She might have killed someone.

Closing her eyes, she wished for some sensation that was bigger than fear, some feeling that was deeper than anxiety. She prayed for that weighty supernatural arm to slip across her shoulders, to support her on jelly legs and guide her to the person she'd launched from that scooter. She could help.

She could help. *Please.*

Nothing. Audrey opened her eyes. The tule fog hid everything. *Tule* rhymed with *Julie.* She shivered.

After Jack left her she was questioned yet again by one more investigator who asked her the same questions repeatedly. Someone who was not in uniform took samples of the blood on her arms and photographs of her. She tried to catch Ed's eyes, to affirm with a mother's gaze that everything would be fine, that telling the truth as he saw it was all he needed to do. But they kept him at a distance from her. Geoff, who'd rushed out of the bakery after the crash and had helped her and Ed look for Julie — or whoever — wasn't allowed to talk with her again until she was released from questioning.

Sunrise came around six thirty, but little sunlight reached the scene. This fog might last for days, or it might lift by afternoon if the temperatures warmed enough or another storm rolled through the basin. Audrey couldn't remember the forecast.

An EMT cleaned up her hands and said her wrist didn't appear to be broken, but she should make an appointment to have it x-rayed for fractures. He wrapped the swelling limb and applied antibiotic ointment to the minor cuts from her fall. She would need an HIV test in about six weeks, he explained. She really ought to wait three months, which was the time her body needed to develop the antibodies that would give the most accurate test results. Then the photographer returned with a bag and asked her to give him her bloody clothes.

Numb — her mind stuck on *HIV test* and *still no body* — she started to unbutton her blouse. It was a clumsy effort with her bandaged wrist. She felt Geoff's hand on her shoulder.

"She can have a little privacy for that, can't she?" he said, taking the bag from the investigator, firm but respectful. The man agreed but asked a female officer to go into the bakery with them.

Geoff held the door open. Audrey took off her shoes and dropped them into the bag.

"Our customers shouldn't see that kind of mess," she whispered.

"We'll close up for today," Geoff said.

"No. All that bread! We've got bread, don't we?" She looked up. The racks and cases were nearly full with loaves of the honey oat and semolina and rye, even though Geoff had been out with her for more than an hour.

Her husband nodded and guided her by the elbow toward the hall with the bathrooms. "Estrella came in a half hour ago. She's got everything under control."

"She's so good to us. Look at that." Audrey gestured to the cases full of pastries.

An overweight woman with a clear, silky complexion and thick wavy hair was seated at a table near the window. The bread basket in front of her held a miniature baguette, untouched. The woman's sad eyes were locked on Audrey's horrifying outfit, and Audrey wished she had come in through the back.

"I'm so sorry about this," Audrey said to her.

The woman squinted in the way one does to hold back tears.

Geoff said, "Let me get a blanket from the truck until I can go home and get something for you to change into."

"I'd rather you stayed with Ed. See if Estrella has anything I could borrow?" Audrey placed her hand on the swinging door that led to the bathrooms as Geoff made his way toward the kitchen.

"I have a shirt," someone said. The woman at the table. She was leaning down toward the backpack at her feet. "And some jeans. They're way too big for you, but they're clean."

She rose, unzipping the bag, and pulled out the clothing as she walked toward Audrey, who found herself thinking that this woman was giving her the only other clothes she owned, which was an odd impression to have of a person who parted so easily with her belongings. It might have been the way

68

she clutched the backpack — close to her breast, like a woman on a sinking ship — or the frayed hem of the jeans she wore, or the unwrapped bar of soap that fell out of the pack.

"That's generous of you," Audrey said, hesitating to take the clothes because she was still such a mess. "Are you sure?"

The woman thrust the articles at Audrey, then stooped to pick up the soap. "Maybe you could use a dish towel or string for a belt? I can ask Mr. Bofinger to find something for you."

"Thanks."

"This is a real nice place you got here," she said, walking toward the display cases.

Audrey watched her go, confused by her conflicting impressions of the woman.

In the restroom Audrey stripped down to her bra and panties in front of the policewoman, peeling off her wet clothes and depositing them in the evidence bag. The officer gave her instructions on where the Bofingers would need to go to be fingerprinted, so their prints at the scene could be identified. "Eliminated," the officer said. But Audrey feared they might somehow condemn.

After the woman left with the clothes, Audrey washed off her legs and torso at the sink with hand soap and damp brown paper towels. The weather had flattened her short, dryer-tossed blond hair, making her wide jaw seem wider than usual, and the fluorescent light made her sun-damaged skin seem more deeply lined and blotchy. Or the stress of the morning might account for that. She stared at her reflection for a minute, sensing that her life had just changed in ways she wouldn't comprehend for a long, long time.

A small pain like a cramp poked just under her belly button. She applied pressure to it with her palm for a few seconds, wondering if her period would start early — oddly early — then the feeling passed.

The woman's flannel shirt hung to Audrey's knees and smelled like dryer sheets. Audrey gripped the size 18 pants in a fist at her size 10 waist and went in her stocking feet to find Geoff.

He was standing outside the restroom door with a cup of coffee and a leather belt she recognized as Ed's.

"That's a new look for you," he said, assessing her baggy gear.

"Compliments of our customer."

"Diane Hall. She was at the window before five. I let her in."

"Of course you did." Audrey said it lovingly.

"I gave her a muffin. Estrella gave her the baguette. She needs something else though, something that has nothing to do with food. Don't know what it is."

"Bet you'll have it figured out before she leaves."

"I don't think she's leaving soon. She's been pacing in that corner since the accident. I keep expecting her to bolt, but she just sits awhile, then starts at it again."

Audrey cinched the belt around the jeans, not bothering with the loops on the high waist, and tightened the buckle over the last notch.

"Hopefully we won't have everyone's pants falling down today," she said, referring to her son's style preferences.

"Ed assures me the world is safe from indecent exposure." Geoff handed her the mug. "How are you holding up?"

She held the coffee in her right hand and raised her left, with bandages on the heel. Her fingers quivered slightly. "Still a little shaky. I'm so sorry about the car."

"I'm not worried about the car."

"Jack," she said.

Geoff nodded. "But I haven't seen him since he talked to you."

"The older I get the less I understand what God is up to." Audrey sipped the coffee and found comfort in the bitter warmth. "Did Jack question Ed?"

"I think someone else did that."

"Good. He said Julie wasn't riding that scooter."

"Which is something to be glad about, but . . ."

"But someone is hurt. Somewhere."

"Looks that way. But I was going to say that I don't think anyone knows where Julie is. Still."

Jack might have been lying to her, though that seemed out of character. Audrey studied Geoff's face to gauge how worried he might be by this unexpected encounter with the Mansfields. When the church had unceremoniously booted their family out the front doors at Jack's insistence, Geoff had shaved his head. He never said much about the gesture, and she didn't nose around in it, sensing it to be something between him and God that might be destabilized if she butted in. Besides, she liked the super short shave. He let a month's worth of growth return, then decided to keep the scruffy look and adopted the new style for his face too. And although the less-than-clean-cut statement made him look younger and less troubled by life's conventions, it had the disadvantage of slightly altering expressions Audrey had come to interpret easily over two decades of marriage.

"Here's what we're going to do," she announced. "We're going to go out there and give bagels to Jack's crew. And we're going to be cooperative, model citizens, and we're going to stay open and sell bread and help Ed keep his perspective on the straight and narrow until all of this is resolved."

"Scared, huh?"

"You're the only one allowed to know it."

Geoff pulled her close to him and kissed the top of her head. "Likewise."

"They said I should take an HIV test," she whispered into his chest.

"I heard. But they've got plenty of the same blood to test first. And it won't take them three months to do it. So let's not jump into a river of worry."

"Okay." She took a breath. "Let's go. Maybe we'll attract a crowd of hungry looky-loos."

"Wait." Geoff held on to her, and Audrey smiled. After all these years, prayer was rarely her first thought, which made her all the more grateful for her husband. Geoff prayed over her like a man who wanted nothing more than to protect his wife but knew he'd need God's help to do it. These prayers, which were different from his "pastor prayers," as she called them, were spoken with such a loving combination of faith, intimacy, and affectionate teasing that Audrey embraced them like a sacred form of lovemaking. *This woman you gave me, God,* Geoff would say, an inside joke between them and their Maker, *this woman you gave me deserves the miracles only you can give, and I'm asking you for them on her behalf . . .*

Geoff prayed for her and their son, and for Jack and Julie, which didn't surprise Audrey at all. But then he added this Diane Hall to his list, and that caught her off guard. Still, Geoff often saw things she missed. He prayed for less than a minute, but by the time he finished, some of Audrey's urgent need to keep the world in perfect order had subsided.

They pulled away from each other. "Maybe I should go over to Julie's house, see if she's there," Audrey said. They walked down the hall.

"I'm sure Jack is taking care of all that," he said.

"I'll call her then. Borrow your phone? Mine's still out in the car."

"Do you know her number? Because I don't."

"Maybe Ed knows it." They pushed out

74

the door into the dining room.

"Have times changed that much? Because when I was nineteen, I didn't give a rip about my ex-girlfriends' mothers' phone numbers."

"That's because no one had cell phones back then."

Ed was standing in the arched entry to the kitchen, staring out through the front windows toward the gray morning light like a sleepwalker. Audrey rounded the back of the counter and went to him. "Ed, do you know Julie's phone number?"

He blinked. "What?"

"Julie Mansfield's phone number. Do you know it?"

"Audrey, it's really not a good idea to call," Geoff said.

"It will give me peace of mind, her being okay. And I need to apologize for the bike. She should hear it from me rather than Jack, wouldn't you say?"

"It's not great timing. You two aren't close. Jack is eyeing you for whatever he's going to call this crime. And Ed doesn't know the number."

"Actually, it's only one digit off Miralee's," Ed said, his tone flat. "I guess it's how their family plan worked out."

"There. See?" Audrey reached for the old

phone mounted on the kitchen wall just inside the archway. "Tell me."

Ed recited the number.

"Do you think she'll be more upset that someone stole it," Audrey asked Geoff, "or that I demolished it?"

Behind her Estrella opened an oven door and slid a baking sheet onto the rack. In the dining room a phone rang. The ring tone was particular and unfamiliar, something rhythmic and international, like African drums.

"Just be careful what you say," Geoff advised. "What if the rider was someone she knows?"

She hadn't thought of that. She clicked off the phone to ponder Geoff's wisdom. The ringing in the bakery cut off midtone. It seemed to be coming from Diane's backpack, but if it was, the woman was ignoring her call, staring out the viewless window.

Audrey decided that chances were slim Julie would answer her phone at this hour. Also, if Jack hadn't been able to reach her, Audrey could start to patch things up by leaving a message rather than putting Julie on the spot. Waiting to address matters like this never panned out well. At least, it had ended very badly the last time they put it off.

"I'll just leave something on her voice mail," she told Geoff as she hit the redial button.

Geoff was staring into the dining room, focused on Diane and her untouched baguette. Audrey's call connected.

Diane's backpack started ringing again. Audrey felt an unpleasant flash of heat pass through her stomach. The ringing ended and a recording began. Julie's voice came over the line, and the African drums in the pack ceased their beating.

In that moment, Audrey couldn't think of what she wanted to say to Julie. She hung up and raised her voice. "Is that your phone?"

Diane gasped and turned from the window, one hand on her heart.

Audrey tried not to sound accusatory. "Is that your phone ringing? In your bag?" She pointed to the backpack as she came out of the kitchen, around the counters, and crossed the room. Geoff followed her.

Diane's eyes shifted as if seeking the definition of each word in Audrey's question. "I don't have a phone. Those clothes are really too big for you."

"They're exactly what I needed. You're kind to let me use them."

"Are you sure you don't have a phone?"

Geoff asked.

Diane blinked. "No, what would I — oh." She bent over the pack and unzipped the outside pocket. "I found one on the way here. In the gutter." She fished it out and handed it to Audrey. "I wouldn't even know how to answer it."

Audrey pushed the button and swept her finger over the display. Five missed calls. She quickly found the log. The bakery number appeared twice, and beneath it, the name *Jack,* three times within a half hour of the accident.

"Where did you find it?" Audrey asked.

"A couple blocks that way." Diane pointed down Main Street. "It fell off someone's scooter."

Geoff put both hands on his head and exhaled audibly.

"Does this have something to do with what's going on out there?" Diane asked.

The phone felt heavy in Audrey's hands. She found her eyes darting to the windows, looking for Jack. Without weighing the pros or cons of what she was doing, Audrey quickly deleted the calls from the bakery in the log. She placed the phone in the middle of the round table.

"All that blood . . ." Diane murmured.

The three of them stared at the device.

Geoff said, "I think it would be best for everyone if you give this to the detective yourself, Diane. Would you mind?"

"The detective?" Diane's mystified tone sank into resignation. She lowered herself back onto the chair. "Why should I mind? I guess death just follows some people around."

CHAPTER 6

When the administrator at Mazy High called Jack to see if he knew where Julie was, Jack left the accident scene. He returned to their modest ranch-style home and scanned the low-maintenance yard in the front: a lawn shaped like a kidney bean, juniper bushes under the windows, several old oaks dropping leaves onto the tar-shingle roof, redbrick walls that never needed painting. Behind the windows that faced the street, the curtains were drawn, as always.

The jack-o'-lanterns that Julie's students had carved and presented to her last month, before she took a short medical leave, were sitting on the porch, wrinkled and collapsing in on themselves, toothless old hags. Jack pulled the police cruiser he had borrowed into the driveway and made a mental note to throw them out before they liquefied. Usually his wife took care of such things, but a lot had changed since Miralee left.

The fog had thinned to a mist and floated beneath the trees.

He parked outside the closed garage, exited the car, and punched the security code into the exterior door opener. The familiar whirring hefted the panel and revealed the empty spot where Jack's Jeep would have been if it wasn't still in the shop. Next to this, on the left, the bay for Julie's sedan was also empty.

He sighed, no longer expecting to find her here.

Jack walked to the rear of the garage, which led to the backyard, and began to speculate: *Someone breaks into the shed, steals the scooter parked there. Julie observes from the master bedroom window, decides to follow.* The theory had holes. Julie would have called the precinct. She wasn't at the scene of the scooter disaster.

At the back of the garage, a crooked flagstone path led to the shed, which looked like an old single-car garage with barn doors padlocked shut. No forced entry. Padlock secure.

The phone inside the house was ringing. After the fourth ring the caller was sent to voice mail. Jack stepped onto the flagstones.

A quiet break-in. Julie wouldn't have heard. She gets up, goes to work none the wiser.

She didn't go to work, obviously.

She grabbed coffee with a girlfriend, forgot about the meeting she was supposed to attend before school. Or took a detour to put cheap gas in the car.

That was another habit she needed to change: Why on earth waste gas money by driving great distances to save a nickel? The math didn't work. She of all people should know that.

When was the last time he'd spoken to his wife? He mentally reviewed. Usually she called him when she needed something. When he was deep in a case, checking in with her rarely occurred to him. Had she called him at all yesterday? Now that he thought of it, no. *She's angry with me about the long shift. Ignoring my calls now because she feels ignored.* Julie did that once in a while. Not frequently enough for him to pay much attention to it. Still, that she was doing it now annoyed him. The circumstances were urgent. This was no time for games.

An affair. A plot to run away, start a new life. Casanova drives the scooter, she follows him out of town. Divine justice intervenes and reduces the interloper to a grease spot. She hauls his broken body into her car and —

Though such an offensive scenario might have been supported by Julie's recently chilly behavior, her doctor had suggested she might withdraw for a time after her hysterectomy. Some hormonal side effect. Also, he didn't need a psychiatrist to tell him that Miralee's abandonment had devastated his wife, even though Julie refused to discuss it with him. She was having a rough time, not an affair. There was also the matter of her surgery, which would throw a wet blanket on any sexual flings, and the not-so-small matter of her not being able to lift more than ten pounds for another four weeks.

The Bofingers had been adamant that there were no other parties at the scene, though they had plenty of motivation to lie to him. Well, that wasn't his fault, was it?

On the side of the shed, the key was hidden above the window on its protruding frame. He removed the padlock, swung the white wood door open on its tired hinges, and reached for the string that turned on the light.

Nothing had been disturbed, not even the scents of potting soils for summer window boxes, or gasoline for the mower. Organic mixed with synthetic, damp air and dry earth. Rusting metal tools on a spongy wood floor, untouched dust and spiderwebs, and the clean-swept spot near the door where the blue-and-white Vespa should have been.

There was nothing wrong with this scene at all.

New theory: *More than one thief, careful people who know my wife's habits, like where she keeps this key. Stalkers? They stole both vehicles, because —*

A new possibility for why Julie wasn't answering the phone struck him, so obvious that it should have been the first to occur to him and not the last. He left the shed wide open and cursed himself as he ran back to the house, through the garage, and — the house door was locked. Julie never locked this door, though he admonished her to. His keys snagged on a thread in his pocket and tangled with each other before he got the right one into the keyhole.

His entrance into the kitchen was confused: rush to find Julie or treat the house like a crime scene?

"Julie!"

The refrigerator hummed.

"Julie, are you here?"

Three options: Julie was gone. Julie was here, clinging to life. Julie was here, dead.

The scooter accident had taken place more than three hours ago. If she was still

84

here, she was probably not clinging to life any longer.

Procedure. Method. Don't do anything that will make a loophole for whoever did this.

It was Jack's house. There was no need for him to cover his hands or his shoes. Prints from both would be everywhere, and he could be easily excluded from the evidence.

The kitchen was like the shed, as it always was: the eat-in table empty except for a bowl of fruit and two placemats, though they never ate in here. The dishes cleaned and put away. The counters were tidy but still bearing crumbs from whoever had made the last sandwich. Perhaps Julie, for dinner the night before. Or him, when he packed a lunch two days earlier.

An inch of cold coffee sat in the carafe of the instant coffeemaker, as he had left it Monday afternoon.

Was Julie eating? He opened the cupboard that held the trash can. It held a clean, dry liner. Trash would have gone out yesterday.

He moved into the adjacent living room, scanning quickly for anything out of the ordinary. Carpets flat, furniture sitting squarely in carpet divots, pictures straight on the wall and organized in frames on the shelves. TV remote waiting for him on the end table, magazines in the rack. In the entryway his eyes alighted on the bench. Julie's classwork, organized neatly in a tote bag, sat on the bench. Beside it, her planner, her teacher's edition textbooks, a piece of lined three-ring paper bearing a note. Jack read it without picking it up: *Mrs. M, Thanks for the great opportunity, but I've decided not to do it. Maybe Colin would? I hope you'll understand. −L*

Julie wouldn't have left these behind if she had headed for the school. He didn't see her purse. Jack's pulse was louder in his ears now than his mental insistence that his wife was fine, perfectly fine.

He rushed past the guest bathroom on the left, the den that doubled as a guest room on the right, and only glanced into the bedroom at the end of the hall that was still Miralee's, though she'd vowed never to return. His goal was the master bedroom, which was where Julie was supposed to have been when Audrey's car demolished that bike, when Jack called and called, when the fog was far too thick for anyone to be slashing through it like some jungle adventurer.

The door was nearly closed. Through the inch-wide crack he saw the unmade bed. His fingertips pushed the door open, and it swung freely, silent onto a room deathly still.

The nightstands labeled which side was whose: by the walk-in closet, his Bible, his reading glasses, his alarm clock. He opened the small drawer. His personal firearm was still there. On the other side of the bed, by the window that overlooked the backyard, Julie's table was nearly hidden by notes, earrings, and lotions. Miralee, frozen in a rare smile, looked out at him from a small glittering frame. A tower of novels on the floor leaned toward the wall. Three bottles of pills — antibiotics taken as a precaution to ward off the postoperative infection, a painkiller, and what Julie had said was an anti-inflammatory — stood capped next to a glass of water. Jack thought this third bottle was an antidepressant, though his wife denied it. He ought to finally look it up.

All her clothes and shoes, except for her favorite pair of walking shoes, which she wore almost daily, seemed to be in the walk-in closet. The suitcase stood in the corner. The dresser was full of pants and T-shirts.

Her makeup was spread out on the bathroom counter. The shower stall held droplets of water.

Jack returned to Julie's nightstand, because something about it seemed off. He studied it the way he used to play memory games, which he always won, when he was a kid. It took a minute, but then he figured out what was missing: an ugly old necklace that looked like it had been made by a child, a yellowish rock surrounded by a silver donut.

A neighbor, an aging man whose wife had died recently, gave Julie the piece just a few months ago. The couple had a soft spot for her. She had claimed it was an uncut diamond, to which Jack had said if it was she should trade it up for something more attractive. Instead, she hung it from her lampshade, where the sight of it would rankle him. He understood perfectly: the necklace wasn't even worth its sentimental value.

In the face of its absence, however, his confidence faltered. Could the rock have been a diamond after all?

There was no other sign of anything amiss except his wife's decision — at age forty-two, after twentysome years of responsible, if unspiritual, living — to abandon responsibility and common courtesy for a day.

But this simple possibility failed to explain the scooter accident and the blood and the absence of a body. Jack rubbed his eyes and sat on the edge of the rumpled bed. There would be no rest for him yet, not until he made contact with Julie.

Where to look next?

He glanced at his Bible, the only book he had never been able to convince Julie to read. It was his sorest complaint about her: a close-mindedness to the things of God, and he prayed daily that God would confront her sins head-on. If she could understand the way the world worked, she would be less depressed from time to time. God said it plain as day: live one way and your life will be rewarded, live another way and reap the consequences. It was simple. They lived in a world governed by spiritual rules and regulations that yielded good or bad outcomes, depending on whether one was a follower or a rebel.

Because Jack had chosen the right way to live, he had great faith that one day Julie would come to church with him, sit next to him, and redeem this one mark against him as an elder of the church, namely, that his wife was stubbornly agnostic. Then they would be complete, the way a husband and wife were meant to be, and their lives would be better, because the half of it that was her responsibility would improve.

Jack stood, because if he stayed seated on the mattress a second longer he would sink into it and not wake for a day, or until Julie leaned over him, shaking him by the shoulder because the precinct needed him.

The landline rang again. The closest receiver was in Jack's den. Neither he nor Julie saw the point of a phone in the only place they could protect their sleep. He returned to the den and answered.

"Yeah."

"Jack, this is Ellen Stone again."

"Hi, Ellen. She still not at school?"

"She's not. I thought I'd check one more time before I get a substitute in."

Jack noticed that the office window was open a few inches. His eyes lingered on the gap while he wondered if Julie would have opened this window — she preferred to work on her laptop at the dining room table, not in here — and if she had, whether she would have left it open.

He said, "I'd go ahead and do it if I were you. I'm just home from work, and all her school stuff is still here at the house."

"Oh dear."

"No, no, I'm sure it's nothing. I was just about to call her doctor, see if maybe something came up suddenly, you know, with the surgery and all."

"Of course."

"I'll let you know as soon as I learn something."

"There's a rumor going around that she

was in an accident downtown —"

"Just a rumor. Someone stole her scooter, got in a mess with it in the fog. But she wasn't involved."

"What a relief. For Julie, I mean."

"Thanks, Ellen." There was nothing to be thanked, but it was a good technique for getting out of a conversation while making the other person think they'd contributed something important.

He hung up and reached for his computer's power button.

The machine was already turned on, though he always turned it off before shifts. Julie had her own laptop. The monitor came alive after he jiggled the mouse.

A document was open on the screen, untitled and unsaved, a sheet of electronic paper, blank except for one sentence: *Some crimes never see justice.*

Jack lowered himself onto the chair. The proclamation was caffeine on his brain. Only a few months ago these words had come from his very own mouth. He spoke them of Geoff Bofinger, on the day he convinced the elder board that their pastor had violated his promise to be their spiritual leader and should be sent away.

The crime: the taking of a human life. When that predator Ed took advantage of

Miralee and got her pregnant, it was Geoff who had given her the money for an abortion. The arrogant man abused his power, thought he could save his son's face, avoid a scandal, send Miralee away. But those spiritual laws that governed the universe could not be denied, and Jack learned the truth the day he found Miralee sobbing on the bed in her room, days before she left Cornucopia.

Some crimes never see justice, he had said to the elders. The seduction of his only child and the murder of his grandbaby would never be prosecuted in this world's courts. He had pointed to Geoff at the head of the table where they had gathered and said, *But that doesn't free us from our moral responsibilities.*

The Bofingers were released from their duties at the church within the week.

The cursor blinked at the end of the line.

Jack reached for his keyboard, then hesitated. Whoever had typed this might have left prints. He glanced at the open window. He would dust that too. Out in the garage he had the powders and brushes he needed from an old kit.

He got up to retrieve these items, then stopped in the doorway. Procedure. What was the best way to close all the loopholes on the monster who had broken into his home and done something to his wife? Sitting here dusting his own keyboard was not it. Someone else could do that for him. He pulled out a phone and placed a call to Rutgers. Jack needed to be out there looking for Julie. Who better than he to bring her back into the safety of his leadership and spiritual shelter?

He had a pretty good idea where to start the search.

CHAPTER 7

Diane had been on her way to liking Geoff, because of his strange decency toward her, but when he told her she would have to give that cell phone to the police officer in charge of the investigation, she wondered if that was his way of telling her he regretted his kindness. Couldn't he see the problem? Couldn't he understand how a police officer would view her, a killer in possession of a missing woman's phone?

She had found her way back to this heartbreak home of hers for only one reason, and that was not so she could return directly to jail. *Do not pass Go, because you are so pathetic you can't even make it one time around the block without getting into trouble. Do not collect two hundred dollars, because you are worthless and undeserving of everything, including your measly hope.*

Though true and familiar, the thoughts angered her as she sat at her little table in the warm corner of the bakery while customers came in and out, gossiping about the accident and finding excuses to linger. Then she decided that her anger was actually about the prospect that she would have to leave this place sooner than she wanted, while what she needed was directly upstairs. So close.

She wondered when the policeman might come inside. Geoff said he would come in to speak to them again before he left, but it seemed the man had already gone. It was after eight o'clock now, and still she had not worked up her nerve to run.

Would *anyone* believe her story, that she had seen the phone fall off the scooter and slide toward the street gutter several blocks away from the accident? Would a detective believe that she had picked it up thinking she could give it back? Would he believe that she didn't even know how to use it?

Of course not.

Diane watched Geoff move back and forth between the kitchen and bakery, filling baskets and slicing loaves of bread. A cute little Mexican grandma ruled the kitchen as if it were her castle. Geoff's son, a handsome athletic type, worked the register, and the wife Audrey made coffee, still wearing Diane's bulky clothes.

Diane wondered about the wife, who had done something to the phone after realizing whose it was but then failed to wipe it off. Bright-shiny device like that was a fingerprint database! Her own prints were visible to the naked eye on the edges where she'd so gingerly handled it. Even Diane knew what to do about *that.* Geoff hadn't touched the thing, then made the mistake of trusting that she would turn it over to the detective on her own.

When was the last time someone had trusted her?

Audrey had seemed startled by the discovery of the phone, and Geoff seemed to be anticipating a disaster he could not prevent. Whatever catastrophe those two were headed toward, she couldn't afford to become entangled.

The detective's failure to appear became a sign to her that she could choose her next steps of her own free will. She'd given him a fair amount of time to show up.

At eight fifteen there were half a dozen customers in the store. When she believed she could leave unnoticed, Diane picked up the phone and used the cotton T-shirt under her sweater to wipe down the edges where she'd handled it. She put her uneaten baguette into her backpack. The tissue liner in her basket was a tiny bit greasy. She shook out the crumbs and wrapped the phone in it, then set the bundle in the pack next to the baguette.

Without the clothes, her burden was light. She left the bakery quickly and slipped into the fog, which was less dense now. The moist air would do what it wished, and though science could explain some of it, no one could control it. She moved away from the scene of the accident. She had planned not even to look at it, but then she thought that ignoring it so totally might be more suspicious than a quick glance.

She looked without seeing. Counted *one, two, three,* then returned to her straight-ahead march.

Five doors down from the bakery storefront there was an alley access through a parking lot on the other side of the watch repair shop. At least it had been a watch repair shop when she and Donna last used the shortcut. Diane had no idea what it was now and didn't care enough to look when she passed it. Her breathing and her pace were too fast. She needed to concentrate on measuring both, even if the fog did shield her somewhat from anyone who happened to be looking.

It was longer for her to go this way, but

safer, farther away from the accident that the baker's wife had caused.

Diane passed through the shadowy parking lot and made her way to the back of the buildings, where she emerged into the alley. In the center of the passage, halfway between where she was and the bakery, was a storm drain with a grate on it that had swallowed many of her precious quarters and Super Balls over the years. Once Donna had even crammed her sister's ice-cream sandwich down the drain, petty revenge for Diane's failure to return a favorite pair of jeans. A bully had ruined them when he ambushed her with a paint gun.

The grate was plenty airy enough to accept a cell phone that was smaller than a deck of cards.

The risen sun still hadn't found its way over the tops of the buildings that shared the alley. But the light was gray enough and her memory vivid enough to allow her to proceed.

Her foot left asphalt and landed on metal exactly where she expected. She knelt, lowered her pack, and unzipped it before she realized that the sieve-like grate had been replaced sometime in the past two and a half decades by a solid manhole cover.

Diane swore.

The cover would not come up. Of course it wouldn't. Not without a hook or a magnet or whatever newfangled thing they used these days to pry metal disks out of the street.

She swore again, and stood, then yelped when a soft weight pressed against her leg. A skinny old cat rubbed its body across her ankles and mewed. Diane shoved it away. "Shoo."

The tabby's affection vanished and he marched off, his erect tail snooty.

She had other options. There were plenty of Dumpsters bordering the alley, though some had locked covers or sat behind secure enclosures. But a Dumpster was not the brightest spot to leave evidence while police were still scrutinizing a scene, and she had no idea when trash pickup was.

She hated the idea of carrying the phone with her longer than she already had. She hated the idea of walking any farther with it and risking being seen, stopped, questioned.

When Geoff noticed she was gone, would he send the detective looking for her? Would he give the officer a description? *Fat chick, dull red hair, middle-aged, ate all my bread and took off without paying me . . .*

An idea came to Diane. A smart idea. She dropped the phone into her backpack and then proceeded down the alley, approaching the rear entrance of the shop adjacent to the bakery. It had something that the bakery did not: a flight of fixed metal stairs that led to its upstairs rooms.

When Diane and Donna were about fourteen, Donna started using that fire escape to sneak out of the apartment when it was necessary for her to be somewhere without their parents' permission. Their own "balcony" had a rusted ladder that was too noisy for a rebel teen who needed to go undetected, but the gap between balcony to neighboring landing was only about five feet — easy enough for an agile teenager to bridge.

Donna was the agile one. Diane, fifty pounds heavier than her twin sister even then, had tried the route only once and nearly broke her neck. Today, in the gray morning light of neediness, a much older and heavier Diane thought the gap looked smaller than she remembered.

The exterior metal stairs were shaded with an orange hue from years of sitting in moist air. They complained about her weight, and her shoes made clumsy noises on the metal steps. Diane feared she'd be heard before she made it even halfway up.

And yet she reached the landing without anyone shouting at her, demanding to know who she was and what she was doing — the same demands bouncing around in her own head.

The moisture that had accumulated on the railing was more dangerous than her foolish ideas. She wiped it off with the sleeve of her sweater, then centered the backpack between her shoulder blades and climbed up on the skinny piece of metal, first one knee, then one slippery tennis shoe at a time. This would have been impossible without the rain gutter that ran down the side of the building. She held on to the hollow tube for balance and managed to get to her feet.

Her weight was hard to center. She had visions of herself slipping off the banana-peel rail and plummeting, or of managing to jump but slamming into the outside of the other balcony. Five feet was suddenly five miles.

Think about it, girl. You're five six. All you have to do, really, is tilt.

She envisioned taking a hit to her midsection, which would be unpleasant regardless of her fleshy padding, or to her jaw, which would likely knock her unconscious. She imagined actually making it into the center of the balcony and then cracking her skull open when she toppled into the rail on the opposite side.

She never had been very good at the positive-thinking, motivational stuff.

Diane jumped without slipping but didn't have enough vertical height to make it to safety inside the other rail. Her knees clipped the outside on her way down, and she felt her toes grab the rim and then pop off as she fell. Eyes closing, head snapping sideways, belly scraping, fingers clawing at air. One elbow hit the side of the building and then her armpits stopped her fall, a jarring emergency brake that brought her teeth down on her tongue. The reverberating noise was ridiculous. She hung there, the pain in her shoulder muscles oozing down her torso and her arms. She smelled the damp metal of the rusty rail. The chill of it stabbed through her clothes in time with her gasping.

Any second now, the spotlight of discovery would cut through the mist and shine on her incompetence.

After a few seconds of frantic jerks, her dangling feet found the balcony's lip and her quivering legs received enough adrenaline to get her up and over into safety, gracelessly as ever. She fell onto her side, her fleshy cheek imprinted by the metal grid of the platform. The backpack shifted.

She heard a tumbling, and a clatter, and got onto hands and knees in time to see the liner-wrapped phone shoot out between two of the bars, chased by *The God of Small Things.* Diane grasped for the backpack behind her to keep the money from falling out too.

A Dumpster beneath the balcony received the phone, barely catching it at the front corner beside a flour sack recycled as a trash bag. The noise startled the tabby cat, who was nosing around the bakery's back door. He made a four-pawed jump to dodge the book, which bounced off the rim of the bin and slapped closed where he'd been standing.

Diane stared, trying to assess what her separation from these two items might mean and whether she needed to get them back. No one knew the book was hers. It didn't even have her name in it. If the phone were discovered, though, Geoff and Audrey would know that it had been in her possession. The Dumpster outside the bakery was the worst possible place for that to have ended up.

Worst for whom? For the Bofingers, not for her. She was merely an innocent by-stander. They were the parties who were truly involved in the mess on the intersection. Should she care about that? On some level, some selfish level, she had to. She needed the Bofingers to be her friends, so she would try to remedy the latest problem she'd created as soon as she could. In the meantime, she'd focus on this window, which led into the room she and Donna had shared as children. It was an old wood window with so much dry rot in the sash that the lock had fallen out of it, yet one more convenience for Donna's adolescent comings and goings. Their parents had never felt the urgency to replace the lock, considering the window's location.

The morning traffic rose in volume on the street. She heard conversations and police radios.

Donna lifted her fingers to the screen.

She groaned.

This window never had a screen, this . . . vinyl window . . . these sliding panes . . . with not one but two locks.

God, will you never answer any prayer that I have ever prayed? Will you never make a way for me to undo the things I wish I'd never done? Are you so heartless that you'll keep sabotaging me every step of the way?

Diane sagged, not expecting God to answer at all, but certainly not to answer in the voice of grinding gears and shifting hydraulics. At the far end of the alley, the lights of a commercial trash truck were jostled as the beast tipped a Dumpster into its upturned mouth, filling the narrow passage with the sounds of bouncing cans and breaking glass.

It wasn't God, of course. Not really.

Her attention snapped back to the waist-high window. She lifted her foot to the side not covered by the screen. She had enough room to hit the pane square on, and forcefully. She had enough body weight to put some power behind a good kick. She'd spent enough time in prison to know what a good kick was.

The truck would need a minute to arrive. She had only one chance, maybe two, to make this work.

Diane reached into the backpack and transferred the few remaining items from the center compartment into the smaller surrounding pouches. Then she shoved her foot inside the bag and zipped the sides up to her thick leg to prevent it from getting cut. She waited for the truck to arrive beneath her, hoping that the driver would stay put in his cab while the automated arms did their work, oblivious to her.

The truck's complaints were louder directly under her than they had been down the street, so loud that she considered kicking even before the dump. The Dumpster creaked as it came off the ground. She failed to make up her mind in time for a decision to matter.

When she heard bags starting to slide, she kicked dead center in the pane of glass.

And bounced off.

Trash was raining into the truck. She stole a look downward. The old Dumpster was rusted through the bottom in three spots.

She focused her mind on her heel, instructed it to go *through* the glass.

Diane kicked again and the pack penetrated. Glass daggers fell into her old bedroom and snagged the backpack as she withdrew her leg. She thrashed a little, losing her balance and falling back against the balcony rail. A few pieces of glass fell to the ground below, shattering.

Two more swift kicks took out most of the shards before the Dumpster was set again to rest. By this time Diane had her leg out of the backpack and her hand inside it. She used the leatherlike reinforced seat of the pack like a glove and swiftly wiped out the remaining glass before the trash truck pulled out of the alley onto Main Street and turned left.

The sour smell of neglect rushed out of the closed-up space, trying to get away.

CHAPTER 8

The first time Audrey had felt the arm of God encircle her shoulders, during their first winter in the Great Central Valley, she and Geoff were baking bread.

They baked bread every Tuesday because it was something they had done together since the early years of their marriage. It was an easy habit to maintain, Tuesdays falling when the church office closed and complaints about the Sunday sermon from the dear hangnails and bunions of their precious "body" had been addressed. Audrey loved the members of Grace Springs Church because they were so unapologetic about their own humanity. On the downside, her role as the pastor's wife seemed like an eternal, unsatisfied audition for the part of June Cleaver.

It took Geoff and Audrey most of the day to bake whatever variety they'd chosen for the week: whole wheat or peasant bread or semolina rounds or sourdough-rye. Ed understood that he was on his own for breakfast and lunch and could enter the kitchen on Tuesdays only after his parents had left it. They rose before the crickets stopped chirping, weighed and kneaded the ingredients, then made coffee in the French press. They carried coffee mugs and walked up and down the rows of the hundred-acre orange orchard behind the parsonage while the yeast did its early work on the dough.

Yeast, Audrey thought, didn't get much good press in the Bible, so she particularly liked Jesus' singular comparison: "The kingdom of heaven is like yeast that a woman took and mixed into a large amount of flour until it worked all through the dough." A good thing, a wonderful thing, a small creation doing great and wide work.

In San Francisco, land of the American sourdough, rumor had it that some commercial bakeries used a yeast starter that had been in existence for more than 150 years. Surely that represented "a large amount of flour."

The words were recorded in Matthew, right after Jesus' remark about the greatness of faith no bigger than a mustard seed, the tiniest of seeds. But yeast, though the disciples couldn't know and science wouldn't be able to explain for another eighteen hundred years, was smaller still: a living, single-celled organism destined to have far-reaching effects. Set in motion by the sensitive fingertips of a woman, no less.

Geoff allowed her the pleasure of getting feminine credit for this. Every Tuesday, their personal sabbath, God's sense of humor and his promises restored them both.

They would return from their walk, punch down the massive glob of dough, and divide it into crude loaves. Then the dough rested, and so did they. Everyone ought to have such recovery time after a pounding, Audrey always thought. The lumps took a nap under kitchen towels, and they returned to bed, stealing half an hour of bliss before their son rolled out of bed and placed his feet on the floor for the day.

Then they gave the loaves their final, intentional shape and ran their empty dishwasher through a rinse cycle, turning it into a miniature sauna. When it finished, they set the loaves inside on a special rack Geoff had made to fit, then closed the door for a final proofing. They preheated the tile-lined ovens, one in the kitchen and, in the garage, two from a refurbished-appliances store. Audrey read the day's headlines aloud while Geoff scored the loaves — her cuts were clumsy and unartistic — just before they'd doubled in size. While she flipped pages he spritzed the ovens' interiors with water, and then the bread baked.

In spite of Audrey's stealing credit for working yeast into the dough, the art of creating bread was Geoff's passion and skill. There was something very biblical and sexy about that ability, Audrey thought. Not everyone could make golden, weightless loaves out of flour, water, salt, and yeast. And though she loved every moment alongside her husband in the close quarters of their kitchen, her love of food had more to do with feeding people.

She planned the evening meal around the scent of rising bread as if it were wine worthy of a perfect pairing. Dense millet-and-oat loaves called for hearty vegetable stew, glossy rosemary-buttermilk dinner rolls for fish, torpedo-shaped Vienna rolls for leftover-turkey sandwiches. This was the family's California-style, midweek Sunday dinner.

Audrey and Geoff had been installed at the Grace Springs church for two months the first time she felt the weight of God on her neck. The sensation was peaceful and warm, and she stopped fashioning the loaf between her palms to experience rather than examine the moment. She closed her eyes and took a deep breath, and then a stabbing headache and upending dizziness took her to the floor, where she blacked out for a few seconds.

According to Ed, who was fourteen at the time and interested in his parents' hobby in the coolly detached way of adolescent boys, she swiped the bread board off the counter when she fell. He rushed in at the sound, helped his dad bring her around, then assured them that he could handle the bread's final stages while Geoff took Audrey to the ER.

The attending physician told her she had high blood pressure, which she didn't believe for a second, and also that she would have a nice bruise on her right knee where she hit the corner of the cabinets on her way down. He gave Audrey a prescription for the hypertension and instructions to see her physician the next day. Geoff made the appointment for her on their way home, against her protests.

When they arrived at the house, three gorgeous *boulé* loaves of blond-colored Tuscan bread were cooling on the counter, and Ed was watching TV as if he'd done nothing remarkable at all. Audrey gave him a double helping of her garlic-white-bean soup at dinner, which was interrupted by a phone call from one of the church members.

Mrs. Dawson asked Geoff to come sit with her husband, who had been hospitalized after a heart attack, a complication of his high blood pressure.

Audrey blinked at this news and let her spoon sink slowly into her soup. "Take the Dawsons a loaf of the bread," Audrey said to Geoff, rising from the dinner table to wrap one up and wonder. "The Tuscan is made without salt — it'll pass muster with his doctors. Tell them Ed made it. They'll love that."

Audrey took the other loaf to her own doctor the next day. She'd hoped it would be something of a joke to lighten her disbelief in her own diagnosis.

"But this is salt-free bread!" she insisted, holding out the loaf to him when he came into the room. "There's no way I can have hypertension."

"I'll second that," he said, looking at her chart. "Your blood pressure is as low as any athlete's."

This was confusing news. "Then how . . . ?"

"Probably stress," he said. "You're new to town, new to the church. Family-size transitions take a toll on go-getters like you. We've seen anxiety mimic hypertension like this from time to time."

"I haven't felt stressed at all. And yesterday I was *baking.* For me, that's like getting a day off. It *was* our day off. From the church."

"Try to pay attention, then, or fluke events like that can become a regular thing. Thanks for the bread. It'll get the wife and me through a few meals without going to the store. She's off her feet for a while — had a misstep yesterday and injured her knee."

For five years the Bofingers baked bread and Audrey tried to pay attention. Not to the high blood pressure, which never reared its head again, but to God's leading with a gentle touch, especially while baking.

Most of the time she felt the way she always did. Content, focused, and accomplished at the end of the day. After the blood-pressure incident she talked Geoff into making six batches instead of only three. It was important for her to be giving more of their bread away. She'd put up two loaves for her family, then slip the other four into muslin pouches, tie them off with colorful grosgrain ribbon, and decide whom to give them to.

Sometimes she knew who'd receive them

long before she got to this stage. During a sleepless night she thought of Katie Thompson, who was taking care of four children during her husband's third deployment. That morning Geoff and Audrey made sweet sugar-dusted stollen for the Thompsons and three other families with young kids. After twisting her ankle during one of the Tuesday morning walks, she limped home thinking of Billy James, her son's basketball teammate who'd torn a ligament in his ankle and been sidelined for the season. She and Geoff made cinnamon rolls for the team, and a dozen just for Billy. One winter morning when the fog was so thick it was unsafe to wander in the orchard, the gloom filled Audrey with an irrational sadness, and she thought of Richard Mickey, whose wife had passed the week before, the day before their forty-fifth anniversary. Geoff agreed to help her make loaves of dense multigrain sunflower bread that day, heavy and sustaining, because that's how sadness felt to her. She gave Richard two loaves divided into six freezer bags for him to eat when his appetite returned.

Come Tuesday evenings, she grew used to sitting in warm kitchens or on breezy back porches sipping whatever drink had been offered, talking one-on-one with people who never seemed to lack for words when there was a loaf of bread sitting between them.

Geoff knew about these places where it seemed her life intersected with others. Except for the sure sensation that the Lord was guiding her, she might have feared she was looking for connections that didn't actually exist. But Geoff called her sensitive, and admiration filled his voice when he said it.

For five years the kingdom of heaven was like the life she had. And then it changed.

In March, when Cora Jean Hall's grief over the old family portrait had become her own, Audrey took a step back. After that, she entered a person's pain only from a safe distance. She realized she was doing it, but she felt helpless to fully engage. She was kind, a good listener, and that should be enough. For her own well-being she needed to hold suffering at arm's length.

Then in June, Jack accused Geoff of the unthinkable. On the Tuesday after the church body took a public, nearly unanimous vote asking Geoff to step down, the couple rose at their usual time because it seemed dangerous to avoid doing what filled them with hope and pleasure. They made a dark sourdough rye in the morning, the usual six loaves, and Audrey silently prepared corned beef for supper.

That night, Ed didn't touch the food on his plate. Geoff ate only politely. Spontaneously, as sometimes happened around a basket of bread, they took calm turns asking questions none of them had dared ask during the prior week, because of the heartbreak the answers would cause.

Geoff said to his son, "Was the baby yours?"

Ed leaned on his elbows and covered his eyes with his hands. "I think so."

Geoff nodded, and a ball of chewed bread jammed deep in Audrey's throat.

"Did you know Miralee wanted an abortion?" Geoff asked.

Ed shook his head. "Not until after she'd done it. Spring break. She didn't even tell me about the baby until after the fact."

"That's why your grades took such a hit in the last quarter," Audrey said, understanding something that had perplexed her for months.

Ed exhaled noisily. The slide had cost him his planned entrance to the state university. "I'm really, really sorry."

Geoff said, "Why didn't you tell us?"

"I thought . . . I don't know what I thought." Then after a minute, "I thought it wouldn't ever affect anyone but me." Still unable to make eye contact with his parents, Ed asked his father, "Is it true, what Miri said? Did you pay for it?"

"No."

Audrey never again wondered how Jack had been able to produce a cancelled personal check made out to Miralee Mansfield and signed by Geoff in the exact amount charged by the clinic to end the baby's life. Asking how it had happened seemed both unanswerable and pointless. Audrey wept for her son, and for the grandchild she'd never know.

It was harder to feel sorrow for the baby's mother. Audrey felt the pain of injustice run like a spear through her husband's career, through his very heart. And hers.

Audrey believed Geoff. And Ed. Someone was lying, but not anyone under her roof, and that was all that really mattered at the time. She wasn't so sure that the men of her household had the same faith in each other though.

That night, no one returned Audrey's voice-mail messages asking what might be a good time for her to stop by to deliver a loaf. She felt foolish for having called at all.

The following week they made only two loaves of whole-wheat sandwich bread and, during their walk through the orchard, decided to give God as much time as he needed to point them in a new direction. She would support this by looking for a job. While the sandwich loaves proofed in the dishwasher, she browsed Craigslist, which took her to a most unexpected venue: the old Yummy Crumb bakery had filed for bankruptcy, and the bank was looking for a new owner.

By September the Bofingers owned it, in part because Audrey dropped everything in order to present Geoff and God with a seven-year business plan explaining how it would work.

"Okay," Geoff said after she'd spread all the papers in front of him at their dining room table and walked him through each one.

"Okay? Just *okay?* You don't need to pray about it first?"

"Already did." The sad countenance he'd been wearing since the excommunication was overtaken by a grin.

"When?"

"When we stopped baking."

And that was when Audrey realized she and her husband hadn't placed any bread pans into their ovens for more than three weeks.

"We did, didn't we?" She laughed. "Didn't

mean to scare you."

Geoff said, "I'll recover. Where do I sign?"

In Audrey's opinion the bakery would have been the end of them all if not for the good business sense of Estrella Torres. Geoff had the entrepreneurial spirit that had informed his vision as a minister, plus magic fingers that could turn any grain into life-sustaining food, and Audrey had the passion of a caregiver, but it was Estrella's crazy obsession with perfection that convinced customers to forgive the Yummy Crumb's spotted past of weak coffee and dry pastries and tough loaves.

They found Estrella when they found her husband, Cesar, a local wheat farmer who also milled his grain and agreed to sell it to the Bofingers for a reasonable price. At the time Estrella worked for a commercial bakery that sold bread to retailers throughout the valley and Southern California.

"You are *loco*," she had sternly warned Audrey after their introduction to each other lasted more than an hour. When the Bofingers told Estrella they proofed their loaves in the humid dishwasher, the grandmother threw her hands in the air.

"Thees bakery thing ees no hobby. Commercial baking ees not what you do at

120

home. A dishwasher! Where ees your controlled temperature — you let the water heater do that? How can bread rise nice and slow in such heat? You get different result every time. Bread is an art, yes, but a successful bakery ees a science, *sí?* You do what works, you follow the formulas, you sell bread. You can do art in your spare time, which you will not have. You learn what you can, you make new bread. But you don't sell thees new bread, no. You don't sell it until you can turn it into a formula."

"Maybe we're in over our heads," Audrey admitted.

"Ah, no no no. Your Geoff has good talent. And you have the right amount of crazy to make thees work! When I call somebody *loco,* ees a compliment. But you need help. You want help? My employer doesn't want my best help. He wants me to be just robot. I have my own head, *sí?*"

Audrey said to her husband, "I think we need to hire her away."

"Can we afford her?"

"We can afford two full-time employees," Audrey said. "I think she's worth two."

CHAPTER 9

On the foggy Wednesday in November just after Audrey collided with Julie Mansfield's scooter, Estrella tried to show her the proper technique for laying fuel in the wood-fired oven. Audrey had wanted to learn for some time, mainly to lighten her employee's load, but had she known what the morning would hold, she would have picked a different day.

Estrella saw no point in postponing the work when there was little else for Audrey to do.

"Thees will take your mind off things," Estrella said, pushing a wheeled bin full of oak wood to the far side of the kitchen where the oven stood. "A hundred thirty pounds of fuel for our oven, no more, no less."

"I feel like I should be helping outside," Audrey said, hiking up Diane's pants, unwilling to leave the bakery for something as unimportant as a change of clothes. Her husband and son were here. Jack was out there. It was warm in this bakery kitchen, and safe.

"They haven't found the person who was riding the scooter," Audrey rambled. "It's been hours. I should help look."

"And what can you do, *mija?* Are you better than police? Are you police dog?"

"No, but —"

"No! You are not — you are *baker.* Or will be when you learn thees oven. Your Geoff ees already good at it. So here." Estrella gathered twigs the size of breadsticks and handed them to Audrey. "You stay with us, watch over your family until police tell you what else you can do. If you don't, they will be angry."

Audrey couldn't disagree.

The jazzy choreography of wood-fired baking was quite different from the breezy waltzing that the Bofingers did around their little ovens at home. The wide brick structure with the small mouth was a complement to the bakery's industrial ovens, but because of its demanding nature, they used it only a couple of times a week. To run the oven, someone had to rise in the dead of night, build the fire, wait three hours for it to heat the bricks to 800° and then burn to ash, and then have the right dough ready at the right time for baking while the residual heat dissipated across the hours.

"We build fire today just for example," she said to Audrey, "and then later I teach you the rhythm of getting the doughs ready at the right time. That ees much harder than building a fire."

"It's complicated," Audrey murmured.

"You only *think* ees complicated. Really, bread is simple — water, flour, salt, yeast. But you say, 'How many ways can four ingredients go wrong?' Too many! Even so, we make them work, and when we do, we see that nothing in life ees really so complicated after all. Ees a matter of paying attention."

"Paying attention to what?" Audrey said, noting Estrella's choice of words.

"What you mean, 'what?' What you think? Time and temperature, technique, good ingredients —"

"You were talking about life."

"No, I was talking about bread."

"You said *life* gets less complicated."

Estrella raised her eyebrows as if her friend had dared confuse the conversation on purpose, and this made Audrey laugh.

"Okay, let's play with fire," she said.

"*Sí.*" Estrella ignored the log she'd given

124

to Audrey and fished a handful of dry tinder, pine fire starter, and sticks out of the side of the bin. She piled these together in the mouth of the oven and then lit the crude haystack with a match. "You no build it all at one time, like ees your fireplace at home, right? We start small, like Rise and Shine. We do just a few things, and we do them better than anyone else, and then we grow."

She blew gently until the tinder had shriveled into glowing red curlicues, and flames tickled the twigs. With the patience of an artist, and while moving bread in and out of the conventional ovens, Estrella allowed the fire to swell and burn down into a bed of glowing charcoal. Then she grabbed a rod like a poker, but with a rectangular plate welded to the end, and pushed the burning pile into the center of the oven.

"Now bigger," Estrella instructed, motioning for Audrey's collection of logs that were about two to three inches in diameter. Estrella stacked these atop the coals and fed the fire until Audrey could see it was ready for the baguette-sized logs in the bin, and then the ones as large as torpedo loaves.

The flames licked the higher bricks and made them sooty. Soon the other bricks closer to the floor began to turn white-hot.

"We let thees burn down," she instructed.

"And when that ees done we will sweep out the ash and seal in the heat." Estrella pointed to a removable wood door that was soaked in water. The temperature of the oven would be measured up high at the flue. It would be a hundred degrees hotter there than on the floor of the oven. When the logs burned to ashes and were ready to be cleared out for the bread, that floor would be around 600°. This fire was the most satisfying source of the bakery's warmth.

Ed passed them, hauling a bag of trash out to the Dumpster in the alley.

"You just missed them," Audrey said. "I heard the truck a few minutes ago."

"I'm sure it'll keep until next week."

He placed his backside against the crash bar on the rear door and pushed it open. Audrey saw Jack Mansfield standing outside before Ed did.

"Geoff," she called in the direction of the register, where her husband was taking a customer's order. She caught his eye and motioned to the door. Then to Ed, "Go take the counter."

By the time Geoff reached her at the back, she was holding Ed's trash bag and evaluating Jack's expression. Jack was hard to read even before their families had clashed. Afterward, he'd become downright hard-boiled, in Audrey's opinion. Now it appeared he was one degree away from boiling over.

A black-and-gray striped cat darted through Audrey's legs before she could move to stop it. The stray had been showing up regularly since Estrella started putting down bowls of cream for it.

"Estrella, your cat," she called into the kitchen as she passed Jack to throw away the trash. Geoff caught the door as it drifted closed behind her. Glass under her sneakers made a grinding sound. She tossed the bag into the hollow Dumpster. The boom of it landing resounded in the alley.

Geoff said, "Front door's open to you. No need to lurk back here."

"No one's lurking." Jack pointed upward. "Saw that on my way in. Came back to have a peek."

Audrey craned her neck. The window in the upstairs apartments, which they used for storage at present, was missing one of its panes.

"That must have happened recently," she said.

Estrella appeared at the kitchen door and tossed the cat outside. He rushed back in, eluding her outstretched hands.

"When was the last time you were up

there?" Jack asked.

Audrey looked at Geoff. "This morning, first thing," he said.

"I'll have a look around, see if anything's missing, damaged."

Jack made a move as if to walk into the bakery, but Geoff stepped out and let the door behind him close before Jack reached it.

"No need. You've got more important things to do right now. We'll take a look when things slow down in here."

Jack crossed his arms, still looking upward. "I'd hate to see you two be the victims of a crime, after all you've already lost."

Audrey held her tongue. If someone had turned her husband's car into an oil spot on the road and *he* were missing, she'd be a little cranky too.

"Because some crimes never see justice, do they, Geoff?"

"So you've said," Geoff answered. Audrey cringed.

"It's a catchy truth," Jack said. "Thought you might have picked it up and claimed it as your own."

"What?"

"Throwing my words back at me now, are you?" Jack asked.

Geoff cleared his throat. "I'm not sure

what you're saying."

"I think we understand each other."

"No, I'm afraid we don't."

" 'The Lord is known by his acts of justice; the wicked are ensnared by the work of their hands.' "

Audrey shivered at the sound of scripture coming from Jack's mouth. The words were right, but they sounded backward. A threat to her husband instead of a thanks to God.

Geoff said, "I can imagine how concerned you are for your wife —"

"No, you can't. Don't suggest that you know what's on my mind while this conniving, reckless woman stands right next to you."

"Don't talk about my wife that way, Jack."

"Don't talk about *my* wife then, unless it's to tell me where she is."

"How could we possibly know?"

Jack turned his face to the sky and opened his arms. " 'Lord, who may dwell in your sanctuary? Who may live on your holy hill? He whose walk is blameless and who does what is righteous, who speaks the truth from his heart, who does his neighbor no wrong, and despises a vile man.' " He pointed a finger at Geoff. "You, Plain Geoff, are a vile man. And I have never spoken anything but the truth."

Geoff shook his head at Jack's pointed insult.

Audrey stepped closer to Jack and laid a hand on his arm. "Tell us what we can do, Jack. How can we help? You came by here for a reason."

"Which of your prints am I going to find on the keyboard in my home office? Yours?" He shook off her hand. "Or yours, Geoff?"

"We've never been inside your home," Audrey said, and a vision of the day she had walked across the Mansfield lawn popped into her mind's eye.

"Come back inside, Audrey. When he has something more substantive to talk about, he'll be back, I'm sure."

It seemed impossible that she could feel sorry for this man who had made their family suffer so much, but at the moment she believed he was only acting out of his own anxiety. The gray smudges under his eyes seemed dark and drooping today, like his mouth. She credited Geoff's graciousness for preventing her from speaking to Jack's mean delusions with devastating retorts, because plenty were stockpiling in the back of her mind. Geoff opened the door, and she stepped across the threshold.

A phone rang with music like drums. Audrey spun toward the sound.

Jack was walking briskly to the Dumpster as if he expected Geoff or her to intercept him.

He hefted himself up over the lip, enough to lean into the nearly empty can and retrieve the bag Audrey had dumped. The phone stopped ringing. Jack threw the sack on the ground, leaned over it, and pulled the sides apart.

Trash scattered in the alleyway as Jack shook the mess out.

He kicked around in it with his shoe, and when he didn't see what he was looking for, he returned to the bin, looked inside again, then leaned against the outside until it shifted on its rusty wheels and rolled a foot or so away from its original position.

An object wrapped in paper lay on the ground. One long side had been torn, peeled back just enough to reveal a glossy black phone. Audrey recognized it as the one Diane had pulled out of her backpack. She looked at Geoff, questioning, and he shook his head.

Estrella appeared at the door holding a bowl of cream. The cat, tucked under her opposite arm, was already lapping at it. She set them both down in the alley and glanced at Audrey, then at Jack, before slipping back inside.

Jack withdrew his own phone and placed a call requesting someone with a camera. After he hung up, he pulled a paper-thin glove from his pocket and slipped his right hand into it. The material snapped at his wrist. He crossed an arm across his midsection and propped his elbow on it, striking a pose of thoughtful curiosity.

He mocked them, Audrey thought. They should tell him about Diane.

"What's your explanation for this?" Jack said.

Audrey's lips parted, but Geoff spoke first. "We don't have one," he said, and he gently pulled Audrey back into the bakery and shut the door firmly on Jack's self-satisfied grin.

CHAPTER 10

The apartment over the bakery was small and predictable. Two bedrooms shared a wall and backed up to the alley. The hallway in front of these led to a tiny bathroom at one end and the door to the bakery's back stairs at the other. Through the passage opposite the bedrooms was an eat-in kitchen that shared plumbing with the bathroom, and a square living space with the apartment's only real feature: a wide corner window with a padded bench seat.

The view looked down onto the intersection of Main and Sunflower and all the simple lives that passed through it every day. Diane's parents had been married fifty years ago in the well-kept park across the street, kitty-corner from the bakery. Many, many couples had been married at that park across the years.

Diane estimated that she had spent at least half of her childhood sitting in that window, and then she spent more than half her life in a windowless cell. Even so, she didn't realize until she entered the room how much she had longed to see that view again. She came in from the hall, stepping lightly to avoid being heard below, and saw the curtains drawn and the space in front of them stacked to her chin with cardboard boxes four or five deep. Reaching for the wall switch, she flipped on an overhead bulb. Boxes, plastic storage tubs, empty flour sacks, and outdated kitchen equipment filled every inch except for a foot-wide path through everything and into the kitchen.

The shut-down view was no less disappointing to her than her shut-down life. Even if she could get through this wall of heavy boxes and pull the curtains back off the view again, she feared the exercise would be pointless.

No view, only a silver mirror of fog.

No new life.

No diamond pendant.

It was the pendant that she needed most of all. It was more important than the view or her life, because it was the pendant that was responsible for everything that had happened and was about to happen. Recovering it and returning it to its rightful owners was the only solution that had endured these twenty-five years, though she feared the rock would be long gone by now. For that matter, she didn't even know if the people it belonged to were still alive.

What did she know at all, really? In that moment, her own stupidity smacked her into awareness. She might have kicked in that window over a baby's bassinet, or dropped into the crib of a drug gang armed to the teeth. She might have frightened an old lady into her grave.

She might have come face-to-face with her own parents, and what then?

Diane sank onto a red plastic tub between the kitchen and the living room. She was not thinking far enough ahead to keep herself out of jail for very long. The Bofingers would find that broken window and the police would find the phone, and they'd all march up those stairs, cuff her up and cart her off just like last time, only now with a breaking-and-entering charge attached to yet another death. Because the person who had dropped the phone was most certainly dead; Diane's bad luck dictated it.

She sat there, a dumb lump, within ten feet of what she'd come for. Even if she had time to move all those boxes, where would she put them?

She rested her cheek on her fist, weary

and indecisive.

Diane had a vision of Geoff and Audrey Bofinger standing in the apartment's open doorway, arms crossed, scowling at her as she sat in the mouth of the dark kitchen.

"I'm sorry for breaking your window," she said to the illusion.

"Why didn't you use the stairs?" Geoff said, and Diane shrieked at the sound of his voice. The couple were truly standing in front of her! Not scowling, but — she didn't know how to read the serious expressions. Anger? Acceptance? Audrey propped the door open with a smaller cardboard box. Maybe she was afraid of being shut in with Diane.

"Please don't call the cops," Diane said.

The corner of Geoff's mouth twitched, but she thought it was friendly rather than mocking. "I think the police will be in and out of here long after we wish they were gone."

Diane stood. "They're coming up here?"

"I was referring to their being in the bakery."

"It was locked," Diane said.

"The bakery?"

"The front door. Downstairs I mean. You asked me why I didn't use the stairs."

"Ah. That's right. But why were you so

136

desperate to get in?"

"I'll pay for the window. As soon as I can."

The kitchen counter formed a prop for Geoff's backside as he crossed his ankles. "I'm not too worried about the window for now. Why didn't you tell me what you needed the first time you tried to come up here?"

"I told you I just got out of prison."

Audrey looked alarmed. "You didn't tell me that," she said to her husband.

"I didn't think it was important. But I'm sorry."

Both Diane and Audrey stood there blinking at him. Diane waited for one of them to ask what she had been in for, and for how long.

When they didn't say anything, Diane filled the silence. "Sort of 'just.' It was two months ago, actually."

Geoff said, "I'd like to hear the story sometime. But for now, why don't you tell us what it is you need. Maybe we can help."

Audrey said, "Geoff, she has a record *and* Julie's phone. We can't —"

"I don't have that phone. Anymore."

"But you didn't give it to the detective like you said you were going to," Geoff observed, and Diane wondered why his remark didn't put her on the defensive in the same way that Audrey's body language did.

"I'm trying to get back on track. I told you, I found the phone in the street, and I picked it up. I was curious. But no one will believe that. They'll think I did something that I *did not* do. It's always that way."

Audrey said, "Were you trying to hide the phone up here?"

Diane decided that she would only talk to Geoff from this point on. She looked at him. "No! Not up here. But it fell out of my backpack and into the trash can, right before they picked it up. It's just as well, right?"

"Not exactly," Audrey muttered. At a glance from her husband, however, the woman softened.

"I needed a place to stay," Diane said. "It looked like there might be rooms up here, someplace I could . . . get out of the cold."

"It was an apartment at one time," Geoff said. "But you can see we use it for storage now."

"I can pay rent. Work a little? Wash your bathrooms, your dishes?"

"We really can't afford —" Audrey started.

"No money, just a trade. Just for a little while. Until I can . . . move on."

Geoff said to Audrey, "Maybe we can

138

clean out the back bedroom. Make enough space for her to use the bathroom and the kitchen."

"I really don't think that's wise."

"I won't steal from you, if that's what you're worried about."

Audrey's eyebrows went up. "That wasn't top on my list of concerns."

"Let's give it a week," Geoff said. "It won't hurt us to help her out."

"She's already hurt us! Jack thinks we took that phone and killed his wife."

"He hasn't said that."

"Geoff!"

He laid a hand on his wife's shoulder. "This bakery is a place for second chances," he said. "And not just for us."

"We're being fools," Audrey said, glancing at Diane.

Shame flushed Diane's cheeks. She had to agree.

"For all we know *she* had something to do with what happened to Julie."

"I didn't do anything. I don't even know who Julie is!"

"Her name is Julie Mansfield," Audrey said, and her teeth bit the words at the ends. "And she's the detective's wife. Jack Mansfield."

Julie. And Jack. A good couple-name. Still,

she didn't know them.

"I'm really sorry," Diane said. "But I didn't have anything to do with it. I'll . . . If you let me stay — just for a week? — I'll talk with the detective and try to clear this up for you." With any luck, she'd find the necklace and be gone before she had to do that. But if not, she would tell the truth. Maybe this one time, the truth would work in her favor.

Diane doubted her own thoughts and Audrey seemed to know it.

"I think you need to talk with Jack about whether you can stay."

"But if you stay" — Diane believed Geoff emphasized the words for Audrey's benefit — "it seems we might all be able to help each other out."

Audrey licked her lips and backed off. She looked at her feet and nodded.

"I'm reliable," Diane said, not sure why she picked that particular word.

"Good. Now, come on down with us and I'll show you around, and tonight Ed and I will clear out the back room. I think we have some spare sheets for the bed that's still back there, don't we, Audrey?"

Audrey nodded again and, maybe because of her husband's insistence that Diane was deserving, seemed to have a change of heart. Audrey took a step toward Diane and held out her hand.

"I'll bring towels too, and I'll wash your clothes." Audrey indicated the shirt whose tails hung almost to her knees. "Please forgive my . . . reservations. This hasn't been a typical morning for me by any stretch of the imagination."

Diane matched Audrey's firm squeeze, though she worried about how icy cold her own fingers were in Audrey's warm grip.

"I understand," she said. "If I were you I'd feel the same way."

CHAPTER 11

Within hours of Julie Mansfield's disappearance, business at the bakery was noticeably up. As the trend stretched out into Friday morning, it was hard for Ed Bofinger to avoid thinking cynically about why. People who before had bought only a loaf of bread now purchased a pastry and a cup of coffee too, then bombarded Ed with repetitious questions and suspicious gazes.

"Just keep doing what we set out to do," his dad instructed Ed when he grew impatient with a girl who asked for a spare paper cup with the Rise and Shine logo. "It doesn't matter why they're here, only that we're good servants while they're our guests."

Come on, Ed thought. The girl wanted the cup for a souvenir "in case the owners did it after all."

Groups of gossipers gathered, speculating like nosy small-town bloggers. A few people took pictures of the view of the intersection from inside the window, or the view into the window from the intersection, and sometimes of his parents working behind the counter. Sometimes his parents even dared to smile and pose with their guests, then offered to post prints on their wall, as if the place were a celebrity hangout.

Someone started a rumor that the upstairs apartment was haunted, that someone had been murdered up there, and that perhaps it was the place where Julie Mansfield was tied up and being starved to death. Or worse. Even though Detective Mansfield and other investigators had been upstairs for a look at least twice, the Bofingers and that new employee — well, volunteer — Diane, had to be vigilant about keeping the door to the rear stairs locked.

Diane was a hard worker and washed the cups until they were spotless, but she didn't say much and never looked Ed in the eye.

But perhaps the worst rumor, and the shortest lived, because it proved to be terribly true, was delivered to the bakery on the quiet lips of Leslie Wood, one of Julie's calculus students at Mazy High.

Ed was behind the counter putting a loaf of honey-wheat through the slicer midmorning when he noticed the high school senior at a table at the edge of the room. She sat like a resting moth, silent and inconspicuous, preferring no attention. She'd come in every Saturday since the bakery opened and always took the same table. After placing an order for a croissant and espresso, she'd eat, drink, read, and leave, all without saying another word.

He noticed her today because it was Friday, and because she'd settled in without ordering anything. He supposed the disappearance of her teacher might have disrupted her routine. Her gaze rested on him while he worked, as it had often in the year before his graduation. Her studious attention had always suggested to him that she thought she was invisible. She stared flagrantly, innocent and childlike, mainly because he ignored her. No senior basketball star would give her the time of day, especially not one like Ed, who was dating someone like Miralee. This is what Ed thought Leslie thought, anyway. So he pretended not to notice the brainiac's crush, even though it did feed his ego.

Today her admiration made him uncomfortable. Her relative innocence was superior in most ways to his life experience. A girl like that needed to be protected from a guy like him.

A heavy textbook lay open on the table in front of her.

Ed's mother came out of the kitchen and noticed Leslie immediately. "Good morning!" Audrey called out. His mom was a little more cheerful than average, Ed thought, which was usually only the case when she was feeling under the weather. He looked at her face. It did seem strained, but days of trouble this complicated could do worse to a person.

Leslie took Audrey's cheer as an invitation to approach the counter. She scooted her chair back and tried to avoid the woman who had ordered the loaf Ed was bagging. "It isn't really," she whispered. "Not for Mrs. Mansfield anyway, wherever she is. I thought you needed to know. Hi, Ed."

"Hey, Les."

"The team really stinks without you this year."

He thanked her by smiling. He knew that the team was already 3 and 0, which was a better start than they'd had last season. Ed sealed the sliced and bagged bread with a twist tie. His mother wiped down the espresso steamer with a wet rag.

"Know about what?" Audrey asked. "Is there news about Julie?"

"I think she's dead," Leslie said in such a

low voice that Audrey left the coffee machine to stand closer.

"What did you say, honey?"

"All that blood was hers."

Ed's customer took the bread, laid it on the counter, returned her wallet to her purse and then slowly zipped it closed. The women at the table in the center of the room were silently examining the crumbs in their baskets. Talking to each other would have drowned out Leslie's voice.

"Bit early for lunch break, isn't it?" Ed said lightly.

"It's a teachers' in-service day."

The conversation stalled until the woman at the counter ran out of things to do to cloak her eavesdropping. She departed slowly while Ed scooped a croissant onto a plate for Leslie.

"I love those," she said.

"I remember," he answered, which was a dumb thing to say because it struck the poor girl speechless.

"Who's saying Mrs. Mansfield is dead?" Audrey finally asked, freeing Leslie's tongue.

"Oh" — she tore her eyes away from Ed — "Casey Wilson, who you probably don't know because he was a freshman last year, well, he's a sophomore now and he's also the son of Captain Wilson, who's Sergeant

146

Mansfield's boss at the police station. He put a rush on the forensics because it affects one of their own — you know how they are about that kind of thing. Well, Casey said that his dad said that the blood they found in the street Wednesday is most definitely Mrs. Mansfield's, they matched her DNA and everything, and Dr. Wheeler, who consults for the force sometimes and was out here last week when they needed a reliable measurement of how much blood there was, he said there's no way someone could have lost that much blood and lived."

"That's terrible news," his mother said, and she looked even more pale than she had a second ago. "I really hope it's not . . . the whole story. I'm Audrey Bofinger." She leaned out over the counter, extending her hand to Leslie.

"This is Leslie Wood," Ed said. "Senior at Mazy. Math whiz."

"I've seen you around," Audrey said. "Nice to finally meet you."

The girl seemed to shake his mother's hand without actually touching her fingers.

"I'm very sorry about your teacher," Audrey said. "This must be a really rough time for all her students, the whole school."

"But your family *hates* her! How can you be sorry?"

"We don't hate her, Leslie," Ed said.

"I thought —"

"You can't believe everything everyone says."

His mom said, "Leslie, do you want an espresso? Then maybe you and I can sit down and talk."

"Yeah, that's a good idea." She turned to Ed. "Can you sit with us?"

"Can't. Customers."

Audrey picked up a demitasse cup.

Leslie leaned toward Ed and lowered her voice. "They're saying your parents plotted to kill Mrs. Mansfield."

"They didn't."

"What can you say to such an awful accusation? But I can see why people believe it. After the whole saga of you and Miralee, and the church and all."

"That'll be $4.48," Ed said.

Leslie pulled a five out of the pocket of her hoodie. "I mean, she's the reason why you're not at college right now, isn't it? Because you couldn't keep your grades up after it came out that Miralee was pregnant, that the whole academic probation thing was killer, and Davis reneged its acceptance of you."

Ed put her change on the counter and pushed it at her. He let his eyes convey annoyance that would've been rude to put into words.

"Oh no. I'm sorry, Ed. I'm a terrible person, the most insensitive in the world."

Her embarrassment was so genuine that he gave her the benefit of the doubt. "No, you're not. You're just supersmart."

"About facts, maybe, but I'm always forgetting how people must *feel*."

"It's okay."

"I'm so, so sorry."

His mother carried the espresso around the end of the counter. She gave Leslie the tiny ceramic cup and started speaking out of Ed's earshot as well as everyone else's. Leslie glanced over her shoulder at Ed. Her eyebrows formed a peak of regret that wrinkled her high forehead.

Ed turned away and went into the rear of the kitchen. His father was carrying a sack of flour from the receiving door into the pantry. Their eyes passed over each other's in that way of people who are pretending not to know, or not to have seen, or not to have heard. Ed had noticed but never understood that look before Miralee's pregnancy. Now he saw it in everyone, and most frequently in his father. Most days he believed his dad hadn't paid for her abortion. His father had never lied to him. And he thought his dad believed Ed didn't know about the pregnancy before it was too late. But Ed had lied to his father once or twice, and that might have affected Geoff's opinion of him.

Ed went back to help heft in more of the fifty-pound sacks, which Estrella's husband would have delivered sometime during the morning rush.

Ed had nearly become a father himself. Or was a father, based on his own belief that life began at conception. And, having become a father, what did that change in his relationship with his own dad? Everything, it seemed. The more difficult question that plagued Ed was this one: was he *still* a father, now that the baby was dead?

It was a question God wouldn't answer, and Ed saw that as part of his deserved punishment. God was holy, and his expectations were high, and his grace wasn't a license to get through life scot-free. Ed accepted this; he was mature enough to own up to his mistakes, even if he still didn't understand how or why loving Miralee Mansfield had turned out to be such a beast of an error.

Leslie was right about that much, at least. If everyone else was thinking the way she was, his mother's simple traffic accident would soon become a twisted melodrama.

With a sack on his shoulder, Ed passed his father, this time not making eye contact. In the pantry he dropped the heavy load of flour onto the floor so that it stood on end in its own little cloud of fine dust. He returned to the kitchen.

"She ees a good girl, *mijo,*" Estrella said as he passed her where she stood forming white dough into loaves shaped like rugby balls.

"What?"

"She say all the wrong words, but she come here for the right reasons, no?"

"Who, Leslie?"

"Who else would fit thees description?"

Ed covered up his anxieties with a weak smile. "And what makes Leslie Wood so perfect?"

"What I say about being perfect? *Nada.* I said your mama needs right now to know some things before the police know she knows. Thees what I said."

"Wow. Okay. I think I know what you just said."

"Ees a nice thing for a girl to do for you."

"I thought you said it was for my mama." Ed elbowed her arm.

"What's for mama ees for the whole family. You should know thees at your age!"

He laughed. "Yeah, I know. But things are about to get complicated."

"*Sí,* I hear thees word a lot lately, *comp-lee-cate-ed.*"

"You say it like it tastes bad."

"Ah no. What can I say? People would feel better if they eat more bread. Like thees one." Estrella waived a flour-coated hand toward Leslie. "Should she ever turn down a warm croissant on a plate, I would know her character immediately. Her heart ees less complicated than most."

Diane stopped at the table to pull the dirty stainless-steel bowls off the lower shelf for washing.

Estrella set aside another formed loaf and said to her, "Thees ees correct, yes, Diane? You agree? One should never turn down warm bread."

From Ed's point of view, Diane seemed to be a mere blink away from tears at all times, though he'd never actually seen her cry. She gave them both a panicked glance as if acknowledging she'd heard the question might oblige her to answer it. She ducked her chin to her chest and marched the pans back to the sink.

"See? She agrees."

"Leslie just has a crush on me, Estrella, that's all."

"Aha! Proof that I am right. And that ees all I have to say about that for now. Do you hear me?" Ed opened his mouth, and Estrella said, "Because if I think you are not hearing me I can talk for longer than I can bake bread."

"I hear you."

"That girl ees worth your attention. Don't pretend she ees not."

"Okay! Okay!"

"So I am done with you now. Go. I am busy, and you have customer." Estrella nodded toward the register.

"And you have a cat," Ed said, pointing at the stray, who had come in with his father's last load of flour. That animal was always looking for an in.

"Breakfast time!" she said. "Here, kitty. Let me wash off thees dough."

The man standing at the counter was tall and trim and completely familiar to Ed. "Coach," Ed said, unspeakably embarrassed to be standing in front of Nolan Henderson in a flour-dusted apron instead of a basketball uniform.

"Ed, how are you?"

"Been better."

"It's been awhile."

"Yeah." Of course, Ed had gone out of his way to avoid anyone he knew since losing his scholarship. That had proven harder than usual this week.

"I'm sorry to hear what your family's going through."

Ed nodded, a little offended that Coach was fishing for information. The man should speak to Leslie. "It can't be easy for all of you at Mazy right now either," Ed said.

"No, true. Everyone likes Julie. We're all worried, of course."

In the silence that followed, Ed could not summon the courage to say *We're hoping for a good ending to this story* or *I'd rather be anywhere but standing here in front of you right now* or *I'm so sorry I let you down.*

"What can I get you?"

"Large black coffee and one of those onion bagels. Cream cheese on the side."

Ed cleared his throat. "You want that toasted?"

"Please."

Coach put his cash on the counter while Ed went through the motions of pulling things together.

"You playing any ball these days?"

"Not much." Ed kept his back to the man while the bagel went through the toaster belt. The glowing conveyor warmed his face. "Heard it was an in-service day for all of you."

"Well, the boss doesn't mind if some of us do our service out. But listen, Ed, there's a men's basketball league that meets Saturday nights at the community center. You ought to come play with us sometime."

"Okay. I'll think about it." But he decided right away that he'd never show up. He placed the items on the counter in front of his former mentor.

The man took them in hands large enough to palm a beach ball. Ed thought they shook slightly. But that was only his imagination, wasn't it? Everyone knew Coach was a recovering alcoholic, and it was low of Ed to wish that someone had bigger problems than his own right now — problems that would divert some unwanted attention. Nolan Henderson was admired by all of Cornucopia for overcoming, for doing good by the kids he trained, and for winning two state championships in the years he'd been at Mazy.

"We all hit tough times now and then," Coach said. "It's easier if you don't go it alone. Speaking from experience."

Ed nodded once. He watched his former coach walk across the room to an empty table and eat his breakfast in solitude. Quite alone.

Chapter 12

Audrey was having a difficult time focusing on Leslie's words. Her period had started early and was accompanied by discomforts that Audrey rarely experienced. She feared the stress of the accident and of Julie's disappearance must be getting to her. The downfall had started with her uncharacteristic rudeness toward Diane. The woman, though shy and a self-professed criminal, had proven to be dependable, even kind. And this girl sitting across the table from her needed comfort, possibly even safety.

"You must be upset about what might have happened to your teacher," Audrey said patiently. She felt an unexpected sweat break out on her forehead, feverish.

"It's terrible. I'm so worried. I had to come here when I heard about the blood."

"Giving us that information is kind, but it makes me worry for you. We don't know what happened — or if someone might hold

it against you if they learn that you're looking into things."

"I'm not looking into anything, really. I
just thought . . ."

Audrey saw the coffee cup tremble in the
girl's fingers.

"You didn't think that you might test my
reaction with that news, did you? Form
some opinion of my guilt by how I reacted?"

Leslie blushed.

"Trying to be an investigator is a lot different from just speculating about what happened. What if you stumble onto something
you have no business knowing?"

The girl shrugged. "So, what if? Are you
saying someone might want to hurt me?"

A hot flush spread out across Audrey's
neck, and she touched it gingerly. Her skin
itched. "Are you feeling okay?"

"Me? I'm fine. You don't look so good,
though."

"Right. It's just that sometimes I . . .
Never mind. Leslie, all I meant is that no
one knows what happened out there." She
gestured toward the intersection. "I guess
I'm saying anything's possible, and you
should be careful."

"Is that . . . a warning?"

Audrey felt overcome by exhaustion. "Of
course not. You're a smart girl. Think about

157

it." She was surprised that her irritation brought Leslie to the brink of tears.

"I would do *anything* to help Mrs. Mansfield. Anything. I owe her *so much.*"

"I know, honey."

"No. You can't know what I . . . It's impossible."

Audrey sighed and scratched the skin behind her collar, her fingertips brushing fine, tiny bumps. She felt the slightest bit woozy. "I'll speak to Jack today, find out if it's true that the blood is Julie's. But you should let it go, okay? The best thing you can do for her is stay focused on your schoolwork."

"Will you tell me what you find out? I'll drop by every day and buy —"

"That won't be necessary. If I were your mom I'd have a fit if you —"

"No, I want to. I need to. I'll come back tomorrow." Then Leslie threw back her espresso and slammed her textbook closed and lifted her backpack to her shoulder without zipping it. She rushed for the door. Audrey twisted her body to watch Leslie leave and saw what had caused her to move like a bird in a snake's presence.

At the entrance, Jack's eyes locked on Audrey's clammy face. He approached the table, the entire bakery focused on him. He leaned down toward Audrey and said, for her ears only, "A word with you?"

Audrey stood. "Of course. Anything you need."

"Not here," Jack said.

The necklace was not where she had left it. Diane fretted. She scrubbed Estrella's bowls in the hot water until the stainless steel became a mirror and the fair skin of her hands turned lobster red. Of course, she should have expected something to happen to the jewelry in the two and a half decades since she'd hidden it.

Geoff and Ed had made space for her in the apartment bedroom by stacking boxes deeper and higher in the living room, so that after an evening of their "help" she was forced to spend several long hours clearing a new path wide enough for her to reach the window seat. And then, sweating and huffing and wielding one of Geoff's flashlights, which weighed about as much as her arm, she'd managed to clear more boxes off the seat and remove the faded green cushion. The hinged lid squealed when she lifted it.

Inside, a wooden brace set parallel to the floor helped to support the wide lid. When she was seventeen, Diane had slipped the pendant into a tiny plastic bag that once held spare buttons. Then she emptied the seat's storage area, wedged herself into the space, and stapled the packet to the underside of one brace, near the front joint where it couldn't be seen from above.

She had gained too much weight to climb into the empty box today, but her fingers should have been able to find the necklace easily enough. Instead, all she found was a jagged scrap of plastic held in place by a bent staple. It pricked her skin and drew blood.

What now? What next? A day after the discovery, Diane still had no answer to that question. She'd stared out the upstairs corner window through the evening and cried through the night and took out her desperation on pots and pans through the morning. If she couldn't complete this penance, she'd be better off dead.

She already was dead to most everyone who mattered: her mother, her father, what childhood friends she once had. Not one of them had made an appearance since her return to this building where they'd once come for Pop Rocks and Red Vines after school.

Maybe all their lives had been altered as dramatically as hers.

Diane put away the dry shiny bowls and hung up her apron and stomped upstairs, not caring who heard her. It was time for her to make another decision, and this one had better not take her another twenty-five years. As grateful as she was for a roof over her head, the spirits that haunted this forsaken home would drive her out in a matter of days. And then she might find herself in an asylum rather than a prison.

The Bofingers had put her in the bedroom where the window was still in one piece. Her parents' old room. To begin her decision-making process, Diane entered the apartment and went directly to the room that had belonged to her and her twin sister, the room where she had shattered the window and, once upon a time, her family. She opened the door and saw, behind the cramp of rearranged boxes, the plywood over the broken pane, and beneath it, the place where there had once been a nightstand between two twin beds.

She wondered where the nightstand had gone. For a whole week after Donna first stole the necklace from their grandmother, the diamond had remained in the table's tiny drawer.

According to the family lore, both the diamond and its crude silver setting had come from King's Riches, a valley in the Sierra Nevada that rose behind Cornucopia. King's Riches was a misnamed location if ever there was one. Miners, including Diane and Donna's great-great-grandfather, had tried and failed to make their fortunes in silver in the place that was now annexed to the national park, a destination for nature lovers. Fortunes were spent and lost in efforts to extract the precious metal from its ore, and winter avalanches routinely demolished the mines. In time, the prince was proven to be a pauper.

As for the diamond, well, no appraiser had ever believed the uncut stone had actually come from King's Riches, because so few of the gems had ever been documented there.

But the family myth persisted, mainly because it couldn't be refuted. Great-Great-Grandpa Hall, it was said, found the two-carat rock in the rubble of the avalanche that destroyed the Ransom Mine. When he found it, he abandoned his duties at the neighboring Dynasty Mine and ran home to his wife, full of secret plans to stake his own claim as a diamond seeker. The day after his unauthorized departure, another avalanche crushed Dynasty.

Though no other diamond ever presented itself to Grandpa Hall and he died an

underweight, working-class man, he believed the stone to be a talisman and refused
to sell it. Until Donna, his descendants
respected his thinking. And until Diane, no
one feared that the pendant might cause far
more trouble than good.

Donna had been less interested in the history of the piece than in its potential to
bring in enough money for the prom dress
and accompanying "night to remember"
that she wanted: that is, the kind that no
one else in Cornucopia could afford.

Diane's discovery of the pilfered jewelry
prompted an immediate fight, the twins
head-to-head in the triangular light of the
nightstand's tiny lamp. Diane's best friend,
Juliet Steen, sat next to her on the bed,
lending courage. Diane dangled the necklace between them, and Donna snatched it
away.

"You *stole* it?" Diane accused.

"No, I said, 'Grammie, I need to buy a
dress. May I pawn the family heirloom?'
You're such a retard, Diane."

Juliet. "That's an immature and inaccurate
accusation."

Donna scoffed.

Diane. "I can't believe you stole it. From
Grandma!"

"Of course you can't. You have no imagination."

"Do too."

"Ugh."

Juliet. "Diane has enough brains to avoid a life of crime. But you'll go to jail, Donna. Be careful."

Loyalty was one of Juliet's many stellar qualities. What she lacked in intuition she made up for in unflagging faith. Also, she was prettier than Donna and also got better grades, which gave Diane much needed clout with her popular sister.

Donna. "Even if I'm found out, the worst I'll get is a lecture."

Diane. "If I were you I'd at least feel guilty about it."

"Big surprise there. You feel guilty about eating cookies. What good is this thing for besides a few boring stories around the Christmas dinner table? We don't even need it anymore. We have pictures of the thing. We've heard the tale a gazillion times. You and I both could tell it in our sleep."

"It has sentimental value to Grammie. And maybe even . . . good luck."

"Tell me you're not superstitious."

Juliet. "Of course she's not. She's compassionate."

Diane frowned, angry at her sister's complete lack of common sense and respect. "It

164

wasn't yours to take."

"Please. Miss Holier Than Thou."

"You're being selfish, Donna."

"Hardly. Do you know how much this thing is insured for? Grammie will report it stolen and the insurance company will pay her at least as much as the pawn shop will pay me for it. I've just doubled its value! Grammie will still have her pictures and stories and I'll have my dress and we'll all be happy. All of us but you."

"I can be happy. Buy me a dress too."

Juliet. "Diane! No!"

Diane ignored her. "You'll still get enough money for what you want."

"What do you need a dress for? You're not going to prom."

"I haven't decided yet."

"You don't have to, fortunately, because if you *had* a choice, you wouldn't be able to make up your mind in time, I'm sure."

Juliet. "That's just mean."

Diane. "I do too have a choice!"

"Between what? Staying home or going stag? No one's going to ask you. And if you ask anyone . . ." Donna rolled her eyes.

It was no difficult choice at all back then to bring her sister off her high horse by hiding the diamond until after prom night.

That incident, however, was not what gave

Diane pause as she stood in the bedroom today. The memory opening up in her mind was that Juliet knew everything. Telling Juliet of her plans to hide the diamond had resulted in Juliet's court-ordered testimony against Diane when the time came. Juliet had spoken to the jury with tears and compassion in her voice, clearly torn over whether honesty or friendship was the greater value. She'd lied about one thing, though: no one ever did find the necklace buried in the park across the street, where she suggested Diane had hidden it.

This caused Diane to wonder. Had Juliet intervened? She knew Diane had put the diamond in this window seat, and she had access to it, and she seemed to believe back then that Diane was as much a victim as an instigator in the tragedy of Donna's death. Was it possible that she had exercised her own justice by taking the necklace away from the Halls?

There were other possible explanations, of course. Even so, Diane's next decision was to find Juliet Steen.

Chapter 13

"Let me buy you a cup of coffee," Jack said to Audrey, pointing down Main to the Honey Bee as they exited Rise and Shine.

"Coffee's free at our place," Audrey said. "We could drag a table into the back —"

"I think some neutral ground is in order, don't you?"

She neither answered nor refused to follow him down the block. Her complexion was pale, though; her forehead shiny with perspiration on this crisp fall morning that had managed to stay clear of fog.

Neither God nor the criminal justice system always operated as reasonably as Jack expected them to. The criminal justice system he could forgive. It was an operation designed by men and run by men and as such was prone to inefficiencies, red tape, politicking, and garden-variety sinful-nature flaws.

God, however, had no excuse. There was

no reason for him not to reveal the location of Jack's wife, to save her from evildoers, to redeem this disaster and rescue her spiritual self from an eternity of damnation. Jack had earned such an outcome for her and for himself. He was a righteous, religious man who obeyed God and repented of all his mistakes. Since his wife's disappearance he had examined his heart and found no darkness in it, no cause for corrective spiritual discipline of this magnitude. Still, there was no sign of Julie.

Heaven's silence on this matter had begun to rankle, and Jack's mind turned to alternative explanations for the woman's disappearance. The most obvious was that someone else had sinned, and he and his wife were victims.

Jack believed he knew that someone's name, but he couldn't satisfy the legal requirement of probable cause. His superior, Captain Wilson, had barred Jack from the case because of his personal connections to it. Standard procedure. Though Jack understood this, he was the city's ranking detective, and removing him from the case was like tying the right hand of the department behind its back.

Jack was respected, of course, and Rutgers and Carlisle and others were happy to keep him up to speed on what little progress they made. But they didn't have enough direct evidence to convince a judge to grant a warrant for Audrey Bofinger's arrest, and Jack didn't think they could secure what they needed without his help.

In the light of the lab's conclusion that the blood belonged to Julie, Jack expected another detective to take Audrey down to the precinct for a repeat round of their previous questions, trying to break open new holes in her story. He was half surprised to beat his colleague to it, and he planned to make the most of his coup.

He was treading on unstable ground in asking Audrey to speak to him. He mentally plotted his defense, should he need one: they were two old friends equally concerned for his wife's fate. She had spoken with him willingly. There was nothing official involved. No hidden tape recorders, only hidden agendas. Jack did plan to get as much incriminating information out of the woman that he possibly could, and then work backward to acquire the correlating evidence in such a way that it wouldn't be excluded from the prosecution's case.

He also plotted a very different line of questions from what he believed they'd ask her at the station.

The Honey Bee smelled of greasy griddle sausages and burnt coffee, and the patrons' chatter buzzed like the name of the place suggested it should. A waitress old enough to be Jack's mother and nimble enough to be a teenager snatched two menus out of a rack by the door when they entered. He requested a particular booth that was in view of the register and the security camera. The amicable nature of their meeting would be on file, should he need to prove it.

He indicated that Audrey should slide into the yellow vinyl booth that faced the camera. He sat opposite her, exposing the back of his head to the lens. A suspect's facial expressions and body language were so important. So revealing.

Her menu remained closed in front of her. She folded her hands on the table and watched him more confidently than most suspects could. Underneath the open buttons at her collar, Audrey's skin was red and splotchy.

"Something to eat?" he asked.

"No, thank you. I can't be gone long."

"Coffee?"

"That'd be fine."

He ordered a three-egg farmer's omelet with a side of pancakes and an order of hashbrowns. He wasn't hungry, but if his mouth was full, she'd be more inclined to fill the silence, and he hoped to keep her talking as long as possible.

"How's Miralee dealing with her mother's disappearance?" Audrey asked, and Jack felt irritated that she'd spoken so readily. He would be the one to lead this conversation. And yet he had to keep it as friendly as a conversation between two enemies could be.

"She doesn't know about it yet," he said.

Audrey sat back in her seat, erect. At least he'd get some baseline body language out of this. "Why doesn't she know?"

"That's really none of your business, now, is it?"

"Maybe not, but it's unexpected regardless. Any daughter would deserve to know about something this bad."

"I think I know what's best for my family."

Audrey nodded in a way that said she disagreed entirely.

"Miralee and Julie haven't been on speaking terms for a couple of months, no thanks to you."

"You mean Ed."

"I meant your family in general."

"What do we have to do with their relationship?"

"Audrey, I've never hidden what I think of your husband and son. Their behavior was —"

"Mischaracterized by your accusations." Her gaze was steady.

"The evidence supported me. As did the church."

"Truth always comes out, Jack. I think you believe that more than anyone."

"Which is exactly why you can help me unravel what happened to my wife."

"Before we move on to her, I just want to say that the truth hasn't come out yet about my husband. Geoff didn't pay for that abortion. I think you know it. Deep in there" — she pointed at his chest — "you know it."

"Show me the evidence that contradicts what I've seen, and you'll have my public apology."

"An apology can't undo the harm you've caused. We're talking about lives here, your family and mine. Our children, our spouses. Our grandbaby. You're relentless, Jack."

He laughed low. "You want to hold me responsible for the damage? You and I are victims of all this. And I'll admit, I'm sorry about that. You're the compassionate one, the well-wisher. If there was a way to separate you from the consequences of what Geoff and Ed did, I would have tried to do that for you."

It was a necessary white lie, a justifiable wrong to gain the greater right. Like saving a life on the sabbath. Audrey scratched at the rash on her neck.

"What happened between Miralee and Julie?" she asked.

"I need to ask you some questions about the accident, Audrey."

"Questions different from what you and dozens of others have already asked?"

"Yes."

She sighed, and he had the conversation firmly back in hand.

"The blood on the ground belongs to the missing person."

Audrey blinked. "You mean the blood belongs to *your wife.*"

"That's what I said."

"No, you . . . I'm sorry, Jack."

"For what?"

"For what you must be going through!"

"You're having regrets for what you did."

"You mean do I regret driving too fast for the foggy conditions? Absolutely. It was a mistake, though. Not a plot."

The waitress brought Jack's plate and a pot of coffee, but Audrey's cup was still full.

"That's an interesting word choice. *Plot.*"

173

He placed a forkful of omelet in his mouth and stared at her. She stared back.

"Audrey, have you examined your soul? If you hide sin in your heart it will fester and become infected."

"You may have legal authority over me, Jack, but I don't recognize your spiritual authority any longer."

"When you avoid questions it makes you look as if you're hiding something."

"I haven't avoided any relevant questions."

"You hid evidence from me. You tried to dispose of it."

"What evidence?"

"Julie's cell phone."

"I didn't hide it! Diane Hall had it. You spoke with her. She found it in the gutter down the street."

"Ms. Hall says she never saw the phone."

"What?" The confidence in Audrey's tone slipped away.

"And your fingerprints were on it."

"Well, yes, that's because she showed it to me."

"Why would she show it to you?"

Audrey sputtered through her responses. "I was trying to call Julie. The cell phone rang right in the shop. Because Diane had it."

"Why were you calling her?"

"To see if she was okay. To apologize for the scooter."

"Or maybe to find the phone you lost after you moved her body."

"No! Jack! I keep telling you —"

"I didn't see your number in her call log."

Audrey paled. "I deleted it."

"That's interesting. Why?"

She turned her face toward the window.

"You hardly knew my wife. How did you have her number?"

"Ed had it! It's — Diane said she's never seen it? If my prints were on it, hers must be all over it."

Jack took another bite and shook his head.

"Think about it, Jack — if I had something to hide, would I put it in my trash can while your officers are searching every crack in the asphalt?"

"If you believed that kind of behavior would seem odd to me."

"I can't believe this is happening. Ed and I tried to help. We called 9-1-1. We looked for Julie. I didn't hurt her."

"We, I. So it's not out of the question that Ed did something you don't want to talk about. Or Geoff."

Audrey's coffee sloshed out of the cup as she shoved it away from her. "I came here with you because I'm worried about Julie.

Maybe you can help prod my memory to recall some detail that didn't seem important at the time. Maybe we can put this puzzle together in a way that makes some kind of sense. But if you're going to sit here and hammer away at your accusations, forget it. Arrest me. I'd rather you do this at the station. Wait — you're not allowed to take me to the station, are you? Because you're not even supposed to be working this case! I'm not stupid, Jack. I'm sick about what might have happened. I want answers as much as you do. We'll get further on this if you treat me like someone who cares."

Jack wiped his mouth. " 'All a man's ways seem right to him, but the Lord weighs the heart.' "

"Well, that goes for you too."

"My conscience is clear."

"So's mine."

"My professional record is spotless. I've met people like you before many times. Your family can't fool me, Audrey. You smile and seethe and lead a deceitful life."

"That doesn't sound like something that will hold up in court."

"Expert testimony can hold a lot of sway. But I like evidence, and I have plenty."

"If you had enough I'd be in handcuffs

right now."

"In due time."

Audrey began to slide out of the booth.

"We have Julie Mansfield's blood —"

"Your *wife's* blood. What's wrong with you?"

"— all over you and your car. We have your fingerprints on Julie Mansfield's missing phone. We have your earring, which was found in the dirt outside my home office window. I'm guessing you lost it when you broke in to type a disturbing message on my computer."

Her hand went to her left earlobe, though she wore two blue glass studs today.

"You know which earring I mean."

Audrey leaned back against the seat, looking flummoxed. He'd thought that bit would surprise her.

"No, I don't."

He believed she was lying. "A heart around a rose?"

"The church gave out dozens of identical pairs to the moms. It could belong to anyone. You even took a pair for Julie."

"Strange you didn't offer to show me your own complete set."

"Show me Julie's first."

"No need. DNA results will come in soon enough. I'm liking you for this more and more, Audrey."

Finally, she looked frightened.

It was Jack's strange emotional distance from his wife that spooked Audrey the most. That and his inappropriate probing of her inner life, his claim that she had sinned and that he had the spiritual discernment to expose her.

For a fleeting moment she believed Jack had killed Julie and was using all his resources to blame the Bofingers. He would manipulate the evidence — not too swiftly or cleanly, for the sake of realism — and sever every last tie that held her family together.

She kicked herself for not noticing where she'd lost that earring all those months ago.

The nausea that had been swelling in her stomach peaked. She closed her eyes and blotted the sweat on her brow with a napkin, hoping the wave would pass. But her illness and her fear were indistinguishable at the moment.

Audrey asked God to give her wisdom, and to give her a favorable exit from this conversation as soon as possible. She opened her eyes. Jack was chewing evenly, studying her.

She wondered if he was capable of killing her too.

"I was at your house once, several months ago." Her voice wobbled and she hated the sound.

"You said you've never been to my house."

"I've never been *inside* your house. And I didn't write whatever you found on your computer. But I was there one day, outside — March I think it was. I heard someone crying — Miralee was upset. But she sent me away."

He lifted his eyebrows and shook his head. The story sounded improbable even to her.

Her hands were shaking. She folded them in her lap where he couldn't see them. "I must have lost the earring then. I didn't notice until later."

Jack didn't say anything.

"I didn't hurt Julie," she said. "I would *never.*"

He leaned across his plate and lowered his voice. "You belong to your father, the devil, and you want to carry out your father's desire. He was a murderer from the beginning, not holding to the truth, for there is no truth in him."

"Stop it, Jack. You're twisting everything."

"You viper, how can you who are evil say anything good? For out of the overflow of the heart the mouth speaks."

Tears gathered behind Audrey's lids. There was fear swimming in them, to be sure, but also something else. "Why would you do this to us? You got everything from us that you asked for. Geoff left the ministry, not just your church. Our son's not going to any college for the time being, let alone the one Miralee attends. We've paid your price. It's time to let us go so that *all* of us can get back to doing God's work."

"Not until justice has been served."

Audrey recognized the emotion that was mingling with her fear then. It was pity for this man who might be, if he was as innocent of crime as she was, even more frightened for the fate of his loved ones.

"Then I will continue to rejoice," she said, quoting one of her own favorite scriptures as she rose from the table. She stopped by his side of the booth and leaned over him. "For I know that through your prayers and the help given by the Spirit of Jesus Christ, what has happened to me will turn out for my deliverance. I eagerly expect and hope that I will in no way be ashamed, but will have sufficient courage so that now, as always, Christ will be exalted."

Jack wiped his mouth and threw his napkin down on the tabletop. Audrey left the restaurant, realizing that she felt, for the first time in twenty-four hours, physically well.

On her return to the bakery, she glanced at Jack as she passed by his window. He watched her, expressionless, toying with his table knife.

CHAPTER 14

Rise and Shine did neither on Mondays. Restless and disturbed by her encounter with Jack, Audrey woke before dawn and shuffled out to her kitchen. She considered making six loaves of bread, something she and Geoff hadn't done since the family took over the "real" bakery.

She had no idea who she'd give them to. Geoff was still sleeping, exhausted. Audrey stood in front of her cookbooks without cracking a single spine. Her thoughts drifted to the bakery, and to the wreck at the intersection, and finally to Julie Mansfield, the woman she ought to have known better — would have known better if Audrey had been a more involved parent at Ed's school. She wondered what might have happened if she had insisted on taking a loaf of bread into the house that day when Miralee was sobbing. Why hadn't she acted? Where had her nerve gone? Audrey hated the missed opportunity to make a bad situation better.

Miralee had never . . .

Wait.

Audrey had always believed the cries she heard in March were Miralee's, but in that particular second on that particular morning in November, she stared at cookbook titles without reading them and wondered if the shattered heart and tears had belonged to Julie.

She lifted her hands to rub sleep out of her eyes, and her knuckles came away wet. The apples of her cheeks were slick. Water dripped off her chin and soaked her cotton T-shirt just above her heart.

Audrey stared at her damp hands. She felt a tickle trace her lip. Her nose was running. The even clicks of the old grandfather clock drew her attention, announcing that she'd been zoning for a full ten minutes, crying without knowing it.

Baking wouldn't bring her the peace she needed today — that much was clear. She needed something more vigorous to settle the distress mounting within her. She needed answers to the questions collecting like snow in a blizzard.

Audrey wiped her face dry with a wad of tissues, booted up the family computer, checked the weather, and decided to drive up to the national park, into King's Riches, for one last day hike before access to the area closed for winter. The forecast looked decent, with rain not rolling in until evening, then turning into snow in the higher elevations overnight. If it snowed hard enough, the Old Gauntlet Road that took hikers to the trailheads would soon be impassable.

She opened the cavernous hall closet and started dragging her hiking boots and winter jackets out of moving boxes that she hadn't bothered to unpack since relocating from the parsonage.

"You want company?" Ed asked. She jumped, then rolled her eyes. He ran a hand over his bed-head and then across his yawn. "Shouldn't hike alone, especially this time of year."

"I don't know if you'll be able to keep up with me, Mr. Athlete," she teased. "I'm pretty energized."

"So that means Dad's not going."

Audrey laughed. Geoff did prefer more lazy weekend walks. When the family went into the park, he preferred to sleep at a cabin or sit in the sun with a book while Audrey tore up the mountainsides. She missed walking with him on Tuesday mornings.

"He's got plans today with Cesar and Estrella. Something about getting a grinding lesson at the wheat mill. Would you not go with me if he was?"

"I didn't say that." Ed pulled a dusty backpack out of the gear box.

Audrey dragged out several lightweight jackets that were good for layering. "Let's go to Diamond Lake."

"You planning to spend the week up there?"

"It's not even ten miles round trip. One long day, not three. Although it has been awhile since I've been up at that altitude."

A yawn stalled Ed's reply. "The memory of my warm bed is really, really vivid right now."

"Okay, okay. If you want to stick to the nature trail —"

"We're not going to drive all the way to King's Riches for a one-mile walk. We can do that here."

"Well, I really don't care how far we go, as long as it's *away* from here."

Ed crossed his arms and struck his favorite cool-as-a-cucumber, FBI-man pose. "Energized, flying solo. You're running from the police, are you?"

"Exactly."

"They've been hovering. What's up with that?"

"They don't tell me anything. You know that."

"You're still a suspect? Don't they have anyone else?"

Audrey tossed a pair of thick wool socks at his chest. "It'll be cold up there. Bring your gloves."

Ed sighed.

"None of this is your fault," Audrey said.

"Some of it is."

"Let's go. Be ready in ten."

"Let me drive?"

"Sure."

Ed made a move to go, then took a closer look at his mom's face.

"What?" she asked.

"Nothing. I'm gonna get dressed."

Audrey watched him go, then realized that tears were dripping off her chin again, and her nose had started to leak.

"I'm fine," she muttered. "Really, totally fine."

Jack slammed his rolling chair into the space under his metal desk. A paper cup fell off the edge and tumbled away, making a hollow popping sound on the shiny floor.

"How can we be at the end of our leads?" His voice was controlled even though his body language wasn't. "No one's heard from my wife for six days, and we're still acting like it's day one."

Captain Wilson sat on one ham slung over the lip of Jack's desk. He was a foreboding man, a lifelong resident of Cornucopia who was respected first for his unapologetic efficiency and second for his physical size. They were nearly eye to eye as Jack stood and Wilson leaned.

"If you can name a trail we haven't chased, you say the word, Jack, and I'll check it out myself."

"Now I'm a consultant? Are you telling me they're not doing their jobs?" He gestured to the other desks in the precinct.

"Until we uncover something new, we don't have anywhere to go. It's a temporary holdup. You've seen it happen. Eventually, the tree will drop more fruit."

"If she dies, it's on your hands, Wilson."

There were two other detectives in the open office. One of them, a woman, had the courtesy to leave the room. Rutgers eavesdropped over busywork.

"How many heads do you have on this case?" Jack demanded.

Wilson kept his volume low and even.

"Everyone we've got. Even the ones not officially holding Julie's file are working overtime for the two of you. A little respect wouldn't hurt your cause."

"I respect results."

"No one here wants to be in your shoes. These people would go to Atlantis and back to get Julie if that's where she was, you know that. They're not dumping the case, right? I'm just saying that we don't have much to go on right now."

"Not true. Her phone, the fingerprints, the computer —"

"We all wish it was more clearly connected."

"You can't get more clear, Wilson. That Bofinger woman is guilty as Judas. She had motive and opportunity. She had two men who are looking to me like really nice accessories — two men who blame me for the sorry state of their lives."

"So far, Mrs. Bofinger isn't guilty of anything but a traffic violation."

"Says who? The DA?"

"You know how this works, Jack."

"She's good for it. I swear it. I'll find out what she did. She was *covered* in Julie's blood."

Wilson held up a hand. "Everything we have on her is circumstantial."

"I want the FBI in on this."

"Can't get it approved for you right now. I'm sorry."

"What? Why not?"

"What do we call them in for? No contact, no demands, no ransom — it doesn't look like a kidnapping. We've got no indication anyone's crossed any state lines. We don't even have enough evidence to prove a crime was committed."

"Unbelievable. We have at least two quarts of blood poured out on the middle of the street."

"But no body. And not a drop of blood outside the impact zone."

"And yet everyone here is asking me to prepare myself for the possibility that she's dead, saying no one could have survived that kind of hemorrhage."

Wilson nodded, somber. "It's a high possibility, Jack."

"If it's not an abduction, it's murder."

"There are . . . other possibilities."

"Like?"

"Julie's credit cards are silent. No purchases, no cash withdrawals from your bank, no checks written on your account."

"Which would align with her being dead. I'm not following you."

"She left her car in town."

"I *know* that." He had discovered Julie's Honda when he went to pick up his Jeep at the tardy mechanic's. She had dropped off the sedan Tuesday afternoon and asked them to give it priority over the Jeep. She insisted she needed a new fuel injection system. They thought nothing was wrong with it but did the work anyway and slapped Jack with an overpriced invoice. Rather than pay the bill, Jack left the Honda behind. Julie would clear it up when she returned.

The captain got off the desk and smoothed his pants. "What are the chances someone else is taking care of her?"

Anger like a beast behind bars rattled Jack's ribs.

"Is it possible that your wife was going behind your back?"

"No." His reaction was visceral even though the same question had run through his own mind. He grabbed a jacket off the back of his chair and moved swiftly toward the exit. Wilson followed.

"Was she acting out of character lately? Withdrawn? Distracted?"

"I am telling you, she did not run off with some Don Juan. Think about it." Jack faced off with his commanding officer. "If your wife was doing someone else, would she bother with a big stage production? How does a person pull something like that? Get up every morning waiting for thick enough fog to pull a fast one on a woman with close

190

connections to her family? And where would the blood come from? Who wouldn't just leave?"

Wilson seemed to assess Jack's irritation silently, the way they evaluated persons of interest. He finally said, "Her colleagues at the school seemed to think she wasn't herself. She was late to class a couple of times the week before she vanished, didn't follow her usual routines."

"She's been recovering from a surgery. It took a lot out of her."

"Is that all?"

If Jack had been one to take the good Lord's name in vain, he might have done it then. "She loves her job, she loves those kids more than our own."

"Really?"

"From where I sit."

"Would she confide in your daughter if something were wrong between you?"

"No sooner than I would."

"What do you mean?"

"Miralee's gone."

"Freshman at UC Davis, right?"

"She might be in Arkansas for all I care. She makes her own way now, doesn't need us for anything."

"You want to tell me what happened?"

"No, Captain, I want to end this conversation and *do* whatever it is you think can't be done. She would have left me a note. I'm talking about Julie. About your wild ideas. She would have sent an e-mail if she ran off, left a voice mail. She needs to have the last word that way. When she's angry."

Jack interpreted Wilson's nod as an effort to appease the offense rather than an agreement. He exited the building and crossed the parking lot. Wilson followed.

"Had you been arguing? We've put you through some long hours lately — that last case —"

Jack swore. "Look, the only thing your theory explains is the missing body. That's all. It doesn't explain the blood, the threat left on my computer, all the evidence pointing to those imposters who can't decide whether they're going to run a church or a *bakery.* I'll believe they killed her and cut her to pieces on the spot and threw her into that medieval oven in the back of their kitchen before I'll believe some jerk made a fool out of me."

"Most people who lose their jobs don't also lose their minds."

"You want case histories on the few who do?"

"Our station is within blocks of the accident. There wouldn't have been time —"

"We don't know how much time actually transpired between the collision and their call." Jack was yelling now. "It could have been a half hour, an hour. Whatever they wanted it to be."

Wilson crossed his arms. "I understand how hard it is to think about your wife in these terms —"

"You underestimate me. I am the best detective you have. I know the victim better than anyone in this building."

"The victim?"

"Yes, *the victim.* It's what we'd call her if she wasn't mine, isn't that right? Why do all of you assume I've left my brains on the side of the road and jumped off a cliff? Is that what you do when a crisis is fanning flames up your nose? I can work this case. You need fresh eyes. Let me do what I'm good at."

"No."

Jack kicked a tire before he yanked open the car door and slipped behind the steering wheel. Wilson prevented him from closing the door. He leaned in over Jack's left shoulder.

"You are my best, Jack. But it's impossible for you to do your best work in this moment. I put you on this, and we run the risk of screwing up the most important case of

193

your life. You'd tell me the same thing."

Jack put his key in the ignition and cranked it.

Wilson continued. "Also, you're locked onto only one possibility, and the evidence just doesn't support it."

"Your evidence is even thinner than mine."

"I'm not making a case, I'm just asking questions."

"You're making a mistake not to let me in on this."

"I'm protecting you."

"From what?"

Wilson eyed him carefully, gauging his response.

"You think *I* had something to do with her disappearance?"

"I don't think anything. The best investigators pursue all the angles."

"Well, then let's just ask if she was abducted by aliens, or sucked into the space-time continuum, or sliced and diced by a jealous avatar who escaped the high school computer lab!"

Wilson's face was unreadable. "I want you to trust us. No one in the world will work harder to get to the truth for you than we will."

"Says the man who keeps one corner of his mind for believing I did it."

Jack pulled the door out from under his boss's hand. His professional reputation and his spiritual confidence were on the line. He would prove every liar wrong.

CHAPTER 15

The fifty-five mile trek into the mountains took almost two hours. Audrey let her son drive for the first thirty minutes; she took over against his protests at the Old Gauntlet Road, a one-car lane twisted as an old telephone cord. She didn't make Ed surrender the driver's seat because he couldn't handle it, but because the five-hundred-plus turns on the twenty-five-mile stretch required her full attention. Applying that kind of focus to a task had a way of bringing new clarity and direction to her thoughts.

"I think God likes hanging out up here better than in town," Ed said, looking out at the slender lodgepole pines, stately sequoias, and frilly red and white firs. Their flat, agricultural hometown had its own beauty, but it was unremarkable compared to these sloping mountainsides.

"Maybe. It's probably no contest to say that he creates prettier stuff than we do. But

I think he likes to be where we are."

"That can't be true of everyone," Ed said.

"What do you mean?"

Ed shrugged one shoulder. "I just think some of us are disappointing."

"Disappointing to God?"

"Not only to him. But if he's holy, and holiness can't tolerate sin, then logically speaking, he can't stand some of us."

"Those are much stronger words than *disappointing*."

"I'm just saying that we might live on a sliding scale of approval. Puffed-up proud on one side, disgusted on the other."

"You think God's disgusted with you?"

Her son didn't answer.

"Ed, God hates sin, but he loves us. He's rooting for us to succeed, giving us the tools and the people and the grace we need to do that. You remember the story of the prodigal son. The guy's father spent every day at the window, waiting for him to return so they could all celebrate, not so he could punish his son."

"Do you ever wonder if the son left again?"

They moved off the paved road and onto dirt that was loud under the tires. "Until now, that thought never crossed my mind."

"That part of the story isn't in the Bible, I

noticed. How we redeemed prodigals are always leaving again."

"You think you're a prodigal because of what happened with Miralee?"

"Call it what you want."

Ed's grief was an ache in Audrey's heart. Her son was no rebel. He was a good young man who was sorting out life and wasn't going to get it all right the first time. Or even the second time. Who could?

Audrey said, "You ever ask your dad what he thinks about that? About the prodigal leaving again?"

"We don't talk much these days."

It was her opinion that the distance between the men in her life had more to do with each one's sense of personal failure than with disappointment in each other, but such thoughts had to wait for the right time for sharing, or else they'd be rejected.

"Well, I'd have to say that the father's character probably didn't change in the long run. If his son left more than once, he probably kept waiting by the window. Kept throwing parties."

This made Ed laugh, a bittersweet sound. "Today, shrinks call that enabling."

"Also, there's a difference between leaving and falling down, even though God forgives both."

"I don't know."

"You're so hard on yourself. Much harder than you think your dad is."

"If we told ourselves the truth, Mom, we'd have to say that none of this would have happened if I hadn't slept with her — Dad wouldn't have lost his church, I wouldn't have lost my scholarship. Jack wouldn't be looking at you for his wife's vanishing act." He shook his head. "The baby wouldn't have lost his life."

"As bad as you feel, and as noble it is of you to take responsibility, life is too big to think we understand it all. Some things don't happen the way we want them to, and we don't have anything to do with it."

Ed dropped the conversation then, so Audrey didn't press.

"Maybe we'll hike Silver Gap today?" she said, offering him another conversation. "A good midrange hike?"

"Fine," was all he said.

They encountered no other cars on the winding way. Even in ideal conditions, the road was treacherous enough to prevent King's Riches from being heavily trafficked. Occasional autumn rains had been falling for weeks, and the snows were imminent. Soon enough, maybe even tomorrow, the road would be shut down. But today the skies were clear and the air crisp, a pale gray-blue.

Silver Gap, one of the shorter trails at the end of the Old Gauntlet Road, followed an old wagon road and ended with views of the Great Forked River to the north and the tall Snaggletooth Peak to the east, pointy like a drill's spade bit. The trail led toward the ruins of the Dynasty Mine, though one would have to go off trail with a compass and quite a bit of experience to find the ruins themselves.

Four miles before they reached the end of the Old Gauntlet Road, Audrey and Ed passed through Miners Rest, a multicabin resort that had once been a real home to silver miners in the late nineteen hundreds. The cabins here were updated and refurbished, still rustic but transformed into an organized, romantic notion of life clustered around a small general store.

They passed the turnoff, and Audrey's body was overcome by a chill that made her shudder. A cold sweat broke out on her forehead. The unexpected rush was so startling that she stomped on the brake. Ed braced himself on the dash.

"You don't look so good."

"I'm okay." In seconds, the chill waned and was replaced by a low-grade headache that started between her shoulder blades and moved upward like a rising sun, hot and glaring, up the muscles of her neck and into the base of her skull.

"Want me to drive?"

"No, I'm good." A matching ache the size of a golf ball blossomed behind her belly button and pulsed there in time with her heart. Audrey took the wheel in both hands and lifted her foot off the brake, allowing the car to creep forward. "We should talk your dad into renting one of the chalets there sometime."

Ed was turned in his seat as if he expected her to lose control of the car; he looked ready to pounce on the wheel and twist it out of her hands. "You mean at Miners Rest?"

"Mm-hmm."

"Expensive for a place that doesn't have electricity."

"Some of the cabins are wired. You pay for the experience of the place."

"Miralee stayed there once. Said it was nice. A high compliment, considering the source."

"Miralee doesn't know her mom's missing," Audrey said. Her headache inched its way toward nausea. She couldn't remember if she'd packed any candied ginger or peppermints, which would help to settle her stomach.

"How do you know that?" Ed asked.

"Jack told me."

"Miralee isn't really interested in anyone's reality but her own. Jack probably knows that better than anyone."

"What makes you say that?"

"About Miralee, or about Jack?"

Audrey rolled her window down an inch and took a deep breath of clear air. "I meant what's the rift between her and her parents? Jack won't tell her what's going on, and he said she and Julie hadn't been getting along either."

"I don't think Miralee gets along with very many people. It was one of the reasons I . . . I was just being nice to her at first. She has a thing against Christians, church, you know. Like her mom. I thought I could convince her we're not all . . . like her dad."

"Like her dad how?"

"Uptight. Rigid." His laugh was sad. "I guess my behavior was so completely at the other extreme that it only proved her point."

"Well, Jack's a lawman. Her mom's not like that, is she?"

"Not so much when she's teaching. That's all I know."

"Miralee didn't talk about her?"

"Nope."

The air took the edge off of Audrey's strange symptoms. She took another deep breath.

"Do you regret your —"

"Mom. C'mon. It's embarrassing."

"I didn't mean that, Ed. I wondered if you were sorry for trying to be nice to her. It was a decent thing to do. You had good intentions."

He shook his head in a way that seemed to say *I can't believe you're asking me this.* They traveled the last few miles of the kinked road without sharing their thoughts.

Audrey passed the ranger station on the north side of the road and the campground on the south, where the looping nature trail started. The other trailheads met at a parking lot a little farther down.

"Okay, different thought," Audrey said. "If I went missing, would you want your dad to tell you about it?"

"That's a totally unrelated situation."

"I think Miralee should know what happened to her mom. Maybe she has information that would help."

"Let Jack make that decision."

"Jack's already made it, and I can't say I understand. It even makes him look suspicious. I think we should call her."

"Don't."

"Why not?"

Ed shook his head.

"Look, Ed. When things go wrong for somebody, we can't just sit by and watch them get hurt. We have to do what we can to fix the situation. Like you tried to show Miralee that not all Christians are as bad as she thinks."

"That's the worst example you could have come up with. Also, I don't think you want to do this to help Julie."

"That's not fair."

She pulled into the main parking area opposite two cars, a red two-door and an old gray pickup with a long radio antenna arcing over the cab. Maybe Ed was right. Maybe her true motive had more to do with proving Jack wrong. Maybe her anxiety over having injured the woman was being overtaken by resentment. She stopped the car and turned to her son. The movement strained her aching neck.

"Okay. Maybe my intentions aren't as pure as I'd like them to be. But if something terrible — something that could have been avoided — happens to Julie Mansfield, I would regret it for the rest of my life. That's the truth. I have to do what I can."

"You can't do everything, Mom. And not

everything that's broken can be fixed."

"Does that mean we shouldn't try?"

"Yeah, I think it does. Sometimes we have to let things go. Jesus said it: 'In this world you will have trouble.' That stinks. And I don't think we can avoid smelling it."

Audrey stared out the windshield at the beautiful valley that had been cut by glaciers — the cold hand of God — eons ago.

"So what does letting go look like to you? If we're not supposed to try to fix it, what do you think we're supposed to do?"

Ed stared at her.

Audrey smiled back. "Oh, the mysteries of the world. Maybe a walk will sharpen our minds. And when we get home, we'll call Miralee."

He put his hand on the door handle. "We?"

Audrey smiled and opened her own door, turning to get out. She placed her feet on the ground and pushed herself out of the car, and the earth seemed to slip out from under her as it had when she'd slipped in Julie's blood. The pain of a hot blade sliced through her hips, severing her body's nerves in two.

She doubled over and fell down.

CHAPTER 16

Monday afternoon Diane walked the few short blocks to the county library. It was a decent day, free of fog, though rain had been forecast for the afternoon, which meant the fog would soon follow.

Over the weekend, while thinking through how to go about finding Juliet Steen, Diane felt her ignorance acutely. She wasn't sure which government office kept track of who lived where — when it came to law-abiding citizens anyway — or if that kind of Big Brother thing was even constitutional. Now she thought she should have taken advantage of all the educational opportunities the penitentiary had to offer, and not merely the bare minimum.

So she decided to start with the library and a simple question: did Juliet go on to graduate from the same high school they'd attended together? If Diane could figure out where Juliet had received her diploma, she'd know what to do next.

Because Juliet's twenty-fifth high school reunion was right around the corner, and the committee would have its ways of finding her, wouldn't it?

Diane envisioned herself sweet-talking some nice, middle-aged, former class cabinet officer into giving her Juliet's latest address.

Well, she'd have to practice that.

Worst-case scenario: the librarian would at least be able to tell her where a smart person would have gone to start this search.

Diane passed by a hair salon. She wondered if Juliet still had her silky hair and her rosy marionette cheekbones and her ready laugh. She had envied Juliet's ability to make such a musical sound, and tried to mimic it in moments when she was alone. The effort was ridiculous, the result a fake giggle that was more mockery than merriment. But she had always believed that people who could laugh so freely were predestined to live long and happy lives. She couldn't envision them any other way.

For a sickening second as she mounted the steps to the library, Diane doubted that Juliet would have kept the diamond. What if she had taken the pendant and then sold it as Donna once planned to do? Diane gripped the rail and worried.

Or . . . Juliet might have returned the jewel to the Halls. But Diane's family would have contacted her if Juliet had given it back.

Wouldn't they?

This rabbit trail was short, though, and after a few deep breaths Diane was able to move on. When she entered the library and asked the reference librarian for help locating the Mazy High yearbook from what would have been her senior year, she expected to rediscover her best friend as the young woman preserved in her own memory.

"It doesn't appear we have that particular yearbook at this branch," the librarian said, studying her screen. "You can get these digitally, but not that far back."

"Oh," Diane said. What would she do now?

"I see a copy over at the Exeter branch. Would you like me to have them hold it for you?"

"I don't have a car."

"They could send it here."

"Uh . . ."

"Why don't you tell me what you need from the yearbook. Maybe there's another way we could get to the information."

"I'm trying to get in touch with a classmate. We haven't seen each other for a while."

"Ah!" The woman got up and came around her desk, indicating that Diane should follow her. "Are you on Facebook?"

"Um, no." She had heard of the book but never seen a copy.

"That might be the most popular place to track down people you know — or total strangers!" The woman laughed. "But I know several websites that can find school friends, if yours is registered with any of them. You can use our computer stations. All you need is an e-mail address so the sites can respond to your requests for information."

"I don't have an e-mail address either."

The librarian paused and turned around. "Okay. Well. If you like I can show you how to sign up for a free e-mail account."

"It sounds . . . more complicated than I can handle right now. I'm not that up to speed with computers."

"Have you tried Googling her? You don't need e-mail for that."

Diane's face felt hot. She could have received training at the prison that would have kept her in touch with accelerating technology, but she had avoided anything that might give her a sense of freedom.

The librarian placed a hand on Diane's elbow and gently guided her past stacks of books. "It's okay. A lot of people hate computers. I use them every day for my job, so it's not so intimidating as it was at first."

"I know how to use some computer programs. I just don't have a lot of experience on the Internet."

"I see. So, you've brought me a challenge, and it's been a long time since I've had one. This is excellent. If I hadn't started a career as a librarian, I might have become a private investigator! Let's do some sleuthing." She steered Diane back toward her scattered desk. "In the old days, before the world was downloaded to a gazillion computer servers, we used to use this high-tech device." The woman pointed to her telephone. "Let's call upon some humans. What's your friend's name?"

"Juliet Steen."

"And she graduated from Mazy High when?"

Diane reiterated the year. "But I don't know if she graduated from there. That's what I'm trying to find out."

The librarian swiveled back to the computer to look up the school's phone number. She typed and clicked swiftly. "Well, privacy laws being what they are these days, I doubt we'll be able to get any personal contact information, but we should be able to find out easily enough if she graduated from one of the high schools in this town." She picked up the handset and dialed a number. "And if we're really sweet, we might be able to get someone to tell you if she has a different married name, or maybe if she still lives in the area. Either one of those will help if we have to resort to the big bad computers. But if we can land both, then you might be able to find all you need in the phone book!"

Nothing in Diane's life had been so simple, but that didn't really matter. Finding Juliet — finding the necklace — was her only task at the moment. What were a few more months of delay after twenty-five years?

Her new ally went through the paces of being put on hold twice before she was transferred to the appropriate office.

"Hi, Brenda! How are you today?"

Diane wondered if the chipper greeting was truly familiar or only designed to feel that way.

"This is Selma at the county library, and I'm trying to find someone who might have graduated from your school awhile back. I'm sure you're so busy, but is that something you can help me with?"

Diane shifted her weight and noticed a display of novels that appeared to share the theme of serial killers.

"What a dear! Thank you. Here's the information . . ."

A flat-screen TV monitor behind the librarian's head flashed announcements about a public book group meeting, the children's story hour, and an upcoming lecture on the disputed success rates of reestablishing felons in a community.

"Yes, that's right. Juliet Steen."

The library's peaceful sounds of turning pages and clicking keyboards seemed to belie its more disturbing interests. Diane squirmed.

"Well, is it possible? You would know better than I would." The librarian grabbed a piece of scratch paper from a short pile beside her mouse. "Yes, I can wait." She glanced at Diane and covered the mouthpiece with one hand. "I hate to say this, but I'll be a little disappointed if my chance to do some real investigative work ends before it's even begun."

"What do you mean?"

The librarian held up a finger and returned to the call. She started making notes. "Mm-hmm . . . Well, what a happy coincidence . . . Oh dear. I spoke too soon, didn't I? Why, yes, I'd heard of it . . . Yes, yes. Thank you so much for your help."

Diane leaned over the little counter separating them and tried to see Selma's notes.

"Your Juliet Steen goes by Julie Mansfield now, and she not only graduated from Mazy High but is a teacher there."

Diane tried to think of why the name generated anxiety rather than excitement in her own mind.

"Unfortunately Julie went missing — just recently, in fact. I'm surprised you haven't seen the news?"

"No TV," Diane murmured while the woman's fingers flashed across her keyboard once more. Within seconds a digital copy of a newspaper page appeared on the screen, and the librarian turned it toward Diane.

Juliet Steen, thin and aged beyond her years, stood with the detective who had questioned Diane about the cell phone she had found. The man's stern face, and even more, the badge hanging from his shirt pocket in a leather wallet, had compelled her against her own will to lie to him about having ever seen the phone.

Then he'd shown her this very picture, the couple's arms encircling each other, and asked if she'd ever seen the woman in it. At the time Diane's attention was on the threat of the law, and she'd hardly glanced at her old friend, who was a virtual stranger. Her hair had been cropped short, her pretty cheeks seemed to have sunken, and her expression did not mask the sadness in her eyes — sadness that Diane never would have thought Juliet capable of understanding.

Though Diane's lie about the phone was brazen, her failure to recognize Juliet when Detective Mansfield showed her the photo was completely innocent. Of course, he would think she'd lied.

Diane rushed out of the library without thanking the woman for summoning yet another nightmare into her life.

Jack was still sitting in his driveway, in his car, when the rain started. He watched the drops hit his windshield with polite little tapping sounds that would soon turn more extreme and angry.

The appearance of the rain drew his attention to the juniper bush in front of his home-office window, the bush under which he'd found Audrey's earring. The branches of the juniper formed a green umbrella over the spot, sheltering it. Preserving it for his timely discovery.

The truth quacked like a duck. The Bofingers were guilty. It wasn't merely a job that Geoff had lost, not merely the status of being a pastor's wife that Audrey had lost, the coveted status of sitting at the right hand of a man appointed by God. They had fallen hard, almost as hard as Ananias and his wife, Sapphira, struck down dead for lying to God and the church.

And the Bofingers' lies were even more egregious. The family had stolen the purity of his daughter, murdered his unborn grandchild, then lied about their own culpability.

They might have confessed, even received forgiveness.

Forgiving the trio would have been difficult, but Jack would have done it if their hearts were truly contrite. It was required of him, and he was an obedient man who respected the authority of both men and God. Instead, the family denied and denied, lied and lied.

But the king will rejoice in God; all who swear by God will glory in him, while the mouths of liars will be silenced.

As a man who swore by God, Jack usually found peace in this psalm. After the Bofingers were dethroned, it seemed they had been silenced, even though Jack wished God had struck them dead in the center aisle on their way out the door.

215

But then they had proceeded to silence Jack's daughter — who would no longer speak to him — and then his wife, and their deception had spread even to his colleagues, blinding them to truth! Was this God's justice, that Geoff Bofinger should be standing with his wife and son while Jack's own family fell away?

No. Instead, this must be God's message to him, God's command that Jack Mansfield finally exercise the authority he'd been given by the government and by the heavenly powers to right a serious wrong. The longer he waited, the worse it would get. Would he himself be next to die by the devil's hands? Captain Wilson and others believed the victim's body was rotting, though her spirit was not yet saved.

This was the thought that brought Jack to his religious knees. This was the robbery that was more terrible than his wife's murder: namely, that God had promised Jack her salvation, and this promise had been snatched away from him. Jack would not tolerate the man who would tread on the promises of God.

It was Jack's duty to save his wife's soul.

It was his obligation to bring God's promises to light.

Justice is mine.

Jack got out of the car and stood in the rain, letting it wash his mind until he was clear about what would happen next.

He walked into the house to gather some guns and make his plans.

Chapter 17

By the time Ed had lifted his mother into the passenger seat and careened into Miners Rest, where he could get to a telephone that worked, she was insisting that there was no need to call anyone or take her anywhere but home. She was able to convince him that he'd waste more time and worry more people by stopping to call than if he'd just get on the road.

"I'm taking you to the hospital," he said firmly.

"No, you're not. But we'll call your dad when we get cell reception again."

And by then she was sitting up in the seat, and the tremors in her hands had calmed down. She talked with her eyes closed and her head tilted back against the headrest.

"You're a good driver."

"I think you're too sick to know exactly what I'm doing."

"Ha ha. Strangely, I think all the swaying

has really helped. I'm a baby in a cradle. All I need is a nap. Don't bother Dad for this."

"Right."

Leaving as soon as they'd arrived turned out to be a good thing. The forecasted rain arrived sooner than expected and was coming down evenly at the foot of the mountains by the time Ed descended. They would have been caught in the bad weather before they'd come down from Silver Gap.

Ed called his father as soon as his mom fell asleep. Geoff left the Torres farm right away and was standing in the driveway when they pulled in. As if she possessed some inner homing device that was activated by familiar movements of the vehicle, Audrey woke as soon as the sloping drive tilted the car.

His dad helped her out and into the house, sheltering her from the wet weather with a jacket draped over her head. Ed followed.

"You're warm," Geoff said to Audrey.

"Run-of-the-mill fever. Bring me some ibuprofen?"

Ed went to get it from the bathroom and shook out a couple of tablets into his hand. When he returned to his parents' room with a glass of water, his mom was under the blankets and his dad was perched on the edge of the mattress, holding her hand.

"This hasn't happened for a while," his father was saying, and Ed wondered what "this" was. He couldn't remember his mother ever being sick enough to pass out, except for that time she'd crashed in their kitchen a few years ago.

"It's probably just something I ate, or a bug," she insisted. "Let me sleep the day away and I'll be all better by morning."

"It came on too fast for that, don't you think? You know anyone who's this sick? Is there someone I ought to go see?"

Ed paused at the doorway.

"No idea," she murmured. "I doubt it's what you're thinking."

"Why?"

"Because it doesn't make sense."

"It never made sense, honey."

"I don't have any bread to give anyone. The bread's in the bakery now — do you know what I mean?"

"I don't think your . . . sensitivities were ever about bread."

"Let me sleep on it."

His dad motioned for Ed to come in with the pills. She gave her son a halfsmile. "We should have done the nature trail," she said, then threw them back.

Ed touched his father's elbow as they left

the room. "What were you talking about? Someone this sick — you think she caught something contagious?"

Geoff closed the door without looking at him. "Your mother is susceptible to certain things."

"Is something going on that I don't know about? Is she really sick?"

"It's nothing to worry about. She'll be fine. Let's keep an eye on her today."

The sound of the rain on the roof made the house feel hollow to Ed as he watched his father's back move down the hall, away from him. Ed saw it as a kind of abandonment — his father's refusal to trust him with important information. It didn't feel to him like the kind of shielding a parent did to protect a child; this was the cold shoulder of one man deciding that the other wasn't worthy.

The stark assessment flicked a spark of anger to light in Ed's mind.

Maybe his mother was right. Maybe Jack's refusal to tell Miralee what had happened to her mother was somehow morally wrong, a wrong that could be reversed. Miralee and Ed were both adults, both capable of living in an unsanitary world.

Audrey's day pack was still in the backseat of their sedan. Ed retrieved it and took it into his room, which was at the end of the house opposite the master bedroom. He hadn't bothered to put anything on the walls since moving in. None of the things that had been important to him eight months ago were important any longer, and he hadn't decided yet what values would replace them. He wasn't supposed to be living here, in his parents' home, anyway. He would be moving out as soon as he knew where he was going.

The room was stark: unmade bed, minimal clothes in the closet and dresser, dusty laptop closed on the desk, untouched basketball going flat under the window. The parsonage had a hoop in the driveway; this new rental did not. His Bible, which he hadn't read since Miralee's announcement that she'd aborted their child, sat on his nightstand under a stack of paperback sports-celebrity memoirs.

He sat at the desk and placed the pack at his feet, then rifled through it for his mom's phone. If he used his own, Miralee would recognize the number and probably refuse to answer it.

Ed palmed the old flip-top in his hands and decided what he might have time to say before she hung up on him, or to leave in a message before she deleted it. He dialed, half hoping she'd be in class or uninterested in answering an unknown number from her hometown area code.

She answered halfway through the first ring. "Yeah?"

"Miri, your mom's missing and your dad's decided not to tell you about it."

Her silence dragged on so long he thought she might have hung up. Or he'd dialed the wrong number. Or the person who'd answered wasn't her.

"Ed?"

"Yeah. Hi."

"Is this a joke?"

"No. She's been gone for almost a week."

"What the —"

"Have you had any contact with her lately?"

"That's none of your business."

It wasn't, of course.

"Jack thinks my parents are responsible."

This made her laugh. And laugh. Her amusement pricked his pride, and by the time she finished, Ed had thought of five other things he could have said instead.

"Of course he thinks that. Everything you religious freaks do is so inbred."

"Well said by a girl who doesn't need anyone."

"You're so full of yourself, Ed."

"Look, maybe you don't care about your mom, and that, too, would be none of my business. But I think anyone deserves to know if something like this happens to their mom. I'm calling because I think your dad's wrong to shut you out of it, that's all."

Miralee's laughter had tapered off. "You're going to be a preacher like your dad someday." She said it without the rancor, though. "What do you mean, *missing?*"

"Vanished. Disappeared. Left everything here except the clothes she was wearing."

"She'd never do something like that."

"I don't think anyone's suggesting that she walked off into the sunset." He decided not to tell her about the accident. That might be counterproductive at this point, though she needed to understand how serious things were. "They found a lot of blood. I guess it's hers. I hate saying it that way, but it looks bad from any point of view. I'm sorry."

"And my father couldn't be bothered to tell me this? Tell me what you know."

"My family's under a microscope. No one's saying anything to us. I don't know squat."

"Is *that* why you're calling me? Because our parents are butting heads and you want my help to break up the fight? I left Cornucopia to *escape* that kind of preschool."

"Get over it, Miri. The world is so much bigger than your little universe." He waited for her sharp tongue, but she held it. "If you know anything that will help your mom, tell someone. Doesn't have to be me, okay? Probably *shouldn't* be me. But whatever you've got against your dad can't be worth . . . risking the worst."

"Okay."

Ed held the phone off his ear and looked at it. *Okay?* He didn't know what to say. He waited for her to say more.

"I always liked you best when you were just yourself," she said. "Not trying to be anything else."

Streams of rain flowed down his windows. He thought he should hang up.

"How're you liking Davis?" he said. *I should be there with you.*

"It's fine." Her voice had shifted into a neutral tone, the way she had spoken to him the first time he had dared talk to her.

"I'm sorry about your mom. We're hoping for the best."

"You make it sound like she's got something terminal."

He nodded, glad not to be having this conversation face-to-face. "Has your mom tried to reach you at all?"

225

"Thank you for telling me, Ed."

He coughed, embarrassed by his not-so-subtle hope that he could get his mother off this barbed hook of Jack's. "Sure."

"I mean that. Thank you."

He nodded again, not sure what to believe about her shape-shifting treatment of him. She hung up.

CHAPTER 18

The scent of sweet cinnamon rolls was filling Diane's apartment when she woke Tuesday morning after a few short hours of sleep. Throughout the course of the night, she had gradually arrived at this conclusion: Juliet's disappearance on the very day of Diane's return to her hometown was a sign from God, and not a bizarre coincidence.

Diane didn't understand what the sign meant. But this interpretation of Monday's revelation was the only one that allowed her finally to fall asleep and then get out of bed in the morning, to figure out what she must do next. Sometimes one had to be practical to avoid becoming paralyzed.

She pulled on her clothing, washed her face, and ran a comb through her hair. She went into the living room where she had tossed the blue apron Geoff asked her to wear while she worked, slipped it over her neck, and spent a moment untangling the strings. She could see the front window at the end of the narrow path she had cleared to the bench. A curtain of fog hung on the other side of the glass, giving the world its privacy.

Yesterday's rain — and the high-pressure system that followed it — was responsible for filling the valley with this thick soup. The blinding tule fog was radiational fog, rising from the ground rather than blowing in from a body of water. It was the specific result of climate and geography: Rain filled the atmosphere with humidity. Then the temperatures of the late-autumn air fell fast, and cool breezes slid down off the mountainsides and filled the valley basin. The day's warmth radiated away from the earth as the colder air displaced it and mixed with the moisture like cornstarch stirred into a broth. The warmer air above the mountains trapped it all in, a lid on the soup tureen that would not be lifted except by a strong wind, or some shift in the weather that allowed the air in the bowl to dry out.

When she was a child, her father had explained this more than once as he walked her and Donna to school before opening the drugstore for business. Diane understood the science but found it unable to explain the foreboding such fog created in her heart. The monochrome gray was oppressive, the air measurably more difficult for her to breathe, and she could be certain that the evening news would bring some word of a disaster or death. In the Great Central Valley, this oozing airborne monster was the top cause of weather-triggered casualties.

Donna had died on such a day, though not for that reason.

Diane pulled the apron strings taut behind her ample waist and headed down the dark staircase into the cinnamon scent.

There were only two customers in the dining area when she passed through it, a man in his early thirties and a woman, a girl really, who might have been in high school. Diane thought she had seen them both before, two of the many busybodies who had dropped in during the last week. They were sitting at different tables but talking to each other. He said something about a basketball tournament over the weekend. She said something about a science fair.

Ed was holding a dog-eared paper manual and standing in front of the coffeemaker, which looked to Diane like a Jules Verne time-travel machine, as if he'd never seen one before. Their eyes met as she came around the counter.

"You know how to work one of these?" he asked.

She shook her head. "Your mom always does it."

"She's home with the flu this morning."

"Oh. Sorry."

He was a smart boy. He'd figure it out. She went into the kitchen. Geoff was at the industrial-size mixer pouring water into a pile of flour. Estrella was weighing the yeast. The brick oven was radiating heat from the morning fire. A bucket of hot ashes cooled in the corner of the room, and the soaked wood door had been removed from the oven's mouth, which awaited the next batch of dough.

They all exchanged distracted good mornings, acknowledgments filled with the tension of being shorthanded and a little behind. Diane headed toward the storeroom to fetch plastic baskets and waxed-tissue liners. She'd prep and stack these behind the counter before the morning rush, which would hit in about an hour.

Over the sound of the whirring dough hook in the mixer, she heard the front door open and close. She peeked out to see if she could take an order. No need for Ed to be distracted from the time machine, especially if the customer wanted a latte.

The gray of a man's slacks and the shiny black polish of his shoes were slipping past the swinging door that led to the bathrooms.

Diane returned to the storeroom to collect what she wanted, then scowled at a pile of empty flour sacks that had been dumped on the floor, along with a tub of a creamy cinnamon-sugar mix that had been scraped out and set aside. She stopped to fold and stack the sacks so they'd take up less room in the trash can. She took the tub to the stainless-steel sink and ran hot water and soap in it to prevent the sugar from hardening. Murphy's Law said that because Audrey was absent, today would be the day the health inspector showed up.

For a fleeting moment Diane thought that might have been who had gone directly to the bathrooms upon entering.

She decided to wash the tub rather than let it soak.

That done, she returned to her baskets and liners and carried the supplies out of the kitchen, heading for the service counter. The gray slacks and shiny shoes were standing at the front door of the dining room now, their wearer's back to her. Ed had seen him too. The way Ed lowered the appliance manual to his side caused Diane to look at the guest a second time.

Now she recognized his black hair — his tidy, freshly cut, slicked-back hair — not one strand out of place, as if keeping his hairstyle under control might give him power over life itself. Jack Mansfield was doing something to the door.

She dropped her chin to her chest and spun to the counter. Her hands shook as she set down the baskets and lost her grip on the box, but it landed squarely on the surface. This was a lucky break; she'd have time to leave the room before he noticed her, before he announced that he had discovered her connection to his wife, and that he had deduced that Diane had lied to him about his wife's phone, and that he had looked into her criminal record, and that he was here to place her under arrest for abducting her best friend Juliet Steen and murdering her just as she had murdered her twin sister once upon a time.

Once a killer, always a killer.

Diane set the black baskets and box of tissues on the counter and made what she hoped was a discreet beeline for the door that led to the hallway past the bathrooms and to her apartment. Jack got there first.

"I'm going to need you to stay here, Ms. Hall," he said.

The back door would be her next route

out. It should have been her first choice, of course, because even though it wasn't the closest exit, there was nowhere to go after she got upstairs, which would have been really stupid. But she was really stupid after all, wasn't she? She turned and brushed past Ed, who was staring at the front door.

"The rear door is armed from the outside," Jack said loudly. "Please don't open it."

Diane spun. Jack was holding a gun. The man and girl in the dining room stopped talking. The male stood from his chair, his posture asking a question, and Jack turned and leveled his gun at the man's head. When his eyes alighted on Jack, his expression changed from shock to shocked recognition.

"Look here," Jack said to the guest. "It's the barfly coach. You know my wife. That might be helpful, if you're sober today."

Geoff and Estrella emerged from the kitchen.

Was Jack here for *this* man and not her? In either case, why was arming the rear door necessary?

She looked to the front. The OPEN sign had been flipped so that it faced her. There was a block of something gray and claylike stuck to the seam between door and frame, just above the lock.

Geoff said, "Jack, if you want something from me, I'll gladly give it to you. Put your gun down."

"Let's work quickly," Jack said. "This shouldn't take too long if everyone will cooperate. Ms. Hall, please lower the blinds and draw the curtains." He gestured toward the various window coverings. Diane obeyed. "Young lady" — the girl was clutching a notebook and a fistful of pencils in one hand and a phone in the other — "place your call to the police. Did you know I'm an officer myself? Yes, twenty-one years. Then I'll take that cell phone off your hands."

The girl didn't speak. Diane wondered if her call had gone through. The metallic scraping of curtain rings being dragged along the rods was the only sound in the restaurant. That and the Spanish murmuring of Estrella, praying or cursing, Diane wasn't sure. Jack didn't seem to care, his gun remained at Coach Henderson's temple.

"Jack, please," Geoff said.

"Before we head into the back, a demonstration: everyone, please come over here."

The girl at the table started to cry.

"No tears, girl. You remind me of my

234

daughter, always crying about something. If you knew me, you'd know that I only want the best for you. As for each person here. Except maybe you, Coach. No room for drunkards in the kingdom of God. But that's for another day. *This* day has the potential to end very, very well, no harm done. It's up to you."

The six people in the bakery looked at each other. Only Geoff moved toward Jack.

"Thank you, Geoff," Jack said. "Your life experience has transformed you into a fine role model. It's about time. Everyone else, don't make me repeat myself."

Diane, Estrella, Ed, and the girl shifted by inches.

"Come over here!" Jack yelled.

They went.

"Pick up that string, Coach," Jack said.

The slender man bent and picked up the end of a string lying at Jack's feet. The white nylon cord ran under the closed door and, presumably, down the hall on the other side.

"Pull it."

Coach pulled. Everyone watched through the porthole-style window in the swinging door.

The far end of the hallway exploded, and the group recoiled at the flash of light momentarily obscuring the bathrooms. The door that separated the group from the blast breathed on its hinges. Something like a piece of wood struck its small round window and bounced back into the hallway. Jack nodded, satisfied with the effect. Diane thought the smoke looked like the fog outside.

Except the smoke exited the hall much more quickly, rushing upward past the demolished door to Diane's apartment. It left behind a pile of splintered wood and powdery drywall that now blocked the stairs.

"That," Jack said, nodding at the destruction and then spinning back to the bakery's main entrance, "is what's on *that* door. I suggest you leave it closed. Can't guarantee that it will kill you, but it will mess up your face. Geoff, for the benefit of those who don't live here, please explain that even if the rubble were cleared, there's no exit up those rear stairs."

Geoff nodded, his arms crossed.

"Same thing goes for the kitchen door. Don't open it. Now, to the kitchen."

Jack, keeping his gun on Coach, herded the small group behind the counter half filled with baked goods. They collected in the kitchen in front of the hot brick oven. The scent of something burning came from the electric one.

"Lights, please."

Geoff turned off the switch, and the dining room became dark. Jack grabbed a tall, wheeled rack of warm loaves and dragged it behind him into the kitchen, blocking the entry.

"You" — Jack pointed at Estrella — "no need for a fire. Get whatever it is out of the stove." She moved quickly, arming herself with mitts and grimacing when she opened the door and a puff of smoke escaped. "On the counter." Estrella pulled out two heavy-duty pans of dry muffins. She quickly carried them to the counter Jack had indicated and set them on the shiny surface — then shoved them with all her body weight toward Jack.

He jumped out of the way. The pans crashed into the bread rack and knocked off several of the loaves, then hit the floor, steaming and dumping their contents. Jack found his center, placed both hands on the butt of his gun, and fired at Coach.

Diane flinched. The concrete floor and metal appliances turned the room into a megaphone. The girl screamed and pressed her notebook and pencils over her ears, double bent. Ed grabbed her and pushed her to the floor, shielding her. Geoff was jumping toward Coach. Estrella looked stricken.

The gunshot seemed to hum long after the bullet came to rest.

"That was a fool thing to do!" Jack screamed at Estrella. "I'll kill him next time! Believe me, I have a clear conscience when it comes to his kind!"

Diane looked at Coach. He was crushing his foot in his own hands, and his fingers were red and sticky. He groaned softly. Geoff was kneeling over him with wads of dish towels trying to stop the bleeding.

Jack steadied himself with a long breath. "You" — he indicated the girl — "go into the storage room." She ran in. "And you, Ed, and the cook, before I shove her into the oven myself." They obeyed.

Diane fidgeted beside the rear door, waiting for him to tell her what to do, fearing what he might say. She had stood this close to group altercations before. Cat-claw fights in kitchens and dining rooms, minus the firearms, happened at the women's facility now and then. She knew what was required to get out of the scuffle without being tossed onto some hard surface or sharp corner; it wasn't unlike surviving in a pack of dogs: Stand aside. Don't make eye contact. Be quiet. Obey the alpha.

She kept her eyes low, on the oozing pool of blood under Coach's foot. Jack was watching her. If he thought she might fall against the door and blow them all up, he had nothing to worry about. She took a step away from the crash bar.

"Geoff," he said without releasing Diane from his gaze. "Where's my wife?"

"I don't know." Geoff's voice was as always: level, patient.

"You don't know because she's dead and the vultures have carried her off in pieces?"

"I'll go into the Mojave without water to help you find her, Jack. You don't have to hold a gun to my head, and you certainly don't have to shoot someone who's not involved."

"Sentimental but untrue."

"I haven't seen Julie since the kids' graduation in June."

"Where's *your* wife?"

When Geoff didn't reply right away, Diane glanced at him from the corner of her eye. He was standing, and there was a black stain on the hem of his blue apron. "Hurting her won't tell you what happened to Julie," he finally said.

"I'm not going to hurt her. At least not in the way you mean. Where is she?"

"At home with the flu."

"Ms. Hall, I have a job for you. And I need you to follow my instructions very carefully. I hear you're searching for a way to wash someone else's blood off your hands, is that true?"

Diane nodded once, just enough for him to see. He knew about Donna, about the phone. He knew it all.

"Twenty-five years behind bars can't make a person clean. But I can save you from getting any dirtier. Don't run away now, hear? Because if you run, the blood of these five people will drown your soul."

The people in the storeroom were listening. Now they would know the truth, before she had the chance to do her penance and make her case: Diane Hall had murdered her twin sister and returned to the scene of the crime. What was it to Jack to add five more people to her list of kills?

Jack said, "Geoff, give the lady the keys to your truck."

Geoff fished them out of his pocket and tossed them to her. Jack pointed to the rear door. "Go get Audrey."

"Okay." Her trembling body twisted toward the door and leaned into it before she remembered Jack's warning. But the door latch was already released by the time she caught herself and jerked her palms off the chrome.

"Not yet!" Jack yelled. Diane gasped and froze. She waited for the world to explode.

A rush of cool air slapped her cheeks and a furry cat darted in between her ankles, mewing thanks for letting it in. The door boomed shut again.

"Wait for directions next time." The cat sauntered over to the empty wood bin by the stove. Diane feared Jack might shoot it. "If I hadn't anticipated your stupidity, I might have actually armed the door before you left, and then where would we be? Directions, Ms. Hall, directions. Let's go over them now."

CHAPTER 19

Divine connection. This was the term Audrey had given to the strange experiences that sometimes threw her (and her bread) onto the painful paths other people had to walk.

The last time it happened, she was removing a pan of water she'd placed in the oven to create steam. Her elbow struck the counter and the pan sloshed its contents down the front of her thighs, creating instant blisters that stuck to her jeans when she undressed. Her bread that day had gone to the family of Cody Ryan, a firefighter whose legs had been pinned under a collapsed burning wall. His wife sat with him at the hospital while Audrey sat with the couple's five anxious children for three days, feeding them and reassuring them and helping them with homework.

She let the youngest ones sit on her lap, the pain of that pressure on her burns reminding her not to take their own pain for granted. No one but Geoff, she believed, would understand her willingness to do this and agree with her that it was important, not unhealthy or somehow twisted.

In every situation the identity of the person Audrey needed to reach out to became clear within an hour or two. This was the main reason why Audrey didn't think, even after Geoff suggested it, that her fiery fever and the stabbing pains in her belly had anything to do with someone else.

She feared an infection from the cuts on her wrist, some disease carried into her by Julie's blood. The possibility filled her night with red nightmares.

Diane woke her at six thirty Tuesday morning. She slammed the front door of the house and came in yelling Audrey's name. At the startling sounds of invasion Audrey jerked up in bed, then braced herself on her elbow.

"Audrey!" The bedroom door hit the wall and bounced off the stopper as Diane came through it, shouting as if Audrey were on the other side of the ocean.

"Audrey! Get up. Get dressed." Diane started yanking open Geoff's dresser drawers. "Where are your clothes?"

In *her* drawers, but Audrey was still

dressed from yesterday's journey into the mountains. "What are you doing in my house?"

Diane jerked around with one of Geoff's sweatshirts in her fist. She saw Audrey needed only her shoes, dropped the sweatshirt, and leaned forward to grip Audrey's good wrist. She pulled, and her weighty strength lifted Audrey out of bed, straining at the armpit.

"Jack is holding a gun to your husband's head. He wants us to find Juliet."

Audrey's head was an overinflated balloon. She heard *find Juliet.* She squinted and exhaled hard, as if that might let off some of the pressure. "Who's Juliet?"

"Julie. Jack's wife."

Which was when Audrey finally heard the words *gun* and *your husband.*

"We have six hours."

Audrey's car had no gas in it; the tank was drained after her ride up to King's Riches, but Geoff's truck was idling in the driveway with the driver's-side door open, as Diane had left it.

Audrey grabbed a can of ginger ale from the fridge on her way out in case the nausea returned. The fear, and then the cold fog slapping her face when she rushed out the door, improved her physical symptoms immensely. Her temperature was still high. A vise tightened down on her head, front to back, and sent a drill straight down through the top of her skull. It was not enough to prevent her from reaching the truck and sliding onto the driver's seat. Diane leaped in on the other side.

They slammed the doors and looked at each other.

"Are you okay to drive?" Diane asked. "I don't have a license. I only had one for a year before I went to jail, and the drive over here was almost as scary as Jack shooting that man in the foot, but I'll do it if I have to. I mean, I did it, and I got here."

"I don't know where to go," Audrey said. "Jack shot someone?"

"The man from Juliet's school? I saw him last week once. I think he was one of your son's coaches."

"Her name is Julie. Are Geoff and Ed hurt?"

"When we were kids, she went by Juliet. And no, they're fine. Were fine. When I left."

"You know Julie? Wait — yes, you know her. Story for another time." Audrey placed her hands on the steering wheel and concentrated on the horn. "I need to focus, make a plan." She closed her eyes, envisioning the narrative that had poured out while she pulled on her shoes. "Jack came into the bakery, armed the doors, blew one up, and put everyone in the storage room. Why did he shoot the coach?"

"Because Estrella threw some hot pans at him."

"Are the police there? Besides him?"

"I don't know. I don't know if anyone got a call off. He didn't seem to care if they did. I didn't . . . I didn't think to drive to the station myself. I was so worried about whether I'd be able to find you. The street was kind of familiar, but it's been so long, and the fog . . . Jack made your husband give me his car keys, and Geoff drew me a map. It could have gone so badly if I didn't follow Geoff's directions right on."

Diane rattled on while Audrey picked up her phone from the console between the bucket seats and called 9-1-1. She identified herself as the owner of a bakery where there was a hostage situation and learned authorities were aware of it. She told them she was with a witness who might have information they needed.

The dispatcher got her location and instructed her to stay on the line while she located the officer in charge of the situation. The sun was cresting in Audrey's

246

rearview mirror, and she had a moment of panic. "Did Jack tell you I'm not supposed to talk to the police? Did he give you rules about what I can and can't do?"

"No. Really, nothing like that seemed important to him."

"You're sure? Tell me his exact words."

"He said, 'Tell his wife' — he meant Geoff, and you, it was clear — 'Tell his wife that I expect her to bring mine to me by twelve thirty. Then maybe we'll all go out to lunch.' "

"And if I don't bring her in time?"

A man's voice came over the line. "Mrs. Bofinger?"

"Captain Wilson?" The man had interviewed her more than once.

"Yes, ma'am. It seems things have escalated."

"I don't know firsthand."

"Have you had any contact with anyone inside the bakery?"

"No. I just learned —"

"Who's your witness?"

"Diane Hall."

"Oh yes, it seems we've all met before. Put her on the line, please."

Audrey handed over the phone, put the car in gear, and backed out of the driveway into the terrible visibility. The truck crawled,

Audrey's shoulders tense and taut, like they were the day she and Ed ran over the scooter. This time, she dared not go faster than her eyes could register information.

She listened to Diane's side of the conversation: Jack plus five people inside, back in the storeroom, maybe the kitchen. One man wounded so far. Doors barricaded with some kind of explosive. A demand that Audrey produce Juliet — Julie Mansfield. Until his wife appeared, he wouldn't be talking to anyone.

"Can I talk with him?" Audrey said when she heard this.

Diane shook her head and said to the phone, "When she has Julie, she's supposed to knock five times on the kitchen's rear door."

"I can't talk with Jack?" Audrey repeated.

Diane shook her head again. "The captain wants us to come to the bakery," Diane told Audrey, still holding the phone to her ear.

"What's Jack going to do if we can't find her?"

"I didn't ask. He didn't say. I think he believes you'll just bring her, or her body. I think he really believes that. How long will it take us to get there?"

"In this weather? I hope no more than fifteen minutes."

Diane relayed the information and closed the phone.

Oh, Father, how am I going to do this? How would she react if Jack hurt her husband or her son? The ache in her head and in her lower abdomen became agitated. *Focus, focus. Focus on what you're going to do to avoid ever having to answer that question.*

She said to Diane, "How'd you get out?"

"The back door."

"It wasn't rigged like he said?"

"No. It was lucky . . . well. He's probably done something about that now."

"Did he take everyone's phones?"

"I don't know. Maybe? He didn't ask me for one."

"He knows you don't own one." Audrey frowned at her.

"How'd he know that?"

"He's a detective, Diane. How do you think *I* found out that you lied to him about Julie's phone?"

Diane pursed her lips together and wouldn't look at her.

"You shouldn't have done that."

"People tell me that a lot."

Audrey pointed at her own cell phone. "Here, try calling Geoff. He's on the speed dial, number two." She waited impatiently for Diane to figure out the basic commands of the phone.

"Straight to voice mail. Didn't even ring."

"Try Ed. Number three."

Diane pushed the necessary buttons and got the same result.

"The landline?" She gave her the number. No answer. "I need a way to talk to them!"

The headlights were reflecting off the moisture in the air and glaring back at her. She turned off the lamps so that all she had on were the parking lights, and the pounding in her head eased up just enough for her to choose her course.

"We can't go to the bakery," she said to Diane.

"Why not?"

"Jack's there because he has no idea where Julie is. That means the police don't have a clue either."

"I don't understand why we shouldn't go talk to them."

"If no one knows where she is, talking about what we don't know is a waste of time."

"They might be able to tell you *something.*"

"Like what? Their goal as I guess it is to get Jack under control. They're not going to give me a briefing on Julie's case. I'm a suspect!"

Diane was silent for a few seconds, then she nodded. "Ohhhh. So you think Jack knew you'd go talk to them, and with his demands plus a threat against your family, they'd send you on your way, and then they'd follow you to see what you would do."

Audrey hadn't considered it that way at all. It was an unpleasant possibility. Until then she hadn't thought that the police would be anything but an ally. But she said, "Exactly."

"Maybe it will look really bad if you don't go talk to them at all."

Yes, maybe it would. But six hours wasn't enough time for her to worry about that. When she reached Meridian Road, she turned left instead of right.

"You don't know where Juliet is?" Diane asked.

"No, I don't. I wish I did."

"It's cold out there," Diane said. "Not like in your bakery."

She must have meant something more than what was obvious, Audrey thought. "If you'd be more comfortable I can drop you off at the police station first —"

"What are you going to do?" Diane asked. And through the doubting tone, Audrey believed she heard anticipation rather than fear in the woman's voice. A dare. A hope.

"I'm going to Jack's house."

"Okay." A few seconds passed. "You should expect police to be there, just so you know."

"I don't, actually. We don't have that big a police force in this town."

"Why Jack's house? If he doesn't know where Julie is, wouldn't he have turned it inside out looking for clues? At least his buddies would have."

"Maybe I think he knows where Julie is." That should have been enough of a surprise to drop on Diane's head, but the woman didn't even raise an eyebrow. And so Audrey added, "Also, the last time I was at his home something really strange happened. Maybe I can get it to happen again."

Secretly, she doubted it.

CHAPTER 20

The involved parties have accepted my demands and will comply by 1230 hours. Five souls praying for the safe return of all. Please stand by to aid victim and secure suspect upon arrival. I need no further assistance.

Jack pressed SEND on his phone and delivered the e-mail to Captain Wilson. His methods, while drastic, would be justified as most efficient when it came to ending his wife's ordeal. Julie would come home and return to work; their routines would resume; God would end their suffering and fulfill his promises. Jack's colleagues' hands would be clean; Bofinger's wife would be punished appropriately.

The storage room had a concrete floor with a drain at the center, and walls of cinder block that had been painted white. Floor-to-ceiling stainless-steel racks on wheels were lined up in the space like library book stacks. Jack instructed Ed and the cowering girl, a nerd with her notebooks, to push aside the racks in the center so they might have room to sit. That task would occupy them for a while.

He put the Mexican woman in the one empty corner out of reach of potential projectiles. Jack sat opposite her on an empty five-gallon bucket, which he'd overturned and positioned in the doorway, his back to the kitchen. He attached a silencer to the end of his gun. Wilson, now alerted to "the situation," would only get uptight and start acting recklessly if he heard any guns going off. Jack hadn't expected to send off a round already.

Coach said, "I heard a cat."

He lay on the floor with his foot elevated on a bag of wheat flour. His neck and shoulders twisted so he could see, upside down, through the storeroom door and into the kitchen. A small pile of bloody dish towels was accumulating at his side. Estrella slipped out of her apron and sweater and covered the man with them both, a wasted gesture on this cold slab of floor. Geoff continued to apply pressure to the wound.

"Better not let the health department see this," Jack said to Geoff, gesturing to the red droplets on the sacks. "Or any cats."

A sweat broke out on Coach's forehead.

"I really hate cats."

"Aren't you concerned about what the police department will think?" Geoff asked Jack.

"They're not very interested in your work here," Jack said. "Get the man some Tylenol. Where's your first-aid kit?"

"Estrella, in that cabinet," Geoff said, pointing to the doors behind her.

The set of rolling shelves rattled with cooking utensils as it shifted under the kids' weight.

"The police can't support what you're doing," Geoff continued while Estrella found the white box bearing a little red cross on the lid.

"Drastic methods are hard to support before they're proven effective."

"I would like to see thees man say so to a judge," Estrella said to Geoff.

"If you don't keep silent, you might miss that opportunity," Jack said to her. Then to Geoff, "We can be done with this whenever you say the word. The right word."

Estrella handed Coach some tablets.

"I wasn't lying to you when I said I don't know what happened to Julie," Geoff said.

"Your wife doesn't confide in you? That's some marriage bond you've got."

The phone in the kitchen rang.

"Audrey doesn't have anything to hide." The baker applied one more clean towel to the coach's foot and secured it with some of the duct tape from the roll Jack had tossed onto the floor.

Coach said, "Julie confided in me more than she did in you, Jack."

"When? All those times you took her out clubbing? Did you think I wouldn't find out about that?"

"What? We didn't go clubbing."

"Then what do you call those nights out at The Barley Field?"

"It was a retirement party for the athletic director. *One* night. All the staff from Mazy went."

"But you and my wife were joined at the hip, from what I heard. You know my fellow officers like to end shifts there too? Yeah, I think you knew."

"For crying out loud, Jack. She was just being supportive. Like a sponsor."

"I think the pain is clouding your mind," Jack snapped. "Maybe a little brandy or rum will take the edge off. Any of your recipes call for that stuff, Geoff?"

The baker ignored him.

Coach said, "She's a good woman. I've lost track of how many times her kindness kept me sober."

"Julie has a soft spot for dogs."

"You're the best evidence of that."

Jack called upon his years of experience as an officer to maintain an outwardly unaffected poise. It wasn't good that he'd already lost his cool before he'd even set everything in motion. On the bright side, it seemed that shooting Coach in the foot might have been providential. If the man was belligerent now, how much trouble might he have caused if still standing?

"I'm sure your knowledge of my wife is limited."

"Like yours, you mean."

"You're not lying in a very safe position to insult me."

"Julie is my friend. She and I spend more hours together at the school than the two of you spend together in your home. That's a simple matter of number crunching, Jack."

"But she didn't marry you, did she?"

"All I'm saying is, depressed people need sympathetic ears. Their spouses can't always provide those. Not in the same way someone who's been there can."

"My wife is not depressed!"

"That, right there, is exactly my point."

The girl with the Bofinger boy whispered something to him. They leaned shoulder to shoulder as they pushed a second shelf unit against the wall.

"If you have something to say, let's all hear it," Jack said to her. The girl started crying again.

Geoff said to Coach, "Did Julie ever seem afraid to you? Like she feared someone might hurt her?"

"Fishing for alibis, are we?" Jack said.

"No," Coach said to Geoff. "She wasn't afraid, she was clinically depressed. Diagnosed by her doctor."

"If my wife was sad it's only because she hasn't been saved yet."

Estrella snorted. "Thees man can't be serious."

"As my bleeding foot," Coach said.

All eyes turned to Jack. These people disgusted him. Their hearts and minds were dense. "Depression is a spiritual sickness."

"It's physical," Coach said, "and Christians aren't any more immune to it than the common cold. I've struggled with it — and more."

"Then I question the depth of your faith," Jack said.

"I thought Mrs. Mansfield was depressed." The snuffling teenage girl seemed unable to stop her outburst. "Even though she tried not to show it."

"What's your name?" Jack asked her. He

put a hand on her shoulder and turned her away from Ed. Ed warned Jack off with his superhero laser-eye gaze. Jack pointed at the remaining unit that need to be pushed aside, and Ed went to it. In the corner of his heart, Jack felt sorry for this girl and feared what sins Ed might lead her into if she wasn't wary. That, however, was out of his hands.

"Your name," he repeated.

"Leslie," she said.

"Leslie, even if you're legally an adult —"

"I turn eighteen next —"

"— you have a lot to learn about adult behavior. The age of adulthood ought to be raised to twenty-five and probably will be one of these days. A girl our daughter's age is the last person my wife would confide in. The last."

"She didn't have to tell me anything," Leslie whispered. "I could just see it."

"Well, that's evidence enough for me!"

Geoff couldn't resist derailing the conversation at this point, seeing that Jack was taking the upper hand. "Maybe it would be more helpful if —"

"You've never been very good at saving people from themselves," Jack said. "Stop trying. Stick to playing with your flour and water."

"If you want to know what happened to Julie, consider that all the people in this room know her — everyone except Estrella. If we pool our information, maybe something helpful will open up."

"I know everything I need to know," Jack said, returning to his bucket perch. "I didn't come here to do more investigating."

From somewhere in the dining room a cat mewed.

CHAPTER 21

Nothing about Jack's house appeared as it had on the spring day when Audrey had last come. The sunshine warmth seemed forbidden here, excommunicated from the property. Flowerpots contained only caked soil and dry plant skeletons abandoned at summer's end.

Audrey didn't see any police.

"How are you going to get in?" Diane asked.

Audrey's mind had been focused on how her body might react to arriving here. So far, she'd sensed no change in her previous achy condition.

"I'll look around outside first, see what I see. Stay here."

She got out of the truck and walked around the front, waiting for that firm invisible hand to guide her toward the thing she needed to find. She started across the little bean-shaped lawn toward the window where

261

she had stood months ago and lost her ear-ring in the dirt.

The moist air slipped across her neck, and she shivered.

Your ways are mysterious to me, God, but if you'd give me a map with point-by-point directions to Julie Mansfield right now, I'd be grateful.

She stood in front of the window, looking at the shrubs and the dirt under it, which had become spongy in yesterday's rain. *Or I'll settle for a subtle dose of intuition if you'd rather work that way. That's fine too.*

Diane's arm brushed hers.

"I thought you were waiting in the truck," Audrey said after she got her heart out of her throat.

Diane shook her head and was looking at the windows of the house, all shut against the damp. "Juliet's parents lived here when we were kids," she said. "She and the detective live here now? Really?"

Audrey nodded. "I didn't know you were from around here."

"I was born in this town. So was Juliet. There's a shed in the back. It used to be our clubhouse."

"Did your clubhouse adventures ever include breaking and entering?"

"Oh, Audrey, don't. It's not worth it,

262

believe me."

"Are you married, Diane? Do you have kids?"

"Neither."

"They're worth it. Their lives are worth anything I have to do."

Diane didn't say anything.

"Show me how to get into the back?"

"The gate's over here. Are you okay? You're flushed. Ed said you had the flu."

"Just a fever."

Diane led her over a flower bed and onto the slab walkway between the front door and the driveway. On her way past, Audrey opened the screen and tried the doorknob, jiggling it. The hardware felt pleasantly cool on her hot fingers.

"Locked," she said aloud.

"Jack doesn't seem the type to forget those kinds of things," Diane said.

"No. You're right. He's" — Audrey tried to think of the right word — "systematic."

On the other side of the garage, they gained access through a gate with a simple latch and no lock. They passed between the garage wall and the neighbor's wood-slat fence, a narrow path with precisely placed pavers marching into the backyard. Audrey saw the short chain-link fence at the far end of the property and the storage shed just

263

inside of it, directly ahead. To the right, another small lawn was bordered by fruit trees and a small vegetable garden.

"That's the master bedroom," Diane said, pointing at the short end of the L-shaped house. She continued down the pavers toward the shed. Audrey detoured to try the door at the back of the garage.

The knob turned easily in her hand and swung open into the darkened space.

"Diane," she called, then motioned she would go in this way. The area was attached to the house, and even if the door that led into the main building was secure, she might find something of interest in here — if not a key.

Audrey headed toward the glowing orange light that she guessed was the garage-door opener. When she reached it, she ran her hands along the wall and found a light switch.

A bulb in the center of the rafters shone on an old compact car that Audrey didn't recognize. Maybe it was Julie's.

The interior door opened soundlessly into a clean kitchen. Diane had caught up with her. The women stepped in.

Diane glanced around the kitchen and then quickly passed through the dining room toward the front of the house.

"Look for anything that seems off," Audrey said.

Diane pulled up short and twisted to look at Audrey. Surprise lined her brow. "Right." Her legs took her into the living room though her eyes were trained on the hall leading to the bedrooms. "What do you mean *off?*"

"I don't know what it will be. You knew her — anything that doesn't look right by what you know about her personality, her habits?"

Audrey's eyes quickly moved over the clean kitchen counters as she followed Diane.

"I don't know if I'd catch anything out of the ordinary," Diane said. "We've been out of touch for a while."

She sounded apologetic.

Now that she was standing in Jack's house, Audrey realized how desperate she must seem. Unless Jack was careless or sloppy, which she had never known him to be, she should not have expected to find anything helpful here.

God, you know the truth about what happened. Please, would you show it to me before Jack hurts the men I love so much?

The living room was immaculate and predictable: a sofa, a long coffee table, two chairs, a short coffee table between them. Planters in front of the window, bookcase bearing books, a stereo system, and half a dozen or so neatly organized framed table-top photographs.

She turned down the hallway and flipped on the light. Diane went to look at the pictures. Audrey passed a bathroom on the left and a home office on the right. She heard the sound of Diane opening a drawer.

Audrey paused at the office, turned in at the door. This room overlooked the front yard and would have been the room where she'd heard the heartbreaking sobbing those months ago.

Grief like a whip across her back dropped her to her knees in the open doorway. She rocked forward onto her arms, her forehead meeting the dusty carpet, her mouth gasping, reminded of the intensity that had bent her over the hood of her car.

A cool metal barrel kissed her spine as she crouched.

"Who are you?" a voice demanded.

Between her illness and the devastating emotion, Audrey barely had the presence of mind to answer. "Audrey Bofinger. I'm looking for Julie."

"Oh. You."

The gun came off her back, and she felt

the person's feet pivot near her backside.

Audrey lifted her head and turned her neck. The quick movement filled her ears with ringing and her throat with sickness. She held her breath to hold it down.

When it receded she asked, "Where's Julie?" She directed the question at the person behind her and managed to twist over onto her seat as she looked up. "Miralee."

The name on her tongue was a miracle medicine, a fast-acting remedy that decimated Audrey's pains. The headache evaporated. The nausea slipped away. The grief became a distant impression. Audrey wiped perspiration of a broken fever off her forehead with the back of her hand.

The girl held the weapon down at her side. She was looking down the hallway.

"My friend Diane is in the living room."

"You broke into my house."

"Yeah, well, your father thinks I kidnapped your mom."

"I know. Ed told me."

Audrey wondered what had changed his mind. "I didn't know he called you. Is that why you came home?"

"No." Her tone was flat. "I came because I can't resist a good drama."

"Jack's taken five people hostage. My husband. Ed."

Miralee showed no reaction to that news. "Did you kidnap my mom?"

"No."

"Didn't think so."

"Yeah? That was easy."

"I'm not a difficult person to get along with. It's you churchgoers who are royal pains. My father has been wrong about everything his entire life."

"I don't know about that." Audrey used the doorframe to pull herself up to standing.

"But he thinks you know where to find my mom."

Audrey nodded.

"So there. He's wrong again. This is a dumb place to start looking, wouldn't you say?"

"Will you help us look for her?" Audrey asked.

"Don't know what I can do. She won't respond to my efforts to get in touch with her. I say if she wants to be left alone, we should leave her alone."

"What if someone's got her?"

"Show me a ransom note and I'll answer your question then."

The pretty girl was the same age as Audrey's son and looked more like Julie than Jack, with high round cheeks and a tall forehead. Her features in their natural state were photogenic, attractive. But since leaving her high school years behind, or maybe since leaving her father's house, Miralee had sharpened her appearance to suit her personality with foundation too pale for her true complexion and cosmetics too dark for her youth. Audrey thought she might have dyed her hair as well.

An image of Miralee holding a baby, Audrey's grandbaby, popped into the front of Audrey's mind unbidden. For some reason the child was a girl. She reached out for the bundle without thinking of what she was doing, and at the same time Miralee stomped toward the living room.

Audrey glanced back into the office. The curtains were drawn, the desk clean, the computer shut down. A recliner in one corner of the room was tucked in on itself, waiting for someone to lean back in it and rest. The reading light on the adjacent table was dark.

"Get out of that cabinet," she heard Miralee order Diane.

Now that she was feeling more like her normal self than she had in the last twenty-four hours, Audrey felt anxiety weaseling its way into her emotional state. She needed a

269

better plan. She needed tangible information.

"Is your parents' home always this neat?" she called after Miralee.

"My father's version of it is."

Audrey peeked into the bedroom at the end of the hall — chaotic, Miralee's she assumed — and then entered the master suite opposite it. The large room was as tidy as the rest of the house, clean as a showcase home, right down to the glistening white bathtub. As white as if Jack had committed a heinous crime and then had it professionally cleaned.

The idea was ridiculous. Jack lived by the book — and by the Book. But there he was, just a few miles away, holding her family hostage in their place of business. She wondered which scriptural passages he had used to justify this particular approach to finding "the victim."

Could a man who'd taken a group of people hostage also be capable of murdering his wife and blaming the crime on someone else? Or was he guilty only of desperate love?

On her way out of the master bath she caught sight of the couple's nightstands. On the right side, nothing but a Bible and a pair of reading glasses. On the left, the only disorganized area in the room. The narrow table was stacked with books, a lamp that had been pushed aside and braced between the mattress and the wall, knickknacks, a water glass, and medicine bottles. No Bible in the tall stack.

Audrey wondered if partners who agreed to live by different worldviews commonly found themselves at an impasse. How much strain could accumulate before their bond snapped? How many bricks could one stack on a bridge before the span collapsed?

She picked up the pill bottles. Antibiotics, with several tablets remaining; painkillers; a third that Audrey didn't recognize. All prescribed by a Dr. Reese.

"Was your mom sick?" she called out.

The words left her tongue and entered her own ears and elicited one clear, certain answer: Julie was excruciatingly sick. As sick as Audrey had felt.

She went back out to the living room, carrying the bottles.

"Miralee, what does your mom have?"

Diane was handing a framed photograph to the girl.

"What do you mean *have?*"

"What's this medicine for?"

"How should I know?"

"Do you know a Dr. Reese?"

271

"Yeah. She's Mom's oncologist."

The girl said the word the way one would say *hairstylist* or *tennis partner*.

"Your mom has cancer?"

"Maybe she still does. Ovarian. I first heard about it in the spring, but she caught it early. She had lots of treatment options then."

"But she had surgery."

"Did she?" A light of surprised concern passed through Miralee's eyes, then flickered out. "She was always a bit extreme when it came to her health."

"That's not so extreme for ovarian cancer. You didn't know about it?"

"I didn't know that's what she finally chose."

"Don't you guys talk about this kind of thing? Is it delicate for some reason?"

"Did you want to find my mom or just sit here dissecting the Mansfield psychoses?" Miralee handed the photo frame back to Diane and said, "That's Cora Jean and Harlan. Bitter old folks."

Diane took the image in both hands as if it were more fragile than a newborn.

The weak morning light, filtered by fog and white sheers covering the windows, was just enough for Audrey to glimpse the photograph of a threesome standing in front of an old gray Ford. Julie in the middle was flanked by the aging Halls.

"I know them," Audrey said. She took the picture from Diane's hands. "They're your parents' neighbors. Cora Jean died in April." Harlan's expression was stern and reminded Audrey of Jack's uncompromising sense of right and wrong.

Diane had turned her back to Audrey as if she was studying the other pictures on the shelf.

"Did your mom know them well?" Audrey asked Miralee.

"This is a framed photo in the family living room. Duh."

"Maybe Harlan will know something about what happened to Julie. Let's go down there."

Miralee said, "You think an old man who probably can't remember what he ate for breakfast will have some information about my mom that the entire police force couldn't dig up?"

"He's not that old," Audrey defended. "Or forgetful."

"Have at it."

"You're too young to be so sour," Audrey said to Miralee. "What happened?"

"Nothing you could possibly understand. All you religious people are in one big happy alliance of denial. Go talk to the old man. I'm going to the bakery."

"What will you do there?"

"Talk some sense into the man called Jack."

"He's not talking to anyone, honey. I'm sorry to be harsh, but if his own people can't get through his head, what makes you think you can?"

Miralee crossed her arms, but the lines of her lips softened.

"What did she die from?" Diane whispered. "Mrs. Hall."

"Pancreatic cancer."

A sob broke out of Diane's throat, a startling and terrible sound.

Miralee rolled her eyes. "If my mom doesn't have anyone to help her but you two, she's dead already."

Chapter 22

Ed didn't know the clinical definition of *breakdown,* but he was pretty sure Leslie was having one. She had been sitting next to him for an hour with her knees pulled up to her chest. The neat stack of books at her side had spilled. Her lips moved, but Ed couldn't make out the words.

He had moved once, and she'd grabbed his arm hard enough to leave fingernail impressions in his skin. This bright girl with the good heart, as Estrella had put it, was the most terrified girl he'd ever met.

"This is all my fault . . ."

He finally made out her mumbling.

"It's totally my fault."

He leaned in close enough for her to hear him. "What are you talking about?"

Leslie's head popped up. The pencil froze in her hands. "I need to call my mom. Do people know what's going on here? She knew I was coming before school. I need to tell her I'm okay."

"You don't seem okay," Ed whispered. "She'll hear you don't sound like yourself and worry more."

"You're right, you're right. But no, wait. What if she thinks the worst? There was that explosion, he shot that gun . . . What if she's thinking I'm dead? I should call her!"

Ed put a hand on her knee.

"I mean, I might die. And then what?" Leslie started crying. "I really want my mom."

"Shh."

"Let her call her mom," Jack said. He stood from his upended bucket, and the shift of his pants leg covered the backup revolver Ed had seen in a holster strapped to his ankle. The cordless bakery phone was mounted on the wall just outside the store-room door. Jack took it out of its cradle and extended the handset to Leslie.

She looked at it as if it might be a grenade. Ed scanned the man's face for some hidden agenda. What hostage-taker allowed his hostages to use a phone? Leslie finally snatched it out of his hands and clutched it to her chest. He leaned against the wall.

Geoff got up and took a step toward Jack. "I'll just go get my cell phone," he said to the detective.

"You stay put. You can use that phone if the battery's still working when she's finished. No cell phones. But I don't care if you call the old-fashioned way."

"Why not?" Ed asked, glancing at his father.

"What harm will a simple call do?" Jack said. "I'm the one who doesn't need to speak to anyone. Diane's probably told everyone everything they need to know anyway."

"Be careful what you say," Ed told Leslie.

Jack ignored Ed. "My aim isn't to hurt anyone. Call your mom, little girl. Tell her if you're lucky, you'll be home for lunch."

The phone buttons beeped as Leslie dialed.

"But if I don't get my wife back by twelve thirty, I'll kill this man first. Put him out of his spiritual misery." He indicated the coach, who was still on his back with his foot propped up, eyes closed, brow pinched in the middle. "And then I'll shoot her, because she is annoying." Jack leveled his gun at Estrella. "You have the good fortune of being third." Leslie shrieked when the gun swung toward her. She dropped the phone, and the plastic battery door popped off when it hit the ground.

Ed scooped up the parts and fit them back

together, blood pounding in his temples. His hands were sweaty.

His father took a step between them and Jack. "These people are innocent —"

"No one's innocent."

"— of harm against Julie. God won't smile on you for punishing them."

"I don't think you know what God smiles on. You thought your own reputation was more important than the blood of an unborn baby. Maybe you won't care when their blood is running all over your shiny floor. But it'll make an impression on your son. It's the youth who pay the highest price for sin, isn't it? Maybe I'll do Leslie a favor by taking her life. 'The righteous are taken away to be spared from evil.' Should I shoot her first?"

"Scripture in your mouth is a twisted thing," said Geoff. "You're doing evil here, Jack. At least call it what it is."

"I call it *justifiable force.* Sometimes one has to break the law to save a life. Jesus said that. Not too many ways that can be misinterpreted."

"And yet you've managed to do it."

Leslie was speaking in broken sentences into the phone, whispering frantically as if Jack might take the phone back at any second.

Estrella's tabby cat appeared then, sauntering into the room through Jack's legs. The animal saw his friend and cried for his morning meal. Estrella moved toward the cat with her eyes on Jack, then scooped it into her arms. Ed watched Jack, wondering if he would allow Estrella to indulge her pet.

Jack paid it little attention. *His* eyes were on the coach, who'd rolled onto his belly when he heard the cat's demands for attention, then pushed himself back into a corner, favoring his bad foot.

Estrella turned around and saw him. "What?" she said.

"Like I said, I don't like cats." He rubbed a shaky hand across his brow.

"Lots of men say thees," Estrella said, waving Coach off. "You want cats to be dogs, all worshipping you." She carried the animal to a cupboard in search of a bowl.

Ed thought Coach might have wanted cats not to exist at all. At least not that one.

Jack chuckled. "You're afraid of *cats*."

Coach didn't answer.

Jack's amusement grew. "What is this? A side effect of your sobriety? Part of that 'depression and more' that is *not* your spiritual struggle?"

"It's all . . . it's all related." He held up a

trembling hand to shield his eyes from Estrella's pet.

Ed felt confused at the sight of his confident mentor cowering in the presence of a four-legged fur ball.

Jack laughed. "He's afraid of cats! And he thinks it's a medical condition!"

Geoff said, "A lot of people are afraid of cats."

"A lot of people in service to *the devil*," Jack retorted.

"Shut up, Jack," Geoff said.

One of the fluorescent lights overhead flickered.

"He's partly right," Leslie said. "Hitler. Genghis Khan. Julius Caesar. History shows they might have been ailurophobic."

"Been what?" Estrella said. She had a bowl in hand. The cat batted at it.

"Abnormally afraid of cats." Coach's voice wobbled. Sweat showed through the front of his shirt

"No medication for that, is there, Coach?" Jack was shaking his head.

The cream was out in the kitchen. Estrella seemed caught between Coach's bizarre fear and Jack's imposing figure at the doorway.

Coach straightened his shoulders as if that would help to stop the tremors in his arms. "Therapy —"

"Is an exercise in self-centeredness."

"It works for me. Exposure therapy —"

"Yeah, let's have us some of that," Jack said. In three strides he reached Estrella and seized the contented cat by the scruff, snatching it out of her arms. The bowl fell to the ground when Estrella protested, but Jack lifted the surprised animal out of her reach. It froze in the shape of a C, and its tail went rigid. Its yellow eyes caught the lights overhead as Jack tossed the cat into the center of Coach's sweat-soaked shirt.

Ed found his feet while the animal was airborne. His instinct was to separate the cat and the coach, though the flailing, snarling pair needed no help. The cat drew blood across Coach's chest just by bouncing off of him. The wide-eyed feline pounced on Leslie's books as it escaped and sent papers sliding over the floor.

Coach's limbs jerked for long seconds after the animal had vanished, and Ed feared he was choking on his own air. What was the right first-aid procedure for something like this? Ed crouched next to him, lost, while his father moved in, a calm force able to inject peace back into Coach's body with a simple touch.

"Cured? No? Maybe you should try prayer," Jack mocked.

"Or getting shot in the foot," Coach gasped. "A good distraction."

"There's a reason why people suffer," Jack said. "And it's not because you have the wrong meds. It's because of sin."

Coach tipped his head back into the corner where the walls met and closed his eyes. Geoff placed a hand on his knee.

"God's world is simple. Get it wrong; pay the consequences. Get it right; be blessed."

"So tell me, Jack, where did I go wrong?" Coach placed his palms on his diaphragm and took deep breaths.

Ed's mind was racing, dodging the insanity — not to mention the cruelty — of Jack's argument.

"What about that blind man?" he said. "Someone asked Jesus who sinned and made the guy blind. And Jesus said it wasn't sin that caused it, but that God wanted to show his goodness through the man."

Ed saw the corner of his father's mouth lift.

"You are *loco*, boy," Estrella murmured as she tried to coax the cat out from under one of the shelves.

"You think God caused the blind man's suffering," Jack challenged.

"Caused it? I don't know. But I guess he allowed it. For a purpose."

"Yes, to be healed," Jack said. "And the man was healed. Let's talk about the ones who never get their so-called 'healings.' Who, perhaps, don't deserve them."

"Not all of God's promises are for this life," said Geoff, looking at his son.

"So shoot me," Coach said. "Because I'm getting tired of waiting for God to show up."

Jack fired his pistol through the coach's other foot without measuring his aim. Leslie screamed and dropped the phone. She wouldn't stop her screeching. Frantic cries of another person came through the telephone's earpiece.

This was the chaos that snapped Ed out of his self-imposed wallowing in what he thought had been divine punishment. Senselessness morphed into sense. In the space of two seconds, he had a revelation: What if his own humiliation wasn't divine at all, but merely a distraction from what he was supposed to be doing? What if all *this,* this insane ordeal, was not a consequence of his own sin but a chance for God to do something amazing, if only Ed would participate?

All right, then. What was he supposed to be doing?

CHAPTER 23

Her mother was dead. Cora Jean Hall, gone before she was sixty-five, before her only surviving daughter could find her way back home. Standing in Juliet's living room amid death and threats of death, Diane took the news as a sign: she should go knock on her father's door and beg him to kill her.

Not literally; she didn't believe Harlan Hall was capable of physical harm the way she was, though he could spear heart and lungs with his eyes alone. And she'd hoped to make the request with a diamond necklace cradled in the palm of her hand, outstretched. *Here's the object that took over my life. Here's the thing that made me do it. I'm so sorry, but I think it's best if you don't forgive me.* She only needed her father to agree, to declare the remainder of her existence here on earth a pointless waste. Then perhaps, when she physically died, God might say she had been punished enough,

284

though she would understand if he didn't.

She hadn't considered that her parents would stay in this small town and steep in the family tragedy. She hadn't thought that Juliet would have stood in for her as her parents' surrogate daughter all these years. Had she used the necklace to worm her way into their hearts?

She wanted to stay at Juliet's house and ransack it. Find the diamond. Instead she followed Audrey out the front door of the Mansfields' house and heard Miralee lock the door as she exited too. She didn't care why the young woman had changed her mind and decided to come with them. After they met Harlan Hall, Diane would crawl back into whatever dark corner would have her, and it would be nice if Audrey didn't have to search for the woman by herself.

The fog was thicker here than it had been in the cold alley behind the bakery, when Jack had pushed her out the rear door. The sun seemed so powerless against it.

Diane's feet dragged, and Miralee soon caught up with her.

"Are you one of them too?" Miralee asked.

Diane frowned. "One of what?"

"A Christian. Are you in their camp? Churchgoing, law-abiding, brownnosing?"

"I don't think they . . . I don't think I . . .

It's . . . I don't think so."

"What is there to think about? You are or you aren't these days, isn't that how it works? I hear fence straddlers get splinters up their —"

"Then I'm not. No. I definitely have fallen on the wrong side of the fence."

Miralee held out her hand as if they'd make a pact. "Glad to hear it. One more soul taking a stand against hypocrisy."

Diane didn't take the girl's palm. She couldn't fathom what Miralee was talking about. "Your mom isn't a Christian, is she?"

"No more than the Dalai Lama!" Miralee laughed.

"I remember her as pretty opposed to religion in general."

"To this day. She says there's too much suffering in the world for religion to do anyone any good. I guess I have to agree with her there. How do you know her?"

"It seems like you're not very interested in finding out what happened to her."

"And that's related to religion how?"

"That's what I'm wondering. What are you holding against her, if it's not faith?"

"Oh. Easy. My mother is a hypocrite of a different flavor. Christians are the worst, you know. They have a canned answer for every hard question and don't seem to care

286

when their philosophies don't hold up in real life. But a person doesn't have to be a Christian to be a hypocrite."

"So you don't care what happens to her?"

Miralee picked up her pace and passed Diane without looking at her again. "I didn't say I don't care."

Her father was standing in the open doorway five houses down from Juliet's, and Audrey was speaking with him when Diane reached the corner of the property. Her resolve to face him ebbed away.

He looked much older than he was in her own mind, even taking the toll of difficult years into account. His hair had thinned to gray wisps surrounding his crown, and the sagging skin under his eyes was visible from where she stood. She didn't think she'd have recognized him on first glance if she saw him in a lineup.

He might look at her with the same lack of recognition. She was a young woman when he'd turned his back on her. Did he know she'd been released? Had he counted the calendar? Thought of trying to find her?

The walk down the stretch of sidewalk in front of his home was a marathon. She went up the driveway, unable to lift her face toward his, though the girl and Audrey had his full attention. She looked in his direction and saw behind him in the bright living room a mess of card tables bearing radio boxes, components, and tools.

"I've wondered why Juliet hasn't come 'round," he was saying. "She's usually over here a couple of times a week since Cora Jean passed. But she had some surgery that took a lot out of her by my reckoning. I figured she maybe had some complications, got laid up a bit."

"Was she complaining about being sick?"

"Oh no, not that one. I don't believe she ever complained about anything."

"That's the truth," Diane heard Miralee mutter. "The rain never fell on her, not even when we all could see she was soaking wet."

That was Miralee's definition of hypocrisy?

"When did you see her last?" Audrey said.

"Well, now, Tuesday I think. She had me pick her up at the mechanic's. Something wrong with her car."

"No one has seen her since then," Audrey told him.

"Is that so? What happened?"

"Don't you watch the news?" Miralee said.

"You know we don't, child."

Miralee looked over her shoulder toward the street.

"Hardly read the paper anymore neither.

There's just nothing there to keep my spirits up, as if I need any more to bring us down. Just yesterday —"

"Her husband is very upset, as I'm sure you can guess." Audrey looked ready to burst.

Harlan hadn't given any indication of noticing Diane.

"I guess he is. He's wound tight, that one. To be expected, living in the line of duty the way he —"

"Did Julie say *anything* to you about being worried about something going on at work, or someone being upset with her, or —"

Harlan shook his head. "Like I said, Juliet wasn't one to whine. I think we were the ones who did all the moaning. She's a good girl, that one. Yes, she is. A good listener. Probably what makes her a good teach—"

"Was she acting strangely at all? Did she do anything out of the ordinary?"

"Strange, no. Uncommon, maybe. She talked me into parting with my Ford just a bit ago. Said she was ready to give up her Honda, for all the trouble she was having with it. I wondered about that, classy girl like her in the old gray mare. But she liked to ride that scooter of hers too, so who am I to say? It was maybe two weeks back? The truck was older than her and running worse than me, but she said she wanted it, and it was just sitting there useless, now that I have Cora Jean's cruise ship to myself."

Cruise ship? Diane noticed the sleek, late-model Cadillac sitting in the open garage. Her mother had longed for one back when they couldn't afford anything more than a used station wagon.

Audrey looked at Miralee. "The gray truck in the picture?"

"I guess."

"Paid me cash for it. A grand. I wanted to just give it to her, but the woman is generous. Her husband — not so much. She asked me not to mention it to him. Not that our paths cross often. Juliet's always trying to take care of me, I have to say. A fine, upstanding soul in a world full of morons. She's the daughter we lost, once upon a time."

Daughter. Singular. It required no thought to deduce which one he referred to. Diane wouldn't even have to look him in the eye in order to be emotionally leveled. He'd already obliterated the very memory of her.

She allowed the cold blanket of the air to numb her mind.

"This is the worst news I've gotten since my Cora Jean's passing," her father said. "How can I help find her?"

Diane didn't think he could do anything — what were any of them able to do, after all? Poke around her house? Hang out at the bakery with a bunch of police officers who didn't want civilians around?

Audrey was looking past Harlan into his house. "Maybe you could put the word out to whoever's listening," she suggested, pointing at his radios.

"Sure thing. That's a good idea. I'll do that."

"Where's the truck now?" Audrey asked. "The one you sold to Julie?"

"Couldn't tell you. The thing was built long before the days of GPS and tracking devices," Harlan said.

"Tell me the plate number? Maybe the police can have a look for it."

How would a teacher have come up with a thousand dollars and kept it hidden from her detective husband? All the possibilities of what Juliet might have done with that diamond nibbled at Diane's brain.

What Diane really wanted to know, however, was why God ordained life to work this way: that a beloved woman far better than she, who had been the good daughter Diane could not be, would be mysteriously wiped off the face of the earth, while Diane was allowed to wander.

Chapter 24

Coach had passed out from the pain. A waterfall of powdery grain was spilling onto his pants from the split flour sack. Geoff and Estrella worked together to keep him from losing more blood. Geoff was on the phone with paramedics outside, applying their guidance to the wounded feet.

Leslie leaned heavily on Ed's muscled arm. She pored over a notebook, examining complicated equations. The exercise had a calming effect on her. Ed watched Jack sit on the overturned bucket and relax against the cinder-block wall. The detective held his gun across his knees.

Ed wondered if Jack had more than one backup gun, and how they might be wrestled away from a veteran who outweighed him by maybe thirty pounds.

Ed glanced at his watch. It was almost eight. Four and a half hours to go. Forever. Leslie clicked her mechanical pencil and scribbled her way through the pages. Periodically she stopped to flip back through the sheets. Her brow furrowed.

Heat from the brick oven on the other side of the kitchen continued to warm the cold storeroom.

Geoff hung up the phone. "You need to let this man out," he said to Jack.

"Why? You're doing a fine job."

"He needs help. I'm no doctor."

"Who needs a doctor when we have a pastor? Those aren't grave wounds."

Ed tried to focus on Leslie's math. He'd scraped his way through geometry, trig, and the rest. He'd half believed, while dating Miralee, that the reason Mrs. Mansfield gave him the cold shoulder was because he appeared so unintelligent in this area. The other half, he supposed, had something to do with his faith.

He elbowed her gently, eyes on her paper. "What did you mean when you said this was your fault?"

"Mrs. Mansfield wanted me to enter a state competition up at the university."

"College stuff?"

"Yes. High-level math. Calculus. Physics. Quantum theory. She was going to be my mentor. Thought I had what it would take to really wow people, maybe even win."

"It wouldn't surprise me."

"Thanks." Leslie blushed. Her pencil bobbed as she continued to write. "It would have given Mazy some national attention. Win some money for me and for the school, for the math department. They could use it, you know, with all the cutbacks."

"So what's that got to do with this mess we're in?"

"I decided not to enter. I woke up one morning, and it was just too much pressure. I'd do it for her — but for the money? For the whole school? The whole town? I'm supposed to be thinking about prom. Cutting class. Cow-tipping."

Ed laughed aloud. "You'd never."

Leslie frowned at him. "Maybe I want to do that stuff. Sometimes it blows, being the responsible one all the time. People have these expectations."

"But responsible people are influential people. The ones who make great things happen."

"So the opposite has to be true also. Our actions can be . . . terrible. Mrs. Mansfield was counting on me, and I . . . and I . . . went *cow-tipping*." She huffed. "In a sense."

"I still don't get it."

Leslie's sigh was thick. "I didn't even have the decency to tell her to her face. I wrote her a note. The next time I saw her . . . you should have seen her face. I thought she was going to cry. Which made *me* want to cry."

Ed hoped she'd connect the dots soon.

"Do you think she killed herself?" Leslie whispered.

"Over that?"

She recoiled as if he'd slapped her.

"You're not that powerful, Leslie. Sure, she was probably disappointed. But do you think you could single-handedly drive her to jump off a cliff?"

Jack's attention swiveled in their direction.

Estrella applied a fresh cloth to Coach's foot and tied it firmly in place with the necktie he had taken off earlier. Geoff sat on the ground next to Coach and was talking to him in low tones. He must have come around.

Jack returned his attention to Leslie. "As much as I hate to say it, I have to agree with your friend on this one. Children don't get to set the course of their authority figures' lives. That's not how God ordained it."

"But she was so sad."

"If she was sad, it was only because she hasn't found the courage to accept the one true faith that can make her happy. In due time. I have faith."

"Blind faith," murmured Coach. "You can't see what's in front of your own face, Jack. We're trying to help."

"Fine. What did she tell you about this little girl's power over her? Put the child out of her misery, please."

Coach didn't answer right away.

Jack said, "Maybe you didn't know Julie as well as you claim."

Coach's voice lacked strength. "She said some days made her question whether being a good teacher made any impact on the world at all. It wasn't about you, Leslie. We all feel that way from time to time."

Leslie sniffed and looked slightly relieved. Her pencil was flitting across the paper again.

"Your wife's a great teacher," Coach murmured.

"Of course she is. If she put as much effort into her spiritual life as she puts into her vocation she'd be —"

"— all but a saint," Coach provided. "She told me you say that a lot."

"Thees woman has run out on you," Estrella dared. "With some man who ees not so backhanded."

"No, no," Coach said. "She wasn't seeing anyone on the side. I asked her, and she laughed at that."

"I have another idea," Leslie said, lifting her pencil off the paper to get Jack's attention. "Let's say someone stole the bike —"

"We've been over all that," Jack said.

"But you haven't solved this problem about not being able to find . . . evidence of the rider. What if there was no rider?"

Jack leaned forward over his knees.

"I've been working on this problem for a few days, and it's not ironclad because the math is just way too complex, but something about the whole scenario is really bugging me." She turned to a fresh piece of paper and made a quick sketch of an intersection, a car entering it, and a scooter crossing it. "We think the bike was crossing on Sunflower, and Mrs. Bofinger T-boned it. Then everyone starts looking for Mrs. Mansfield out here." Leslie drew little arrows fanning out in the same direction the car was headed.

"Like an arrow shot from a bow," Ed said.

"Sort of. She would have sort of bounced off your mom's car, but she's not a rubber ball. She couldn't have been thrown far if your mom was only doing thirty."

"She wasn't going any faster, I swear."

Jack said, "Look, the child does physics too. Does your math take into account how much time this yahoo had to drag her body away?" He pointed at Geoff.

Leslie's eyes widened. "Is that possible? I heard the police didn't find any blood anywhere other than around the car."

"How did you hear that?"

Leslie opened her mouth, then clamped it shut again.

Jack said, "It's true, though."

"That eliminates a few options, then." She continued to write.

"Now she's an accident-reconstruction specialist. Amazing."

"Are you interested in what she has to say or not?" Ed asked.

"Well, we lost ours in budget cuts last year."

Leslie ignored them. "We've been assuming that Mrs. Bofinger and Mrs. Mansfield were both in motion." Leslie drew a line up Main Street and another coming in from Sunflower until they met in the middle. "But what if the scooter wasn't moving?"

"Why would she stop in the middle of the street?" Ed asked.

"I don't know why, I'm just saying *what if?*"

"You tell us."

"Here's what happens to the body: there's no mechanism to impart any velocity to it, but being seated on the bike puts her center of gravity pretty high off the ground. Have you ever seen a car hit a bike?"

Leslie didn't wait for answers.

"A ton of things can happen, depending on the velocities, the masses, angles, centers of gravity, and so on, but usually the rider and his ride will be separated. If the body has a high center of gravity but no op-positional velocity, it's going to slide up onto the hood of the car. And if the car doesn't slow down —"

"Mom didn't hit the brakes until after the collision."

"— the car will pass right under the body, which will tumble over the car and land in almost the same place from which it was launched."

"Behind the car," Ed said.

"Yes."

Jack said, "Well, that didn't happen."

"Exactly," Leslie said. "So that's problem number one."

Ed could think of a million more.

"Hear me out. The other problem is what happened to the bike. If Mrs. Mansfield is driving in from Sunflower —"

"Just tell me where else my wife could have landed," Jack said.

Leslie held up her pencil. *Wait.* "If she's

driving perpendicular to the car and the side of the bike is facing the car when it hits, the energy is distributed across the scooter, making it more likely to bounce off the car, or come apart."

She looked at everyone as if this should make sense to them. Ed raised his eyebrows and shook his head.

Jack said, "The bike collapsed under the front fender. Completely crushed — who is leaking this stuff to you?"

"I told her that part," Ed said.

Estrella stepped in. "You think ees a head-on collision," she said.

Leslie nodded.

Jack snatched the notebook out of Leslie's fingers, looked at it, then handed it back to her. He jiggled the gun at his side, frowning.

"Why would she be riding on the wrong side of the street?"

"She's trying to say that no one was riding it," Ed said.

Leslie brightened. "Yes. It was just parked there."

"This makes less and less sense," Geoff said.

Estrella offered to Jack, "Ees best explanation yet for why you cannot find Julie."

"Why?" Jack said, his volume rising a

notch. "Why would she park it in the middle of the street?"

No one had any theories.

"There ees nothing in physics to explain human nature," Estrella said.

"But her blood was everywhere!" Jack barked.

"Which takes me back to my original point," Leslie said. "Let's say someone stole the bike. Anyone could have parked it there. Maybe someone killed her and then —"

"Why go to the trouble?" Ed said loudly to prevent her from saying anything more. His mental alarms were going off. "What's the point of hurting her and then setting up a complicated scene like that?"

A light had gone on in Jack's eyes that looked like the yellow of a predator about to pounce. "I like this girl's thinking." He glanced at Leslie. "I have lots of reasons now to hope Audrey gets back here before you're in line to die. Save you as a witness for the prosecution. How many people would it take to set this up, if my wife was murdered before the accident?" His gaze traveled between Ed and Geoff. "How many to subdue her, kill her, steal the scooter, drain her blood —"

"You're nuts!" The pitch of Ed's voice became a screech. "Listen to you! Do you seriously think we'd do that? Oh my gosh. If we really did have it out for her, I promise you we wouldn't be dumb enough to run her over with our own car!"

Ed was vaguely aware that he sounded like a lunatic and looked like one too as he lunged at Jack.

"Ed! Ed!" The weight of his father's body held him back.

"He's going to level us with lies." Ed's breaths came hard.

Geoff's hands were firm on Ed's shoulders, forcing his son to focus. "No one's going to believe anything this man says after today."

"Evidence talks louder than the person who delivers it," Jack said.

"I'm more interested in the truth," Geoff responded.

"You don't think they're same? That's interesting."

Ed threw his hands in the air and broke away from his dad, invading Jack's personal space. "Aren't you the *least* bit worried about Julie?" he yelled.

"Of course I am. Why on earth do you think I'm here?"

CHAPTER 25

Warmth like two large human hands gently squeezed against the sides of Audrey's head and turned her face toward Julie Mansfield's house. Again, Diane and Miralee followed her. Harlan's house was swallowed by gray fog before they were halfway back.

While walking she called Captain Wilson. She told him about the truck Miralee had purchased from the Halls.

"It might not mean anything," he said to her.

"Except that Jack didn't know about it. And no one knows where it is."

"That kind of secret doesn't bode well for him, if she was making plans to run off with someone."

"I've never heard of someone abandoning a family and leaving so much blood behind," Audrey mused.

"If she wanted Jack to think she was dead —"

"Well, if I'd had an invasive surgery *and* a lover, I wouldn't have run off with him until I was completely healed. And I wouldn't have left my medications behind."

"You found prescriptions?"

"Jack didn't tell you?"

"No."

"You should speak to her doctor."

"We did. There was nothing out of the ordinary about the procedure or Julie's prognosis. I hope you're not about to tell me that you broke into that man's house."

"Her daughter let us in," Audrey said, casting a look at Miralee.

The girl smirked.

"Mrs. Bofinger, you'll be more help to your family if you come down here right now."

"I don't think that's what Jack had in mind, Captain. But I'll come as soon as I can." She hung up before he could argue and waited for Diane to catch up to them. "Harlan Hall shares your last name."

Diane nodded.

"Are you related?"

"My father."

Audrey nodded, surprised that she wasn't surprised. But she was able to quickly add up in her mind everything she knew about Cora Jean's death, about that faded family

304

portrait that held so much pain, about Diane's imprisonment and need for a place to live, and about her silent and aloof posture at the end of Harlan's walkway. "I'm so sorry about your mother's passing," she said. "She was a gentle woman."

Diane's chin twitched. "Thank you."

Then there was Diane's unexpected connection to Julie, and her even more startling appearance at the bakery on the very day of Julie's disturbing disappearance. "I'll understand if you don't want to keep helping," Audrey said.

"But I want to."

"I'm glad for your help, but why?"

Diane took a deep breath. "I think Juliet has something of mine. I need to find it."

"Great," Miralee muttered. "Now my dad's a killer and my mom's a thief."

Audrey laid a hand on Miri's arm as they reached the front stoop. "Back in March," she said, "I dropped by your house. The week after spring break. Do you remember that?"

"You never came to see me."

"I didn't come to see you on purpose. We talked through that window." Audrey pointed. "You wouldn't invite me in."

"I probably wouldn't have, if we'd actually talked, which we didn't." Miralee wriggled out from under Audrey's touch.

"Could you at least pretend to want to help me?"

"Oh, sure. Let's all hide our true selves. We'll cope better with life. It sure worked out well for my parents, didn't it?"

Audrey paused at the front door and held the screen open while trying the knob. It was locked. Miralee inserted her key.

"I never had the chance to raise a daughter," Audrey said. "But I've got a son I'm really proud of, and his dad and I take a little credit for that. So I'm going to tell you something we told him."

"I can hardly wait. The preacher's son, waving his Bible with one hand and unzipping his pants with the other. Do you take credit for that too?"

Audrey grabbed hold of the knob to prevent Miralee from eluding the confrontation, and also to funnel her anger into a controlled, harmless action.

"We told Ed that being a good person is about loving other people well. It's not about having all the right answers or doing all the right things. That's where dishonest living comes in, don't you think?"

Miralee's disrespectful glare invited Audrey to be blunt.

"You're the one who lived dishonestly

with my son. He's the most honest human there is, right down to his last imperfection. You aimed to bring him down just to prove yourself right."

Now Miralee looked away.

"I'm afraid for my family, Miralee. And I'm afraid for the other people in that bakery, and for your father and for you. But I'm also here because I care about your mom. Even though I hardly know her, I can choose to care. It's better than the alternative, don't you think?"

Diane was standing close enough to overhear, and she came closer at these words, looking at Miralee.

"I believe you care about your mom too. Even more than I do. So let's just agree to that much, okay?" Audrey opened the door into the dim and empty house. Miralee stalked in, passing through the living room.

Diane went back to the cabinet Miralee had told her to get out of earlier. Audrey started touching Juliet's things as if she were blind. She ran her hand down the arm of the sofa near the front door. She picked up Juliet's tote bag on the bench in the entryway and put the straps on her shoulder. She fingered the stack of papers, flipping through them and then hugging them to her chest. Then the baker's wife went across the room to the framed photographs on the bookcase. She picked up each picture that included Juliet — there were three or four of these — studied it for long seconds, then set it back down. It was creepy behavior, as far as Diane was concerned.

But it gave her time to do some searching of her own. The cabinet held several small stacked boxes. She opened each one. Candle holders, napkin rings, loose snapshots, drink coasters, furniture coasters. No necklace. She should have started in the bedroom.

Miralee had gone into the kitchen and was opening and slamming cupboard doors.

Diane wasn't sure how Audrey wanted her to help find Juliet. She was unskilled and barely educated. It was unreasonable to think that she could help to save a life or solve a crime that had kicked a respected detective off the ledge of sanity. The sensible part of Diane's brain was leaning against a shade tree and chewing on a piece of wheat, preparing to nap under a floppy hat. *No point in trying,* it muttered to her. The irrational part of her mind was pacing in the meadow, staring at the horizon of her life, wanting to help, to reverse, to repair.

Then again, just finding the cursed family heirloom would have been enough.

As she watched Audrey go through mysterious motions in search of a woman she hardly knew, Diane thought of a children's picture book she had once borrowed from the prison library. It had been donated for those who were learning to read, but she took it because she liked the story, which she thought was a Japanese folktale. It told of a great fire that tore through a jungle, driving all the animals out. Weeping and disbelieving, lions, elephants, monkeys, and serpents watched the massive blaze destroy their home. The smallest creature among them, however, a hummingbird, flew to a nearby lake and filled its tiny beak with a drop of water, then returned to the inferno and tossed its drop onto the flames. It evaporated before it touched the ground.

The animals mocked the bird. How pointless. How stupid. What do you think you will accomplish? But the bird flew back and forth, lake to blaze, blaze to lake, lake to blaze.

I'm doing what I can do, the bird said to them as they stood by and did nothing.

Diane would do what she could do. She headed for Juliet's bedroom.

"Do you believe that a person can ever really know how another person feels?" Audrey asked as she ran her fingertips over

Jack and Juliet's wedding photo.

Diane paused in the hall. She wasn't sure Audrey was talking to her, and she was even less sure of the answer, so she said nothing.

"What I mean is, do you think someone can truly walk a mile in another person's shoes, or put herself in someone else's place?" Audrey looked at her this time.

"No."

"Why not?" Audrey asked. She followed Diane and took the wedding picture with her.

"It's just a figure of speech."

"Sometimes I wonder." Audrey paused as she passed the dining room area and pulled a note card off the stack of Juliet's papers. She directed her voice to the kitchen. "Miralee, do you know who 'L' is?"

"Of course not," the girl snapped. Then she leaned out past the room divider and said, less snippy, "I mean, I'd need more information."

Audrey read, "Mrs. M, Thanks for the great opportunity, but I've decided not to do it. I hope you'll understand. Maybe Colin would? –L."

Miralee shook her head.

"Decided not to what, I wonder?" Audrey said as she turned away and walked down the hall. Diane led the way.

The first door on the right was an office. Audrey stopped outside the door, clutching Juliet's books and picture frame, and leaned forward as if to move into the open room. She jerked back as if the space were a hot oven. Diane stopped to watch, her curiosity in Audrey's strange behavior deepening.

Audrey pursed her mouth and lifted her heel, then tapped the toe of her shoe on the ground once, contemplative-like. She balanced like that, one foot flat, one on toe, for a few seconds, then lunged into the office.

When Diane looked in, Audrey was in the recliner, squeezing Juliet's belongings by the crooks of her elbows, the book bag hanging awkwardly from her shoulder, straps twisted, across the arm of the chair. Her closed eyes were wrinkled at the corners. The knees of her rigid legs touched each other.

"You don't look very relaxed," Diane ventured.

Audrey didn't answer. Was she crying? Silently, tearlessly? That wasn't real crying.

"What can I do to help?"

Miralee had gone quiet in the kitchen. The curtain hanging in front of the window seemed to breathe. Lift, fall. Only once.

Perhaps ten seconds passed.

Miralee approached at the top of the hall.

"Audrey?" Diane ventured.

As suddenly as Audrey had plunged into the chair, she bolted out of it, electric-quick. "I'm okay." In a smooth movement she found her feet and let them carry her out of the room. She pushed Diane out of the way. "That is a very, very sad chair."

She didn't elaborate but went straight into the master bedroom. Diane looked to Miralee for theories, but the girl offered an expression of boredom.

The walk-in closet ran the entire length of the far wall and seemed overstated for such a modest house. Audrey placed the school papers and wedding picture on the bed and kicked off her sneakers. Juliet's pill bottles rolled across the bedspread.

Audrey walked into the closet and put her feet into a pair of women's slippers.

"What are you *doing?*" Diane demanded.

"Walking in Julie's shoes," Audrey said, scanning the feminine side of the closet for . . . for what?

"This won't help us find Juliet."

"It might not work, I realize that. But I have to try."

"You have to try what?"

"Miri!" Audrey called out.

"I'm right here."

"What's your mom's favorite sweater, or

sweatshirt, or whatever? What she wore most often?"

Miralee came toward the closet as Audrey pulled a sun hat off the top shelf and rammed it down onto her head.

"You shouldn't do that," Diane whispered. "Those are her *mom's* things."

"Why do you need to know?" Miralee asked, starting to slide hangers across the bar.

"It will take too long to explain. Just show me what your mom liked to wear more than anything else."

"Not that hat, that's for sure," she said. "A plum-colored vest. A fleece thing, light-weight. Zipper-front. She wore it all the time at home and layered it with other stuff when she went out. Through the school year anyway. She was probably wearing it when . . ."

Diane only noticed that Miralee hadn't finished her sentence because Audrey stopped looking for the vest and turned her body toward the teenager. Miralee's handling of her mother's clothing was nearly violent as she shoved each piece aside. Audrey took off the sun hat and put it back on the shelf.

"I know, Miri. I'm so sorry. We'll find her."

"It'll go one way or the other, won't it?

Fifty-fifty. There's a part of me that hopes we don't find her. Sometimes the truth is worse than the mystery."

Audrey said, "I promise you that I —"

"Don't!" The sea of fabric parted and the purple vest appeared, and Miralee stripped the hanger of it and held it out toward Audrey.

Audrey's fingers closed on the jacket, but she waited for Miralee to let go. "Then I won't make promises. I'll just keep telling you the truth. Deal?"

Diane thought Miralee bit back a disrespectful remark.

"Do you know how many tears your mother cried for you?" Audrey said kindly.

"What would you know about that?" Miralee said.

Audrey turned toward the mirror on the closet door and slipped her arms into the openings. "I'm not sure if this is a good sign or a bad one, finding this vest still here." She said this to Diane as she tugged the collar close around her neck.

A bad one, Diane thought. *On all counts.*

"Why do you call her Juliet?" Audrey asked.

"Because that's her name."

"Julie is a nickname?"

"I guess. No one ever called her that when

we were kids."

"Dad always called her Julie," Miralee offered.

Audrey left the closet and crossed to the bed, which she sat on. Miralee threw herself back across the foot and stared at the ceiling while Audrey picked up the framed portrait. It had a brass plaque embedded in the base of the cherrywood frame. "Says Juliet here too. So the formality lasted until her marriage at least."

Diane shrugged. Something like that couldn't really matter.

"Do you know when it changed?" The question was for Miralee.

"Her name? Never asked, never offered."

Audrey said to Diane, "How do you know her?"

"We went to school together."

"How long?"

Diane approached the bed. "Since the fourth grade. Through . . . through high school. I really don't like that you're wearing her clothes. What are you going to do next? Eat her food? Use her toothbrush?"

"I'd like to see that," Miralee said.

Audrey's eyes brightened. "What does Julie like to eat?"

"I don't know!" Diane said. "Why are you asking? It was a long time ago. People change." *People drastically, permanently change.*

"Almonds," Miralee said. "Mom is crazy about almonds."

"Is that why your family lives here? All the almond groves?"

"Of course not. We're like, generational types. Miners on Mom's side, as she tells it. We were here before Steinbeck was. Practically before the Native Americans."

Audrey blinked as if that amount of history was overwhelmingly greater than the little connections to Juliet contained in this small bedroom. Insurmountable stuff. She sighed and shook her head, scanning the room, maybe for something smaller and more tangible.

"We don't have a lot of time," Diane said. "I don't understand what you're looking for. Can you tell us more?"

"I'm not sure, really." The optimistic Audrey looked pale now, as if aware of how much time she'd wasted on something pointless. She placed a hand on her stomach and closed her eyes.

"You people are the worst investigators I have ever met," Miralee scoffed.

"Quit talking to us that way! What are you doing to help?" The strength of Diane's own voice frightened her. Even the girl seemed surprised. Why had she said it? She didn't deserve respect from anyone, not even this kid.

Audrey groaned. Her face had gone green. "Excuse me," she murmured, and she pitched forward toward the bathroom.

Miralee flopped back across her parents' bedspread. "That woman is nuts, if you ask me."

Well, I didn't ask.

CHAPTER 26

Audrey stumbled into the bathroom wearing Julie's vest and Julie's slippers and placed her palms against the edge of the tile counter. She felt the irritation that is the partner of exhaustion. And she also felt hopeful. This was as close as she'd come to recreating her connection to Julie since Diane's jarring wake-up call. What was the explanation for the feverish flare-ups, the nausea? Logically — if Audrey defined the term loosely — Julie was ill. Perhaps injured from the motor scooter accident.

A memory came to Audrey: the ghostly image of a figure floating on the periphery of the intersection of Sunflower and Main. Had Julie stumbled away from the accident, delirious, on the brink of something awful?

But no — Audrey had seen that shadow before striking the scooter. Wasn't it before? Now that she thought of it, she couldn't remember, and she supposed it didn't really matter. Audrey needed more than illness to guide her. She needed that strong arm.

C'mon, c'mon.

What time was it? She couldn't just stand here. *Move, Audrey. Make a plan. Your family needs this.*

She took a deep breath. She swallowed the nausea. She leaned over the basin and ran cold water from the tap and splashed her cheeks. She straightened and looked up into the mirror.

Instead of her own reflection, she saw the angry face of Julie Mansfield, cheeks flushed red and brows drawn together. She clutched the books, the tote bag, the wedding photo, the pill bottles that Audrey had been hauling around the house.

"You have *no* idea." Julie spat the words, and Audrey took a step backward. Her backside hit the closed door of the bathroom. Julie flung her arm, hurling the papers and picture at Audrey.

She raised her arm and closed her eyes as she ducked.

Nothing but the sound of fluttering papers came down on her.

Audrey opened her eyes. There were no papers on this side of the mirror, and Julie's hands were free of them. She caught Julie's furious eyes. This time Julie launched the tote bag at her. Audrey twisted into the corner as the bag crashed into the door. The noise was real enough, but when Audrey glanced downward, there was nothing on the floor.

"Audrey?" The worried voice was Diane's, out in the bedroom.

"It's okay," Audrey croaked, wondering if anything she was sensing in the moment truly existed. "Out in a minute."

Julie was yelling again. Could Diane and Miralee hear it? "You think you can wear my clothes and go through my things and *be me?* You can sit in my chair and stand in my yard and say you know how I feel?"

Pill bottles like missiles were launched from Julie's hands. This time Audrey didn't duck. She flinched but managed to watch them. They never escaped the plane of the mirror, though the little bathroom filled with the sound of plastic lids popping open and raining tablets and capsules like hail on the tile.

"What do you want me to do?" Audrey whispered.

Julie was wrenching her wedding ring from her finger, tugging against years of increasing snugness. "You smug woman, with your perfect marriage and your happy little family, don't think you can waltz into my world with sweetness and light! Don't sic your trite perspective on me. Don't condescend to my pain." The ring came off in Julie's right hand, and she lifted it like a baseball over her shoulder.

Audrey raised her voice to match Julie's. "What do you want me to do!"

"Dare to own it," Julie said, and she sent the wedding band toward Audrey's face.

When it hit Audrey square between the eyes and glanced off, Audrey gasped and felt smarting tears swell near the bridge of her nose. The jewelry sounded a sorrowful note when it hit the countertop and bounced once, then landed in the sink. The ring rolled around the circumference of the bowl, collecting water droplets, swirling downward toward the stopper in the drain.

It collapsed against the plug.

Audrey picked it up. Her fingers were trembling. This wedding ring was solid and heavy. It was a gold band without a diamond, its only embellishment a swirling scroll pattern stamped into the metal. The grooves were slightly blackened with grime.

"Are you really okay?" Diane was pounding on the door.

Audrey looked up into the mirror and saw her own reflection, haggard and drained. Julie was gone.

Maybe Audrey had knocked the ring off the edge of the sink when she'd splashed cold water on her face.

She didn't believe that herself.

The bathroom door opened.

"Audrey!"

"I'm okay." She turned around and held up the gold band so Miralee could see it. "Is this your mother's?"

Miralee, still sprawled on the bed, nodded.

Audrey realized she was feeling entirely well again.

And then she remembered where she'd seen Julie's truck.

The plastic bucket was the reason he could not get comfortable, Jack decided. His age was showing in his back's intolerance for hard seats.

Geoff was on the phone with Audrey. Ed rose to go stand by his father and listen in on the call. The coach's bleeding seemed under control. The Mexican woman hovered over him. Jack had a brief vision of Audrey sitting on the curb covered in his wife's blood. The smart girl was crouched over her notebooks like a person who needed a mental hospital. Jack hoped she'd be of sound mind by the time Audrey's court date rolled around.

"Turn on the speakerphone," Jack said to Geoff. He was curious.

Geoff complied.

Audrey was saying, ". . . the captain's looking into it."

"Looking into what?" Jack said.

"Your wife bought your neighbor's truck," Geoff told him.

"According to whom?" Jack said. "I would have known."

Audrey said, "It's what your neighbor says. Harlan Hall?"

He pursed his lips and filed away the information in a mental drawer of claims that might be either fact or fiction. *To be determined.* Julie had a close connection to the couple, but she never made a purchase without consulting him.

Harlan Hall. Hall. Hall.

He connected the name to the fat woman he'd sent to Audrey's house. The woman with the record. The sister killer. He chewed on that for a second.

"Ed," Audrey was saying, "do you remember seeing a gray truck yesterday, when we parked?"

"Uh, no. You were sick. I was distracted."

"There was a truck parked in the lot at the Silver Gap trailhead. I'm sure it's the

323

same one in this picture that I found at Julie's house."

Jack didn't know the picture. He'd never paid the Halls much attention, except as was required to be a good Christian, because he'd never paid Julie's friends much attention. They tended not to share his interests, professional or spiritual.

"I'm headed back up there now with Diane and Miralee."

Jack abandoned all thought of the Halls at the sound of his daughter's name.

"Miri's there?" Ed asked, voicing Jack's own surprise.

Jack jumped up from the bucket and grabbed the phone out of Geoff's hands. His child was too close to home for him to lose again, especially not to a woman like Audrey.

"What are you doing in my house?" Jack said.

"Jack, it's a two-hour drive back to that trailhead, and Julie might not even be there today. We need more time."

"No more time. Two hours puts you there by ten fifteen, if you honestly have to go that far. You know where she is. Get her, get out of King's Riches, and then call me and let me talk to her. And get out of my house!"

"Jack —"

"Where's my daughter?"

"There's no phone reception up there. You know that."

"You should have thought of that before all this happened, woman!"

"I didn't take her! Get it through your head, Jack!"

"You're a tool of the devil."

Geoff held up his hand. "Audrey, we're thinking someone might have killed Julie and then set up the accident on purpose. Can Miralee tell you if —"

"Where is my child?" Jack shouted.

"She's right here," Audrey said.

"Put her on."

There was a muffled exchange on the end of the line, then Audrey returned. "She said she doesn't want to talk to you."

The woman's voice was strong, confident. Supremely arrogant.

"Does it matter what a child wants? Is there no respect for authority in this genera-tion?"

No one answered him.

"Miralee!" he yelled.

The line was quiet, the sound of disdain.

"Miralee Wendy Mansfield! Don't you go with this woman! She's a lying serpent. She's murdered your mother. Don't you leave that house!"

"Dad, you're mental."

"If you have any respect for me —"

"I don't."

"Your mother then. You respect her."

"Not really."

"In the name of everything that is holy, girl, then do it for yourself! Don't trust Audrey Bofinger. Or that other woman. They're killers, both of them!"

"No one's killed anyone, Dad. Unlike you."

What did she mean by that? Jack had never killed anyone, not even in the line of duty. Miralee was well aware of it, even if no one else in this gray bakery was.

"If you disobey me —"

"I'm an adult, Dad. Of course, I realize you don't see me that way, and that's part of the problem."

Miralee wasn't an adult by any stretch of the imagination. She was still, despite his raising her to physical maturity, an intellectual adolescent, an emotional toddler, a spiritual infant.

It wasn't his fault she had turned out this way. He had done everything right.

"For the love of God, Miri, please don't leave us again." His words caught in a dry spot in his throat. He swallowed. "I'm begging you. Stay here in Cornucopia. I'll talk to them at The Word. They'd have you back in a heartbeat. It was a good job."

"In your dreams and my nightmares," Miralee said. "You can't go back to your old life after this, you know? You've lost your mind. So while you sit around waiting for someone else to do *your* job, I'm going to go look for Mom, okay?"

This was all Julie's fault. If they'd been united in every way that mattered, this never would have happened.

Jack decided to take the high road. He refused to give her insults any further response. He turned his back on the phone and returned to the bucket.

The Mexican, still gripping the coach's bloody foot, glared at him like a furious maternal bird of prey. Self-righteous Catholic mama. What did she know? She'd find out soon enough. Every generation got worse and worse. God's wrath would fall on them all.

CHAPTER 27

Ed's eyes were on Jack. The policeman sat on that bucket, stupefied. Ed wavered — lunge, take him now, when he wasn't paying attention? As if sensing Ed's thoughts, Jack's eyes snapped to his and the grip on his gun tightened. His eyes contained an emotion that Ed didn't recognize, something deep and cold and pained. But the weapon remained steady on the detective's knee.

"Do what Wilson tells you to do," Ed's dad was telling his mom. "You're amazing, Audrey, but don't try to fix this alone . . . I know that's what Jack wants, but it's not wise. We have to entrust this to God . . . We're fine, everything's fine. Jack just wants to see Julie again . . . Let me pray for you."

Ed spoke to Jack. "I forgot Miri worked at The Word."

Miralee had taken the job at the Christian bookstore after breaking up with him and held the position only until they graduated, when she fled for college. Ed thought the store was an odd choice for her, even a bad fit, but racked it up to her dad's influence. Pressure. Expectations, whatever. Ed had avoided shopping there during those months.

"My dad shops at that store a lot." He said it at the same time that he realized how much that fact bothered him. Something about the timing of events that had tipped over like dominoes from the spring through the summer and into fall — something was off.

"I'm sure he does," Jack said. "As do I, and most of the Christian citizens of this town."

Ed heard his dad say, "I love you too," and hang up the phone.

"Miri must have hated it there," Ed said.

"Few people are blessed to enjoy the work they must do."

"I don't know. I like it here. At least I did before today." He wasn't sure if Jack had heard him. And he wasn't sure if it was the truth, either. Working in a bakery for one's parents wasn't exactly ambitious. *Be happy, aim low,* one of his friends had liked to say.

"Did Miri work in the back?" Ed asked. "Where she could avoid all the high-and-mighty religious folks?"

"Of course not. She's got a better head on her than that. She assisted the accountant."

"She handled the money?"

"Every aspect. Payroll, payables, the day's receipts."

A bridge formed in his mind between his father, a pastor-patron of the Christian bookstore, and Miralee Mansfield, junior accountant.

Geoff turned to Jack. "I'm sorry Miralee treats you that way," his dad said. "That must cause you a lot of pain."

"You wouldn't know pain if it impaled you on a stake!"

The word *pain* came out of his mouth on spit.

"Did you know the French word for *bread* is *pain*?" Leslie said.

All three men glanced at her. She blinked, as if she'd come into the conversation without realizing it.

"It's not pronounced that way," she said. "It's like saying *pan* with a really stuffy nose, but I always thought the spelling was interesting." After a few seconds of silence she said, "With us being in a bakery and all . . . I just thought . . ."

She stared at her paper.

"You wrote checks when you bought books at The Word," Ed said to his father.

"What?" Jack asked.

"Miralee had access to my dad's checks." In an era of electronic transactions in which Ed sometimes wondered if real money actually existed, his dad continued to write checks because he believed that filling in all those blanks longhand made it just a little harder to spend money foolishly.

Geoff's eyebrows made a tent shape over his nose. "That's a hefty accusation, son."

"I haven't heard any accusation yet," said Jack.

"Miralee forged my dad's check. For the abortion. It's not hard to do these days, is it?"

"Why would she do that?" both men asked together.

Were they serious? "Uh, because she needed the money, and someone to blame, and a story to tell you." Ed pointed at Jack. "A story to protect your perception of her. Either that or something that would prove her right about what a bunch of hypocrites we all are. That's her thing, you know, cleaning up the world one hypocrite at a time."

"You just can't accept responsibility for anything, can you, boy?"

Ed wasn't sure who was angrier now, Jack or him. Jack didn't care about the truth, Ed thought. Jack's only aim was to make sure no one could prove him wrong.

"I've never said anything like that. I own my stuff, all of it, which is more than I can say for your daughter."

"Miralee would never do what you've suggested," Jack said.

"Maybe you didn't have as much control over your women as you thought you did. Miralee made a clown of you in front of all of us just a few minutes ago, or didn't you notice?"

"Disrespect isn't criminal," Jack said. "Miralee is only in a phase. She isn't capable of a felony."

"You just said she's too smart for what you think is a menial job!"

His father interrupted. "Ed, that's enough."

"He's the worst double-talker I've ever heard! He's accusing Mom of murder, but thinks his little girl is an angel? That scooter was parked in Mom's lane, head-on! I'm starting to believe *he* set us up! What for? Because kicking us out of your church club wasn't satisfying enough, *Jack?*"

"That's not what's happening," Geoff said. "The truth always comes out, Ed. Be patient."

"I've had it with patience. Sometimes the

truth only comes out because we force it to!"

Jack chuckled at that. "A kid after my own heart."

Ed took a swing at him then, hurling his own arm down at the man's head from above as if it were a basketball in his opponent's hands. Ed's height might have been his only advantage. The detective leaned sideways, evading, in full control of his firearm and his wits. Ed's knuckles scraped the cinder-block wall as momentum carried his body through the punch, tipping him off balance. Pain shot up through his wrist, and then his shoulder struck the bricks too. Ed came around, having enough time and sharp reflexes to aim a back kick at Jack's pathetic bucket. He'd knock it over and take the man on the ground.

But his father had moved to intervene, had placed his body between Ed and Jack. Instead of finding the bucket, Ed's foot struck his father square in the kneecap.

Geoff stumbled, and then Jack rose above him, standing over Ed's dad with the gun aimed down at his head.

CHAPTER 28

The fog was still thick when Audrey drove out of town in Geoff's truck at eight twenty. Diane sat on the passenger side with Miralee tucked away behind them. They headed east on the highway as fast as if there was no fog at all, toward the mountains, toward hope.

No one had said much since Geoff's phone call and the exchange between Miralee and Jack. Audrey had placed another call to Captain Wilson as they passed through the city limits. As far as Diane could tell, Wilson wasn't full of encouragement.

Audrey got off the phone and sighed. "Cornucopia doesn't have any helicopters to send ahead. He thinks he can find one down in the next county, but the weather . . . It could be awhile. They'll send a car up, but we're already ahead of them."

Diane looked out at the thick air. Not

good visibility for flying in, and who knew how far a car or copter would have to climb to get out of it.

"It should be better visibility in the mountains," she offered.

"Might be snow," Audrey said. "But I hope not." They'd borrowed jackets from the Mansfields' coat closet when Audrey announced her intentions. Miralee had brought her father's gun. One of many he had, she said. Audrey thought one would be plenty.

The gray moisture surrounding them messed with Diane's perception of their progress. Instead of mile markers clicking by the window, or rows of groves and fields fanning by in a mesmerizing rhythm, all she could see was the dashed white line slipping under the hood, the same broken paint repeating itself.

"What if Jack doesn't give us enough time?" she said.

"Dad's not going to kill anyone, if that's what you're worried about," said Miralee.

"You said he's done it before."

"That he has. Between us, I think if anyone really killed my mom, he did."

"So will he or won't he?"

"Never in a situation where he'd be found out."

"You mean this is all an act?" Diane twisted in her seat to look at Miralee. "The hostage thing is to cover up what he did himself? Oh, Audrey, he's insane. Some kind of mental. Is it possible he can't remember what he did?"

"I didn't mean literally, Diane. He kills the soul of a person, you know? With that better-respect-the-badge attitude. My mom started dying years before the cancer reared its head. Why do you think I had to leave? Yea, there is no one more righteous than Jack Mansfield, not even one."

Audrey said, "Geoff told me he shot Coach Henderson again."

Miralee leaned forward. "No."

"Is he dead?" Diane asked.

Audrey shook her head.

Miralee leaned back and said, "That man's never discharged his weapon anywhere but at a range. Maybe he is going insane."

"It could happen to any of us." Audrey's tone held censure.

"Us. You mean me. Because he and I are genetically connected, is that it?"

"I mean anyone. Your dad is suffering, Miri, can't you see it? Do you know what suffering can do to a person?"

"My father doesn't know the definition of

the word. In his universe there's only reward and punishment."

"I bet he thinks he's going to be rewarded for this stunt," Diane said.

Audrey said, "I was asking whether *you* understand what it is to suffer, Miralee."

"Insofar as it's related to living with a father who is never wrong about anything, yes."

Diane stared out at the cloak of fog. "I thought I'd be rewarded for killing my sister."

Miralee's neck swiveled to Diane. "You killed your sister? I thought Dad was exaggerating."

Diane nodded.

"No way!" The protest sounded almost like admiration. "Why'd you do that?"

"It's none of our business," Audrey said.

"Donna stole an heirloom from my grandmother, a necklace. She planned to sell it for . . . for something worthless. A prom dress, a limo, something like that. So I stole the necklace back and planned to return it, which I should have done immediately — that very day. That very hour. But I waited. I'm not sure why I waited. No. Yes, I do. I waited because I thought that maybe I would buy something worthless for myself, just to spite my sister. I even thought about paying Jason Moyer to be my date, but I was too scared that he might turn down me *and* the money."

She laughed because she was embarrassed. Jason Moyer had a wide jaw and sweeping golden hair that hid his eyes, and three girlfriends at a time. The highway narrowed from four lanes to two, and the truck began its slow rise into the mountains.

"The next day Mom sent me on an errand. When Donna couldn't find where I'd hidden the jewelry, she went to my parents and accused me of having stolen it. Within fifteen minutes, before I was even back, they told Grammie and she confirmed the piece was gone. So I played clueless, which was my role back then anyway, and the only reason I didn't get in trouble was because it was her word against mine. No diamond, no proof."

"It was a *diamond.* You didn't mention that small detail," Miralee said.

"It's not an important one."

"How much was it worth?"

"Then? I don't know. I was a kid. It wasn't even cut. I don't know if it was ever appraised."

"So for all you know it was worthless."

Diane didn't understand what Miralee was getting at.

Audrey said, "The value of a thing rarely ever lies in its sale price, Miralee."

"But even I'd know to —"

"Miri. Zip it."

The girl was too excited to pout. She was sitting behind a convicted murderer who might be mistaken for a Cabbage Patch doll. "So your sister pointed the finger at you, and — ?"

"And nothing, for a while. I sat on it. My grandmother made her insurance claim. She got her money. Then I was even more confused about what to do with the pendant. But Donna . . . We never got along well to begin with. After that, you can imagine.

"So one night after the drugstore was closed and our parents went out — this was back before the Rx was open 24-7 — Donna and some of her friends got plastered in the alley behind the store. They were completely drunk, and loud, and more stupid than usual. Donna started talking about breaking into the safe where Dad kept the day's deposits.

"What was I supposed to do? She was out of control, her friends hated me as much as she did. I thought if she'd just pass out, she'd forget about it. We both knew where Dad kept his keys. I got to them first. I went into the pharmacy. I slipped a few morphine tablets into a shot of vodka and gave it to her after they dissolved. She threw it straight back, didn't even notice them."

"Wow. You are stupid, aren't you?"

"It would have been better for me if the jury believed that."

"They thought you premeditated it?"

"Donna didn't . . . pass out right away. She led her friends into the store and they ransacked it while she tried to remember the combination to the safe. When I wouldn't give it to her she started screaming at me. She said I was trying to ruin her life. I was bigger than she was; I dragged her out of the office and shoved her into the store. She said, 'What are you trying to do, kill me?' — that's what her friends remembered most when it was their turn on the stand."

Geoff's truck followed the weaving road. The air didn't thin but turned slowly from dim gray to veil white.

"I just wanted her to have a chance to get sober so she could think about what she was really doing."

"Girl like that doesn't think much different sober or sloshed," Miralee said.

"I can't believe they sentenced you to

twenty-five years," Audrey said. "You were a minor."

"Tried me as an adult."

"They charged you with first-degree murder?"

"If you were on that jury and heard my best friend and parents testifying against me, what would you have thought?"

"Juliet," Audrey murmured.

Diane nodded.

"You didn't intend to kill your sister."

"Obviously, I failed to prove my intentions."

"Still, it's unmerciful."

"The judge spared me the death penalty. That's legal here in California, you know."

"Not for minors!"

"Poisoning someone is a capital offense."

"Did your parents really testify against you?" Miralee asked.

"They told the truth that they knew, and that was indictment enough to fill in the gaps."

Audrey protested. "It was an accident, though!"

"Was it?" said Diane. "Doesn't take much time behind bars before a girl starts to wonder."

"No one should have to wonder alone," Audrey said.

"Wonder, or wander?" Miralee asked, looking straight ahead.

The truck drove on into the silence of mist mixing with light snow.

The weather delayed them. It was nearly nine by the time they reached the snaking turnoff for the Old Gauntlet Road that led toward Miners Rest, and to the trailheads of King's Riches beyond.

Audrey navigated the narrow fork off the main highway and followed the powdery road around a bend as her cell-phone reception dwindled to nothing. The entryway came into view.

"No no no no no," she whispered. A low-slung gate barricaded the route, and an orange ROAD CLOSED sign dangled lopsided from the top bar.

"They always close this road at first snow," Miralee said. There was no smugness in her tone, though.

Instead she seemed as stunned as Audrey, who knew the same fact but had been hoping for the best.

"I guess that means there's no way Mom's up here, then. Right?" The question seemed genuine enough. "Any other ideas?"

"What better place to hide someone than a place no one else can reach?" Audrey asked as she opened her door and slid off the seat. But she was thinking, *That truck is the only lead I have.*

Audrey approached the gate. She kicked the padlock holding the latch closed on the south side of the road. Her foot turned the frame into a tuning fork that hummed for a few seconds. The women in the truck behind her were still.

Audrey waited and hoped God would strike her with some revelation. Or some physical sensation to confirm that she was closer to Julie than ever before.

Snowflakes teased her nose and melted on her lips. Fingers of damp air touched her cheeks and burned the skin. She smelled the exhaust of the idling truck.

How far are you willing to go?

The voice might have been straight from God's mouth, dropping from the sky into her ears, except the audible words came from a woman, and, well, Audrey just didn't buy into the idea that God was a woman.

She spun back to the cab. Diane and Miralee were talking to each other, and Audrey couldn't hear what they were saying.

How far are you willing to go? Would you take your own life?

"No!" Audrey said aloud, though this time the questions were not audible. They were emotional. A challenge, a dare. And Audrey was less sure that they belonged to another woman. Maybe the thoughts were hers after all.

She was despairing. She had never despaired. Always hoped, always believed, always pressed ahead. But here she was, facing off with a padlock. Was she about to lose faith in the power of God over a chunk of metal?

If Geoff and Ed died, she might.

"How far will I go to do what?" she asked God aloud. "And *no,* I will not take my own life. You'll have to take responsibility for that part."

There is no one to stop me anymore. Please stop me.

A warmth of a cozy fire passed over Audrey's face, taking the bite out of the air and sending warmth out to her fingertips and toes. Her eyelids closed. *Stop me from what?* The question was vague and unimportant. Her frozen skin relaxed, and she felt the tension between her shoulders ease a fraction. She leaned forward and rested her hands on the gate's top horizontal bar. Seconds later, the peaceful illusion gave way to pain.

The flames of this mystical fire were too hot. The tongues licked her, burning the palms of her hands. She smelled the stench of burning hair and felt the mascara on her eyelashes begin to melt. Audrey jumped backward before she had consciously registered these details.

And after she thought those frightening seconds through, she turned her palms up and made sense of the pain. Her left hand was still protected by a light bandage covering last week's injury. But her right hand, bonded to the metal rail by her sweat, lost some skin when she leaped away. Tiny pink patches of raw flesh appeared like fresh calluses across the pads at the base of her finger joints. One of the wounds was bleeding, and the winter air was salt.

Stop me. Please.

Audrey didn't know what the voice meant. Maybe it was God connecting her to Julie. Maybe it was her own spiritual indecision. But what she really needed right now were strong, strong ties to Julie. A rope on a pulley that would draw her closer to the missing woman. Some emotional or physical sensation wasn't going to do it this time. It was no longer enough for Audrey to say kind words to Julie through a curtained window and then walk away because Julie wanted her to. Audrey needed a battering ram that would knock down a front door or a cage or a kidnapper.

How far was Audrey willing to go? She still had time to turn around and get back to the bakery before Jack killed anyone. Even if the road wasn't closed, it was at least another hour and a half to the site where she'd seen Harlan Hall's old gray mare. Even if she found Julie then, she wouldn't be able to get back in touch with Jack in time.

For the sake of her husband and son, Audrey decided to break a law. Two, in fact. *Somebody just try to stop me,* she thought wryly.

She called back to the truck as she walked. "Diane, what happened to Julie's meds that I gave you back at the house?"

"In the glove box here." Diane reached for it.

"Let me have one of the painkillers." Audrey rounded the driver's side door, which she'd left open.

"You sure that's okay?" Diane asked.

"Not legally, if that's what you mean."

"Maybe you'd better not take it, with you driving and all."

"What happened to your hands?" Miralee said.

"I don't need it for my hands," Audrey said, "and either one of you can drive if I

346

get loopy. Let me have that ginger ale."

Audrey took one of the pills and asked God to forgive her. She swallowed and felt silly. Why did she think that taking Julie's medicine might lead her onward?

She gingerly pulled herself up and behind the wheel, then slammed the door shut. "What time is it?"

"Five after nine," Diane said.

Audrey squared her shoulders and focused on the line of fir trees bordering the road on the other side of the gate. A shadow flitted through the trees, low and crouching, floating down into King's Riches. She blinked, and the vision vanished. She'd seen this form one other time, but only now identified the shape, fluid like the billowing hair of a woman on the run.

"Where to now?" Miralee asked, craning her neck to help Audrey back out of the narrow bend.

"Straight ahead," Audrey said. She put the truck in gear and floored the accelerator.

Chapter 29

Ed found murder in his heart. Jack stood over his father, pointing a gun down between Geoff's upturned eyes, but what Ed saw was himself standing in Jack's place, and Jack dead on the ground with a bullet through his head. If Jack killed his dad, that's exactly how this scene would end up. One way or the other.

"Jack, you are a good man," his father said. "You're not a killer."

The senseless words stripped Ed's revenge fantasy off the surface of the scene. *What?*

"I do what God asks me to do," Jack said.

"I know," said Geoff. He lifted his hand slowly toward Jack's gun, and Jack's arm went rigid. He waved the barrel back and forth over Geoff's eyes.

"I'm a blameless man!" Jack shouted. "I've never done anything to deserve what's happened to me!"

Ed's dad gently pushed the gun away from

348

his face and rolled onto his stomach. Jack snatched the weapon out of his reach and lifted it toward Ed, still directing his words at Geoff.

"I am devout! I provide for my family! I'm a leader in my community! Things shouldn't have turned out this way! There's only one explanation: my family is a victim of other people's sins! Do you understand me?"

Geoff rose to his good knee and pushed himself up. "Yes, I do. I've made the same claims for myself."

"Your sins are responsible," Jack said to Ed. "And yours," he aimed his gun at Leslie, who scrambled away. "And yours, and yours, and yours." Jack walked around the room, pointing at Estrella, and Geoff, and Coach. He stopped over Coach's reclined body, cocked the silent gun over the sleeping man.

"Christ already died for their sins," Geoff said. "And yours. No more death required, okay?"

"You don't know squat about the things of God."

Ed's father held up his hands, palms out, a calm request for reason. "I know about his love and his mercy."

"All I ever tried to do was protect my wife and daughter from people like you," Jack said. "And look at what happened to them. Is that my fault? No. I am Job. I am blameless!"

"Jack, you're going to lose your job, your freedom, your respect. And you won't be able to blame anyone else for that."

The truth of Geoff's words seemed to penetrate Jack's mind. Slowly, his breathing evened out, and the bright blood under the skin of his neck receded. He lowered the gun to his side and took a deep breath.

"My actions will be justified," Jack said. "God will restore everything to me, twice as much as I had before. And your wife will get what's coming to her."

Ed's murderous heart pounded loudly in his own ears. He sat back down beside Leslie. The cat had curled up in the nest of her crossed legs while Coach slept, and she stroked the top of its head, more calm than he'd seen her since the ordeal started. He sat slightly in front of her, placing his body between hers and Jack's. If Jack shot them all to pieces, he might at least die trying to protect someone. It was better than being responsible for getting them killed.

His dad was watching him. Ed's attention flickered to his father, who gingerly put weight on the knee Ed had kicked, then put his fingertips on the wall for balance.

"Dad, I . . ."

Geoff shook his head. "I'm fine."

Jack started tapping his gun against his thigh. The small room wasn't big enough to contain the detective's restlessness. He circled once and drifted into the kitchen, gun smacking his leg in a driving rhythm, footsteps pacing in sync.

Estrella followed him out and asked for permission to get milk for the cat.

"I'm sorry," Ed said to Geoff.

His father responded in an equally low tone. "It'll heal."

"Not that. I mean, I can't believe I kicked you. But I'm sorry I ever thought . . . that I ever wondered . . . that money for the abortion . . ."

Geoff's pained face relaxed slightly into a soft smile. "Ah. That. Any smart man would have wondered."

"I didn't have any reason to. You've always done the right thing."

"No. Not always."

"Well," Ed conceded, "maybe it would have helped if you'd put up more of a fight when Jack started pointing fingers this summer."

A metallic gong sounded as Jack walked by the oven and struck it with the butt of his pistol.

"A fight, huh?"

"You kind of rolled over."

Geoff nodded. "When I was your age I was more of a fighter."

Ed tried to picture his pastor-father throwing punches in a makeshift schoolyard ring. Couldn't see it. Estrella returned with cream for Leslie's new friend. The cat got up at once and started lapping.

"I got carried away at a protest once — all that moral indignation creates its own kind of high. I threw a punch aiming for some guy's kidney, hit his spine instead, kicked him when he was down."

"You never told me that."

"The time never seemed right."

"What happened?"

"He lost the use of his legs and decided not to sue me."

"What? Why?" Ed couldn't imagine anyone not wanting justice for something like that.

"Because sometimes mercy is the best weapon against evil."

Jack's tapping reached the industrial refrigerator.

"Sometimes," Ed said.

Geoff sighed. "Most of the time."

"But in this case —"

"Maybe it was a mistake. Maybe I should

have fought back. I don't know."

"There's still time to fight. We should do something."

His father shook his head. "Trusting God is what I do best. I don't have all the answers, as much as I always wanted you to think I did."

Jack had circled the kitchen and was coming back around to the little room.

"God will lead you, Ed. You'll make your own mistakes and find wisdom in them. He'll give you answers that your mom and I don't have. And we'll watch and be amazed."

Ed looked at the floor. The others in the room were pretending to be deaf.

Jack came back in. The weapon slapping his thigh missed a beat and Ed felt the man's attention on him, suspicion that some conspiracy against him was brewing.

Maybe it was. Ed lifted his eyes to Jack's gun and, with the same intense concentration that Leslie had applied to her math, began to make some calculations of his own.

The gate across the road to Miners Rest was good for deterring law-abiding citizens and maybe some opportunists. Otherwise, it was no match for Geoff's heavy 4×4. Audrey looked in the rearview mirror at the twisted frame dangling from its support pole.

"You don't hold your meds very well," Miralee observed.

"That had nothing to do with meds," Audrey said.

A bend in the road put Audrey's driving violation firmly behind her.

"What's your plan to find the truck?" Diane asked.

"I don't think we'll see it from the road," she said. "Or even in any obvious place. The rangers wouldn't have closed the gate without checking for vehicles first."

"I'll bet vehicles get stranded up here all the time," Miralee said.

"We'll have to follow my gut."

"We're following an intoxicated gut," Miralee said to Diane.

The snow on the road to Miners Rest wasn't enough to slow them down, but the journey was more precarious than ever, with plunging slopes and no guardrail to the south. Audrey looked at the clock on the dash, feeling more anxious by the blinking second. If the truck was still parked at the trailhead (which it wouldn't be), and if Julie was sitting in the cab waiting for them (which she wouldn't be), it would be nearly eleven by the time they arrived, and it would take more than an hour and a half to get back to cell-phone reception.

Audrey begged God to stay Jack's hand. To give Wilson or Geoff or Ed some kind of divine inspiration.

"I was here just yesterday with Ed," she told them. "He told me you'd stayed in the cabins at Miners Rest, Miri."

"My mom and I did once, during her summer break. She likes it up here."

"When Ed and I were driving by there, I started to feel sick."

"O-*kay*," Miralee said.

"I think your mom and I are connected spiritually."

Miralee squared off her shoulders with the front window. "I can't believe this. My dad was right. You two are psychos. You *know* my mom's up here because you *brought* her here, didn't you? Did Ed help you? Are our families going to be locked in some tit-for-tat war until we wipe each other off the map?"

"Absolutely not. Listen to me."

"I can't. I can't believe I am even here. You know, I come across pretty cold sometimes, I'm aware of that, but deep down I suppose I had some kind of little-girl-needs-her-mom moment, and I was sorta hoping you might be telling the truth about being very highly motivated to find her, about how deeply you care about her and all that religious mumbo jumbo. I've had it. Let me out!"

Miralee tried to climb over Diane's side of the front seat and fought her for the door handle. Audrey slammed on the brakes, and Miri rocked over into the dashboard.

"Stop it! I need your help . . . I need you to tell me everything you can think of about Julie and how she spent her time up here. Do you hear me? Because if I can't find her, and Jack keeps his word, I'm going to lose the only thing that really matters to me. Okay?"

"I assure you, losing your family is entirely survivable! You'll get over it, no need for my assistance!" Miralee scrambled again.

Audrey expected Diane to all but fall out of the cab getting out of Miralee's way. Instead, she squared her wide back against the exit and blocked the girl's escape, unflinching even when Miralee's fingers caught in her hair and gripped the silky auburn strands. Diane gripped Miralee's wrist and drove her own thumb into the soft spot at the joint, forcing her to release the rope of hair. The teenager cursed and threw herself back toward Audrey's seat. Diane held on.

"Where are you going to go?" Diane asked her. "We're thirty miles from anyone who can help you."

"Does it matter?"

"For you, yes."

"You're going to kill me!"

"No one's going to kill you, Miralee." Diane looked at Audrey, who could not have been more surprised by Diane's boldness. "Why do teenagers always think I'm trying to kill them?"

Audrey stared.

"Miralee," Diane said without compassion, "you haven't lost your family. You've just walked away from them, and the thing that made it survivable for you is that you know you can walk back home whenever you want. You don't lose your family until you walk back and learn that they've forgotten you. And few people actually survive that."

Miralee wrenched her arm out of Diane's grip.

Diane continued, "When we can't find your mom because she's dead, and your dad goes crazy because he's lost her forever, and gets shot up by his own people when they try to stop him from a slaughter, then we'll see how you do."

Miralee clenched her teeth together and

faced forward. Audrey placed her hands back on the wheel and felt the sharp pain of her raw blisters. The wheels of the truck started rolling again like millstones.

"Tell Audrey where your mom liked to come up here."

Miralee muttered something.

"Speak up," Diane ordered.

"I don't *know.*"

"Then tell her where the two of you stayed that one time."

"In Miners Rest, in the cabin at the back of the property."

"We'll start there, then," Audrey said. The truck took a slow grinding turn around a hairpin corner.

"They'll be locked up for winter, won't they?"

"Maybe."

"What did you mean by *spiritually connected?*"

"I think your mom's alive, and that she's sick. Sometimes I feel things, physical sensations, that seem like they should belong to another person."

"I don't buy it."

"Remember when I asked you about talking to you through the window? I was led to your house —"

"Led. You are *way* out there."

"I felt this deep, deep sadness. I thought I was talking to you, that you were upset about the breakup —"

"I wasn't." Miralee crossed her arms.

"Right. It wasn't you after all, Miri. I think it was your mom."

"You believe her?" Miralee said to Diane.

"Yes."

"She can't know this stuff. It's impossible."

"Maybe it's only impossible for people who don't want to know," Diane said.

"But that was eons ago," Miralee said to Audrey. "Do you stay connected to people forever or something?"

"No. Usually I bake them a loaf of bread and stay for a while, and then I go home."

Miralee laughed.

"But we never got to that point. That was my fault, probably. I should have done more."

"Done more? What did you do?"

"Nothing. I left her. I walked away. And now her pain won't let go of me."

Diane was looking at Audrey's hands. "When was the last time you felt something?"

"At Julie's house. That nausea."

"What about those blisters on your palms?"

"You saw me get those," Audrey said.

"But they remind me of something. This time . . . this time Donna and I went up to Mammoth to ski with some friends. When we were in line for the lift, Donna took off her gloves to fish some Chapstick out of her pocket, and she didn't have time to put them on again before the lift came around. Her hands were sweaty, she sat down and grabbed the bar to pull it over our heads." Diane gestured to Audrey's bandages. "Same thing happened."

"You think Julie might have hurt her hands?"

"You'd know better than I would," Diane said.

"How could something like that happen out here? No skiing, not even any sign poles to lick, not really."

"There are snow-marker poles," said Diane.

"A car door handle," Audrey said. "Or a bumper. Any part of a car."

"Buried treasure and a medieval sword," Miralee said through downturned lips.

"An outdoor water pump," said Diane, and her face paled.

Miralee said, "None of the cabins at Miners Rest have outdoor water pumps *or* swords."

"Not those," said Audrey, "but the old cabins. The ones from the mining days. Problem is, there are dozens."

"My grandparents had a cabin up here," Diane said. "They said it belonged to Great-Great-Grandpa Hall, the one who found the diamond in that necklace. I have no idea whether it's still in the family, or even if it's still standing."

"But do you know where it is?" Audrey asked.

"Off the Silver Gap trail," Diane said. "I can take you there."

"I know that trail," Audrey said. "It's where I got sick yesterday. That's where you said you and your mom used to go all the time, Miralee."

"She never took me to any special family cabin," she said.

Diane muttered sarcastically, "I wonder why."

CHAPTER 30

Audrey wasn't sure whether it was the pain medication or the supernatural peace of God that was preventing her from feeling panicked, but by the time the women left the Silver Gap trail for the off-map cabin, she had come to terms with the fact that she couldn't get back to Geoff and Ed in time. It might have been the first stage of grief she was feeling, that denial of reality that would give way soon enough to anger and depression.

The Halls' gray truck wasn't in the trail-head parking lot. Diane led the way up the uneven ground slowly, more slowly than Audrey wished. In fairness, fresh snow and the passage of decades had transformed landmarks once familiar to Diane. And though Audrey knew the trail well enough, she wasn't one to go wandering far from it.

So she followed Diane, and Miralee straggled behind her. "Are you sure we should have left Geoff's truck running?" Miralee asked when they went over a hill and the parking lot dropped out of sight.

"If Wilson can get a helicopter here, they'll see the condensation from the exhaust," Audrey said. "I hope."

"What if we run out of gas?"

"One question at a time, Miri. Right now I'm still working on what's going to happen if we can't find your mom."

"Are they allowed to land a helicopter down there?" she asked.

Audrey didn't answer that. Surely an emergency vehicle could be set down in a vacant parking lot. The snow clouds had cleared out here, though it was impossible to say where they had gone or what skies they might be clogging up elsewhere. The white winter rays of sun glancing off the clean earth gave Audrey a weak sense of hope and ears straining for the sound of thumping rotors.

"I haven't seen any footprints but ours," she said to Diane's back.

"I'm sure we're going the right way," Diane said. "That's Snaggletooth Peak over there." She pointed east. "And there's Pinpoint Lake."

A glittering sheet of ice that Audrey would have called a pond was directly south of them, lined by a tight row of trees.

"The cabin's behind the windbreak."

"Good place to hide a vehicle if someone wanted to," Audrey said.

"I don't see any route a car could have taken," Miralee said.

"Farther east, along the old mining road," Diane said. "Trucks can come and go the same way horses and carts used to."

She trudged ahead, hugging herself for warmth. Audrey saw that her generic sneakers were soaked through.

It took the trio another ten minutes to drop into the valley and reach the frozen drinking hole dusted with powdered-sugar snow. Numbness had settled on Audrey's nose and ears, and her spirit as well. This was what despair felt like, she thought, the absence of heat, the belief that it would be impossible ever to feel warm again.

At the windbreak Diane paused and placed her hand on the trunk of the closest tree as if it were a weeping friend.

The cabin was a one-room shanty, really, a four-walled box with a weak sloping roof, one window, and an exhaust pipe for what Audrey assumed was a woodstove. A split-rail fence with a few fallen crossbeams poking the earth surrounded a plot barely large enough for a summer garden, if such a desolate place could be cultivated. There was a rusty water pump to the right of the door, and ruins of another shack, a shelter for a horse perhaps, a short distance behind the cabin.

It looked abandoned.

"We can't just walk in," Miralee whispered. "If there's a kidnapper, a gunman . . ."

"There's no gunman in this story but your father," Diane said.

Visions of Julie ran through Audrey's mind, of Julie standing solitary in the center of a stage while scenes crash-changed around her. She saw Julie outside of a full church, doors closed. Julie sobbing in her husband's home office. Julie in her cold kitchen without Jack or Miri to cook for. Julie standing in a graveyard. Julie in a hospital room after surgery, no flowers. Young Julie on a witness stand, cheeks streaked with tear tracks.

Julie alone in swirling fog.

"But she might not be alone!" Miralee insisted. She sounded afraid.

"She is alone, Miri," Audrey said. She left the shelter of the trees and moved toward the cabin. "If you don't believe me, you can always trust your dad's gun instead."

"How do you know? How can you really

know *anything?*"

Audrey talked back over her shoulder as she strode to the shack. "I know it in my heart. That's the problem, isn't it? That she's always been alone, that we've all walked away when she needed us most, because we thought she didn't really need us?"

The wind that was pushing the snow clouds out of the valley swept down over the tired plot of land in a chilling gust.

"There's the truck," Diane said.

Audrey turned. Diane was looking uphill past the ruined horse shed. The gray pickup was a mere boulder atop the landscape, balanced on a hillcrest.

At the sight of the vehicle, the first tangible evidence that something terrible had happened to her mother, Miralee's face was transformed. The sharp lines of her picture-perfect angles softened into something lost, the expression of a child who realizes she's lost sight of her guardians in a big and terrible world.

At the same time, Audrey and Miralee rushed to the cabin, all emotion gone but dread of what they were about to find. Miralee beat her there and gripped the tarnished knob, throwing her shoulder into the door. It flew open on oiled hinges. Audrey reached to catch the girl's arm, but her fingers only grazed Miri's jacket.

Miralee shrieked and dropped to her knees.

Julie Mansfield lay facedown in the center of a strangely comfortable space that didn't match the unwelcoming exterior. Her body was sprawled across a clean braided rug, her head pointing toward the gaping doors of a shiny woodstove gone cold hours before. A puff of gray ash awakened by the bursting door rose in the cavity and floated out onto Julie's fine hair. Her outstretched hand touched a slender cut log that had not been placed on the fire in time to keep it going.

Miralee rolled her mother over before Audrey could stop her.

"She'sdeadshe'sdeadshe'sdead."

The inside of the cabin was as cold as the outdoors. Audrey kneeled and touched Julie's hand. It was too hot. She turned over her wrist and saw blisters on Julie's palms, not the shredded skin of a fall onto coarse asphalt or a freeze burn, but the chafing of hands unaccustomed to wielding an ax.

"I'll find wood for a fire," Diane said from the doorway.

"Look behind the cabin," Audrey said. Light filled the space that Diane's shadow vacated.

"My mother's dead!" Miralee's words were distorted by disbelief. "She didn't want me to go the way I did. She begged me to . . . to . . ."

"She's not dead, Miri, she's sick."

"She's going to die because I left!"

"You're here now. Find a cloth and some water."

Illness colored Julie's cheeks bright red. Audrey remembered the heat that had washed over her face while she stood at the gate across the Old Gauntlet Road. If the sensation had been timed with actual events, she could hope that Julie hadn't been here on the floor for too long.

Miralee stood and seemed to look around the space without seeing anything.

"Try the cupboards," Audrey said gently. "Or under the bed. I can use the pillowcase if you don't see a towel. Ask Diane if she brought your mom's medications."

Miralee found what Audrey needed. It seemed Julie — or whoever had brought her — came prepared to stay awhile, with blankets and bottled water and dried fruit and nuts and jerky and canned goods. The food was hardly touched.

Audrey didn't know anything about what Julie needed except that it was out of reach.

The woman's heartbeat and breath were limp but audible. This fever seemed worse than the one Ed had when he was fourteen and his doctor admitted him to the hospital, or maybe it was just that Audrey's fingers were nearly frozen. It was too cold in the room for a damp cloth on the forehead to bring Julie any comfort, but Miralee needed something to do. They all needed something to do.

The stove shared the wall with the bed, its foot pointed toward the warmth. A duffel bag protruded from under the cot. On the adjoining wall opposite the door was a countertop with cupboards built over the top of it and a cutout that held a metal basin, presumably for water. Next to it was a wooden box filled with newspaper and tinder kept dry from the snow. There was something that looked like a chamber pot at the back of the open door, and a lopsided table, chair, and oil lamp on the remaining wall. A trail map was pinned up over the makeshift desk.

With few words the women worked together. Diane built a fire carefully and lit it on the first try with matches from the cupboard. Miralee helped Audrey get her mother off the floor and onto the cot while the room warmed up. They took off her wet shoes and found dry socks in the duffel. The skin of Julie's feet seemed thin and blue.

Her medications were back in Geoff's truck, and Diane prepared to hike back to get them, but Miralee found keys on the desk and everyone thought of the truck. "Dad has a CB on that truck," Diane said. "Unless he took it out before Juliet bought it."

Audrey told Miralee to go help Diane.

The cool cloth on Julie's brow warmed through within five minutes. Audrey rinsed it, wrung it out, and put it back, wondering if this, too, was pointless. She found a percolator and ground coffee in the cupboard, then poured water into the pot. She set the coffee to brew on top of the wood-stove.

The wind outside picked up but didn't penetrate the cabin walls.

Audrey sat down on the only chair and rested her elbows on the wood of the table, praying for her husband and son, and for Julie, and for the miracle they all needed.

She was staring at the desk without seeing it. *God, if you can promise me that there's a purpose in all this pain, and that one day you'll show me what it is, I might be able to endure it.*

There were papers on the desktop. A sheet

torn from a lined notebook, *Dear Miri* across the top. That was all Julie had found in herself to write. Audrey pushed the pages around with her fingertips, reluctant to intrude but hoping for answers. If Julie had come up here alone, why? If she had set up the scooter accident, why?

There was a statement from an investment bank and a short sheet of paper from which a check had been torn off the bottom. A payout of a 401(k) plan, less penalties, for one Juliet Steen Mansfield, plus a letter about taxes that would be owed on the distribution. It was enough to buy an old truck with cash and have plenty left to live on for a while. Audrey hadn't seen any money in the cabin, though. There was a coffee can with a twenty in it on the top shelf of the cupboard, but none in the duffel bag or other obvious place.

Under the statement was a small stack of organized medical statements: hospital, surgeon, anesthesiologist, labs, and so on. *This is not a bill,* the statements announced. *The account has been submitted to your insurance carrier. You may be responsible for any portion not covered . . .* and so on.

One statement, however, stood out from the rest because the bottom right corner was circled in red and labeled *Amount You*

Owe, which was an amount much larger than the cost of Harlan's old gray mare. There was a receipt for this amount stapled to the top left corner of the statement.

Hemato Labs was the name of the billing entity. The itemization was for *autologous donation, self-stored, 4 units.* Audrey rubbed her temples. That would explain all the blood on the street.

"Oh, Julie," she murmured, "what did you do?"

Under these was a letter to Julie printed on stationery from Mazy High. *Though we are grateful for your years of devoted service, we regret to inform you that budget restrictions will prevent us from renewing your contract at the end of the academic calendar year . . .*

The letter was dated in September.

Audrey sighed, feeling the weight of these burdens that Julie had been carrying. Why hadn't Jack said anything about her job loss?

"Because I didn't tell him," Julie said to her from the cot.

Audrey shot out of her seat. "Did I ask that question aloud?"

Julie's eyes were still closed. "What question?" she murmured.

The coffee in the pot was percolating now and made soft bubbling noises. Audrey rose and moved it off the cooking platform, then found a cup and filled it with the drinking water that Miri had located. She carried it to Julie's side, dragging the chair behind her.

"Can you drink some water?" Audrey asked.

Julie lifted her hand, a weak barricade between her mouth and the cup.

"Darn you, Julie. Quit pushing me away. You don't know what this has cost me." Audrey kneeled next to the cot and slipped her hand under Julie's neck to lift it. No doubt Audrey's icy fingers were part of the reason Julie gasped and became more fully aware. She finally opened her eyes and locked onto Audrey, frowning.

"You're that pastor's wife."

"Baker's wife now. Drink this." She pressed the cup against Julie's lips.

"I dreamed about you," Julie said after a swallow. "You were in my house."

"You were throwing things at me."

Julie's delicate, naked fingers were clutching the top blanket. "You dreamed it too."

"Oh, I don't think I was dreaming. Your wedding ring?"

"Left it at Jack's house. He owns it, you know."

"The house or the ring?"

"Both. Everything. The world. I'm so tired."

Audrey pulled the gold band out of her jeans pocket and held it in front of Julie's face.

Julie winced as if it were a bright light. "What happened to your hands?" she asked.

"My hands." Audrey had no care at all for her petty injuries. What were they compared to what her husband and son were suffering right now? "Your blood did this to my hands, Julie. And your husband is killing me. *Killing* me. Tell me why. What happened?"

"I'm so tired," Julie said, slipping back into her fever. "I'm just so tired."

Audrey slammed the cup of water onto the floor by the cot, sloshing onto the wood. She demanded God tell her why her family should die while this woman should live, and in the same breath she begged him to forgive her for not understanding a thing.

CHAPTER 31

Diane knew when her weight landed in the driver's seat that something was wrong with her father's old truck, something off-balance and unstable, but she waffled over whether to say this to Miralee — so she said nothing at all. She turned the key in the ignition and heard the engine turn over just as it should, a high protest settling down into a comforting rumble.

After a moment's hesitation, Diane dropped the truck into gear and stepped on the gas. The tires spun, and the truck stayed in place. She looked at Miralee.

"High centered," she said and jumped out of the car. She peered under the carriage while Miri waited in the passenger seat. "On a big old tree stump. No wonder your mom stopped here." Leaning into the cab, Diane reached for the key and shut off the engine. "I'm going to have to hike back to get the medicine, if we get it at all."

"What if you leave the engine running? Like Audrey did down in the lot. Police might see it if they get up here — the weather's clearing out."

"But it's not as cold as it was. The sun's almost peaked." Even so, Diane climbed back into the cab and started the engine once more.

"Do you think my dad . . . ?" Miri couldn't bring herself to say the words.

Diane shrugged.

"You're the only one of us who saw him, Diane. Could you tell? Was his mind . . . ? I can't believe it. I don't want to."

"All of us are capable of doing things we never dreamed of doing, good and bad," Diane said. "But mostly bad. That's all I know."

"I always thoughts parents had everything figured out, that it's the kids' job to catch up with them. All I wanted was for them to tell me the truth about life as they know it. But they seemed to think they were supposed to protect me, like if they lied to me about their own misery I'd never have eyes to see it."

Diane wondered if there was a way for the two of them to rock the truck off the log. But the girl was too small to break a twig off a branch.

"Who wants to catch up with people who can't tell the truth?" Miralee said.

"You're the biggest hypocrite of all, Miri."

"What?"

"I spent twenty-five years in a prison with women who lie better than you know how to," Diane said. "Even Audrey sees through you, and she's as pure as they come. Let's figure out this two-way radio."

Miralee's eyes were wet. Diane turned on the radio, wondering if her childhood knowledge of how to operate it would come back to her.

"You're not being fair," Miri said.

"You think your mother's a hypocrite because she tried to protect you from her own unhappiness. Think about that."

"Oh, so she's the perfect mom."

"She's as imperfect as the next parent. But if you start demanding perfection in the people you love, you're going to end up lonelier than she ever was. You ought to expect as much from yourself as you do from them."

"I see that's worked out really well for you."

It was pain talking, and Diane let it have the last word. She had no credentials for pep talks or parenting anyway.

The transceiver emitted a static squeal as

Diane searched for a working channel.

"If our cell phones won't work out here, how do you expect that radio to?"

"Cell phones and CBs don't operate on the same frequencies. We're on a hill — no guarantees I can get anything up here, but it's worth a try. Sometimes CBs work where cell phones won't."

"But you just said this is a two-way."

"A CB is a type of two-way."

Miralee opened the glove box. "Maybe your dad stashed a telegraph away in here too."

"If you don't have something positive to say, don't say anything at all," Diane said. Did that line ever work? "Your sarcasm is starting to annoy me."

She started on channel 19, thinking to pick up traffic on the highways, which even then were possibly out of range of their location. If she was lucky she might find another nearby rural CB operator — one who had access to a telephone. On an even slimmer chance, she might butt into a skip conversation, which would be all but worthless if the parties were out in Montana or Mexico or someplace. Asking them to contact one Captain Wilson in Cornucopia, California, would be like asking them to call the man in the moon.

On channel 5 the voices of another party were audible under a heavy layer of interference. Diane adjusted the squelch to reduce the hissing but couldn't manage enough clarity to break into the conversation. She turned slowly through all forty channels, tinkering with the squelch dial and maximizing the mic gain, but channel 5 was the best she could get. She went back to it.

"I'm sorry," Miralee said quietly.

Diane tried to hide her surprise by answering swiftly. "Apology accepted." She brought up the clearest reception she could, which wasn't quite good enough for her to hear a pause in the conversation. She'd have to be rude.

She pressed the transmission button on the mic and said, "Break for emergency."

If they heard her, she was not acknowledged.

"Break for emergency," she repeated.

"Mad Cow, you've been walked on, repeat," one of the parties said.

"That's a good sign," she said to Miralee.

"What is?"

"They can't hear each other because I'm interrupting their channel. Something's getting through."

"Break for emergency," Diane said more loudly. "Ten-seventeen, I think. Please? Ten-seventeen!"

"Go ahead, ten-seventeen."

"Name's Diane Hall. I need to reach Captain Wilson with Cornucopia PD."

"You . . . ten-twenty-one."

"What's ten-twenty-one? I haven't been on here for a while."

". . . use the . . . phone!"

Miralee snatched the mic out of Diane's hands and pressed it to her lips, "Listen, Mad Cow and Dimwit, if we had a phone we'd use it! There's people dying and Wilson's the only one who can help. So do us a favor and call him!"

"We don't even know where these people are," Diane whispered.

"You know where Cornucopia is?" Miralee shouted into the mic.

". . . right . . . Tulare County . . ."

"That's right. You can figure it out. Tell him we found Julie Mansfield. Got that? *Julie Mansfield.*"

"Ten-four, Wildcat. Wilson . . . Cornucopia, Mansfield. What's your twenty?"

My what? Miralee mouthed to Diane. Diane took the mic back.

"The Old Gauntlet Road, one mile due east of the Silver Gap trail."

". . . closed . . . snow . . ."

"Yes, but that's where we are! Send medics. Do you hear me?"

The man's reply was too garbled to make out. ". . . name?"

Which name? "My name's Diane Hall. But that shouldn't matter. Just tell Captain Wilson *Julie Mansfield*. And Silver Gap trail. Okay?"

Static covered the voices.

"They got it," Diane said doubtfully to Miralee.

"Is that the truth? I mean, is that what you really believe?"

Diane recognized the real question underneath the girl's hardened image. "It's what I want to believe," she said.

"I wanted to believe that the Bofingers were terrible people," Miralee said. She leaned across the seats and grabbed Diane's arm. "I wanted to prove it. I set them up to prove myself right — that I shouldn't envy Ed's Norman Rockwell life, that his lovebird parents were only an illusion. That they didn't have anything I needed."

"Did they?" Diane asked.

Miralee's eyes filled with sadness. "It isn't fair that some people should get everything they need while the rest of us get nothing."

"There was a time when I thought that too," Diane admitted.

There was no sarcasm in Miri's tone this

time. "But now?"

True sympathy for this girl filled Diane's heart. "Right now I think your mom needs you, and you should give her whatever you have to offer. Let's go."

The cat would not stop yowling. Barred from the storeroom and full of Estrella's cream, it started looking for a way out of the sealed building. The tabby cried by the back door for a full minute before Jack stomped his foot and yelled at it.

The startled cat darted through the kitchen, scooched under the bread rack barricade, then leaped over the counter into the dining room. It tried a window ledge, missed, and opened a rip in one of the curtains with its claws. Over the next few minutes the sounds of it pouncing on wobbly chairs and rattling miniblinds and swiping flatware to the floor with its tail reached the storeroom. The only other sound was the ticking of the old clock out in the dining room.

Jack paced, as agitated as the cat.

When all its options were exhausted, the frustrated feline started to mew again.

Jack kicked his bucket stool into the cabinets. The whole room thundered. He'd show that animal a way out.

"What are you doing?" Leslie asked as he passed her. She set her books on the floor.

He checked his magazine and his silencer as he stalked through the kitchen. He rolled aside the bread rack just enough for his body to slip through, then entered the service area. He braced his elbows on top of the glass pastry case, cocked the hammer, and saw the cat's erect tail weaving through the legs of a chair. Jack fired and the wood splintered. The cat became a gray blur. Someone in the storeroom shrieked. Leslie, Jack guessed.

In the slice of light cutting through the torn curtain, a silent shower of fine light cat hairs floated to the ground.

Jack aimed at the trash can where the cat had taken shelter. The pop this time was followed by a thud. The cat squalled and caught about four feet of air as the plastic can fell over. Jack shot again, careful not to hit a window as the cat bounded away over a table and then under the coffee service station. A creamer thermos took the blow this time. It fell off its perch and hit the floor like a failed bomb, spraying white milk in all directions.

He took his fourth shot without pausing, anticipating the cat's direction. *Pfft, pfft, pfft, pfft,* and this time blood instead of dairy spattered across the honey-colored laminate floor.

The cat vanished.

Leslie's shrieking turned to a wail, and Jack saw her yank free of Ed's grip on her at the entrance to the kitchen. She bolted out, behaving as if Jack didn't exist and couldn't put his last bullets right through her heart.

Estrella and Ed were shouting at Leslie to come back.

Jack stopped shooting, as stunned as the cat, which was limping, its body pressed up against the exposed wall. The cat's tail was three times its usual size. The hair on its spine rippled. It was aiming for shelter under a wheeled cart set up for dirty dishes.

Leslie's skinny legs carried her past the end of the counter and straight into the animal, who probably thought she was its fifth bullet, its final hit. She scooped it up and it tried to push off of her, twisting and scratching and hissing and raising a welt on the side of her neck. She was undeterred. When the beast saw that it couldn't escape, it reversed its strategy and clung to her with all its claws, teeth bared and ears laid back flat. The girl held on, her arms a clamp around the cat's wriggling middle. But she directed her fury toward Jack.

"It's *your* fault that he can't get out!" Salty tears ran over her scratches. The cat's blood had made a smear across her shirt. "Only pathetic monsters shoot trapped animals!"

"I almost shot *you!*"

"You couldn't shoot me any more than you could shoot Miralee. You just want us all to think you don't care."

Disbelief made Jack guffaw. "Don't make me prove it."

Leslie buried her nose behind the cat's rigid neck but kept her glare on Jack as she walked back into the kitchen.

Jack rubbed his temples, the gun still in hand.

"Mean, mean man," Leslie cooed. She snuffled, and her voice faded into the storeroom. "Poor kitty, he shot you in the foot!"

Jack fired two rounds into the espresso machine.

Then he reloaded.

CHAPTER 32

How far are you willing to go?

The voice came to Audrey again, male this time, while Julie slept on her cot, murmuring and kicking weakly at her blankets. Audrey stood next to the woodstove, trying to stay warm, trying to figure out what the question meant and how the answer would help Julie, help her husband and son.

At first she had thought God was talking to her about physical distance. *If I asked you, Audrey Bofinger, would you drive through a barrier and down a precarious fourteen-mile road to find a woman who needs you, while your husband and son suffer without you? How far away from them would you go?*

She had gone that distance, though, and the question still hounded her. Maybe if Diane and Miri couldn't raise anyone on the radio, they could carry Julie out. It would be dangerous and guarantee nothing, of course. Not even if they could get back to

Geoff's truck.

Julie clutched the wool draped over her breast and, somewhere deep in a feverish dream, she began to whimper. She twisted away from the cause of her tears, her hips and shoulders rolling in opposite directions. The blanket shifted and Julie's thin cotton Henley shirt opened at her throat, and Audrey saw a blotchy rash there, one that had troubled her own neck in the days after the accident. A pendant on a silver chain seemed to be the irritant, a crude silver circle surrounding a rough yellowed rock — the necklace that Cora Jean had draped over her family photograph where she could see it at all times in her dying days.

The necklace that had separated the twin sisters.

Julie looked more like Cora Jean in that moment than she looked like herself, and Audrey was moved to compassion by her fondness for the dear old woman. Without thinking, Audrey dropped to her knees beside the cot and took Julie's burning hands in her own.

Julie's fever splashed across Audrey's fingers like a flaming oil lamp, spilled. Audrey snatched her hands away. The agony vanished. Julie's tender cries stopped, then after a perplexing pause, resumed with more intensity.

Audrey felt alarmed. She had been here before, helping to bear Cora Jean's heartache in such an intimate, personal way that it was nothing short of embarrassing for her, perhaps for both parties. Julie was no sister, no beloved friend, but a virtual stranger — and not only that, but one who had turned down Audrey's offer of help before. Audrey didn't have any desire to relieve her by sharing the pain; she had enough of her own to deal with at the present moment.

What do you want me to do? Audrey shrieked inside her own head.

Dare to own it!

Own *what?* Whatever it was, she did not dare.

A draft entered the room with Miralee and Diane, who stomped their shoes free of snow before stepping in.

"Did you get the medicine?" Audrey whispered.

"I need to walk back," said Diane.

Miralee was rubbing her hands together over the stove, looking at her mother, her brow rippled.

"Did the radio work?"

Diane nodded once in an unconvincing way. She was staring at Julie's neck.

"So someone's coming?" Audrey demanded. "When? Who did you talk to? Are Geoff and Ed all right? Why do you have to walk back if they're on their way?"

Instead of answering, Diane reached over and touched the exposed pendant.

"Your mother had that necklace before she died," Audrey said to Diane, hoping to offer something good in the fact that the jewelry had made it back home one way or the other. "She kept it in her bedroom, over a family portrait."

"So Juliet gave it back for me. She did what I couldn't do."

And then Cora Jean, with her biological daughters in prison and in the ground, instructed Harlan to give the family heirloom to Julie. It would have been cruel for Audrey to say these thoughts.

"Is she going to die?" Diane asked.

Miralee clapped a hand over her own mouth.

"No," Audrey said. "She's not going to die with all of us helping her."

"What should I do?" Miralee asked.

Audrey didn't know. She didn't close the gap between herself and the bed. "I was thinking we could carry her out. Get her to the truck and the medicine, then go back."

"That could take hours," Diane said. "And the skies are clear now. Don't you think Wilson will send a helicopter even if he doesn't hear from us?"

"And it's so cold," Miralee whispered.

Geoff and Ed didn't have hours, and Audrey preferred to be doing something, fixing problems.

"We could carry her on the cot," Audrey said. She bent over and gripped the corner of the metal frame and gave it a gentle tug to pull it away from the wall. The feet scraped the wood floor as the bed shifted, accompanied by the sound of ripping canvas.

"That won't hold together," Diane said. "It's too old."

Audrey straightened, forced to agree.

Miralee crouched between the stove and the bed and began to rub her mother's feet. Diane used the chair for support as she lowered herself to the floor, sat sideways on her hip, and reached up to stroke Julie's stringy hair.

"I'm worried that she has an infection from her surgery," Audrey said.

"Is she hurt any other way?" Miralee asked.

"Not any obvious physical way."

"But she lost so much blood — wouldn't that take its toll?"

"That blood was your mom's, but it

390

wasn't from an injury."

"Then where did it come from?" Diane asked.

Audrey walked to the desk and picked up the bill from Hemato Labs. "Your mother donated her own blood before her surgery. It was probably something her doctor recommended she do in case something went wrong and she needed a transfusion. The safest blood to get is your own."

"She didn't do that," Miralee said.

"This bill says she did."

"But I know she didn't, because she and Dad had a huge fight about it. The insurance company wouldn't approve it — they said it was unnecessary because the risks for her procedure were so low. Mom was the one who wanted it, and her doctor agreed to prescribe it for peace of mind. But Dad wouldn't scrape the money together, and Mom went off like a firework, said all this stuff about how he cared more about protecting the city of Cornucopia than about protecting her and all that. She eventually let him have his way."

"Apparently not." She handed the paperwork to Miralee.

"That fight was a biggie — The Biggie. I moved out within the week."

"One more loss. How much can a person take?"

"What do you mean?"

"Cora Jean died in the spring. You had an abortion —"

"How's that a loss to her?"

Miralee's tone was defensive. She was so young.

"If you're fortunate to become a grandmother someday, you'll know. It was my grandbaby too, remember. But besides that, it was *your* loss, and a mother bears her children's losses."

Diane was weeping silently. Audrey began her list again, feeling the connections tighten among the women in this one-room cabin.

"She lost her mother figure, her grandbaby, and you, Miri — her daughter. She lost an important part of her body, she lost her job" — Miralee's eyes widened — "and somewhere along the way, she lost her husband's affection."

"If it ever existed," Miri said doubtfully. "She should have told someone."

"If someone's bleeding from the heart, is it her job to ask for help or our job to notice?"

"She lost hope." Diane sniffled.

"A truly hopeless person might pour her

own blood out over a motor scooter and wait for someone to smash it up. That would make a dramatic statement."

Miralee had laid her cheek against the folds of her mother's blanket.

"But why you?" Diane wondered aloud. "What could she have against you?"

"Not me, but Jack. I think she wrote that message on his computer."

"What message?" asked Miralee.

"Some crimes never see justice."

"He's always saying that."

"His colleagues would respond to the scene, tell him the sad story. He'd try to investigate, come up with nothing. But Jack thinks . . ."

There was no need to finish. Everyone understood what Jack thought, and what Jack would do.

"The park where Mom and Dad married is right across the street from your bakery," Miralee said. "I'll bet it never occurred to her that you and Ed would be the ones to cross the intersection first."

Audrey turned slowly to face the trail map hanging on the wall over the desk. "Ed and I hike up here a lot. You know why I love this place? Because it's a land of such huge disappointments, but unsurpassed beauty too. Did you know that the Native Americans who used to live here abandoned this valley? No one knows why, but something bad happened here, something made the place taboo. Then there were the silver-mining failures — you know all about that, Diane — the lost fortunes, the avalanches. Walt Disney even planned to build a massive ski resort here before the land was annexed into the national park. Yes, it's true. He couldn't get it off the ground. All that effort, all that failure — and look at it. We're standing in one of the most beautiful places in the world. It's hard work to get here, but when you arrive, you're met by a peace that reminds me of relief, like the happy exhaustion of a hard day's work. Nothing easy about this place, just hope that has staying power."

These thoughts that had inspired Audrey repeatedly in the past fell flat today. A log in the stove broke in two and thumped the drumlike floor.

"I don't think that's been my mom's experience here so far," Miralee said.

How far are you willing to go?

"I was thinking," Diane said, "about when Jesus went to Gethsemane before he was crucified, and he asked his friends to stay awake with him."

Diane's unexpected observation began to

provide glimpses of an answer to the question plaguing Audrey. She quoted, "My soul is overwhelmed with sorrow to the point of death. Stay here and keep watch with me."

"Why did he need his friends?" Diane asked. "He was the Son of God."

"I . . . don't know. I only wondered why the disciples couldn't stay awake with him. Why they were so tired."

"I think they were scared," Diane said.

"Fear keeps me awake," Miralee said.

"Fear keeps me away," said Diane. "They wouldn't even go with him while he prayed."

These women had spent their lives running away from pain. Audrey's mind opened up to new meanings. *How far are you willing to go? Do you dare to own it? What are you afraid of?*

"I'm afraid of never being forgiven," Diane said. She looked at Audrey. "What are you afraid of?"

The question stunned her.

"She's afraid of losing her family, of course," Miralee said.

But Audrey saw the bigger answer without having to think.

"I'm afraid of hurting so bad that I start to lose my faith," she confessed, staring at the woman who ached precisely that much, and who would not survive it alone.

She closed the gap between herself and the cot, took Julie's hands, and laid her body over the top of Julie's in a protective embrace.

CHAPTER 33

In the back of Audrey's mind, distant and rhythmic explosions pulsed along her blood vessels. They were like lightning behind thunderclouds, illuminating for split seconds at a time the personal scenes of Julie's life that had brought her to this lonely mountain place. And they were like flashbulbs on an old camera, calling attention to the fact that there was a witness to the scenes now, a record of the journey shared with someone else.

The comfort of being allowed to hold Julie's wounded hands with her own scabbed and blistered palms came as a surprise to Audrey.

Julie's pain was as terrible as she had feared but also completely tolerable, divided as it was by four instead of only by one or two. Miralee and Diane held their own at Julie's head and feet, maybe or maybe not having a similar experience. Their presence and their touch were enough. Audrey marveled at God's mercy, delivered by the diverse comforts of diverse women, each doing what she was able to do. No more, no less. The effects were exhausting and energizing at the same time.

Julie's feverish tossing and rambling had quieted. Her hair was soaked at the temples and her blankets were damp. Her breathing had stopped striving.

"Who's there?" she whispered, keeping her eyes closed.

"You're not alone anymore, Juliet," Diane whispered.

"Juliet." A flicker of a smile pulled at the corner of Julie's mouth, then let go. "No one's called me that for a long, long time. Jack stopped" — the muscles of her chin puckered — "the day I told him God didn't make sense to me. I had tried for a long time, for Jack's sake, because I loved him. I was his . . . Juliet. Until that day."

"I'm so sorry," Audrey said.

"I'm not sorry for what I did," Julie said. "He's the man with all the answers. He deserves a crime he can't solve."

Audrey and Diane exchanged pained glances. Miralee said, "Mom —"

"Miri?" Julie's eyes opened.

"I'm sorry I left. I didn't know."

"You came looking for me?"

"Mom, Dad's gone . . . crazy. He's hurt some people. He might kill them."

"You mean like he did his own wife?"

Audrey squeezed Julie's hand. "He's desperate to know you're alive, Julie. He wants you back."

"Who are you?" Julie squinted and frowned.

"This is Ed's mom," Miri said. "I wouldn't have come looking for you . . . if she and Diane hadn't convinced me."

"Diane?"

"Right here."

"Diane Hall?"

Diane continued stroking Julie's hair. "The one and only."

"You left me too." The accusation in Julie's voice shocked Audrey.

After an awkward silence, Diane said, "Thank you for looking after my parents for me. You've been good to them."

"People who've lost everything understand each other."

Audrey was aware of the dwindling time. "We're going to get you home," she said.

"I don't have a home to go to."

"Don't say that," Miralee said. "You have to talk sense into Dad, and then you've got to see your doctor."

.

"I left the medicine . . . so stupid." Julie sighed. "Then I injured something, getting boxes up here. It refuses to heal."

"Mom —"

"I've never been able to talk sense into your father, Miri. It's not going to happen now."

"He's going to murder my husband and son."

"Just let him see your face," said Miri. "You're his sanity."

"No. I'm not going back."

Panic flitted through Audrey's lungs. She sat back on her heels where she knelt, feeling ready to drag Juliet off her cot and through the snow by one arm.

"Don't let Jack harm more people than he already has," Audrey begged.

"I'm not responsible for his behavior."

"That's true, but you can stop him."

Diane said, "I hear something," and got her chunky legs and arms to lift her large body off the floor. She exited the cabin and left the door open. The cool air gave Audrey goose bumps, and Julie cinched the blanket under her elbows, but Audrey decided not to make her more comfortable by closing the door.

"Geoff and Ed don't have to die anymore than you do," Audrey said. "And I'm not going to let them. You're too sick to fight me."

"Then I must be too sick to make an appearance at whatever crime scene he's created for himself."

It was a helicopter Diane had heard. The thumping rotors were like the bursts of relief that Audrey had felt when she'd finally agreed to touch Julie. They empowered her now, with rescue in sight and the hands of the clock not yet vertical.

"There will be a radio on the helicopter," she said. "You can talk to him, that's all. You won't even have to look at him."

"No," Julie said.

"Why not?" Audrey demanded.

"He can't beat me," Julie said. "I have to win at least one round. I have to get something out of this. Something for myself."

Audrey felt new fury rising in her. It wasn't right that one person's injury could cost bystanders so much! She leaned over Julie and took the diamond necklace in her fingers, then yanked it toward her and broke the chain. Julie protested but Audrey easily kept the jewelry out of her weak reach.

If Wilson couldn't justify handcuffing Julie and rolling her into Jack's presence on a gurney, Audrey could only hope that Jack might accept this evidence. "If you give in to this pain, Jack wins. You don't want that."

Julie barely had the strength to roll onto her side and face the wall.

Miralee watched, lips parted and eyes wide. "Mom, we can start over. Everything will work out."

Her statement was a plea that roused Audrey's protective maternal senses.

"You should have let me die," Julie said.

"Why?" Audrey said. "So you can beat Jack by behaving as badly as he does? What kind of win is that?"

She questioned in her heart what she might feel about this woman if Geoff and Ed didn't survive the hour. Would she also be reduced to wanting nothing but death for herself and others? Audrey grabbed Miralee's hand to keep herself anchored to another person's life. Julie Mansfield was like a bright star, exploded, dead but still living as a black hole.

She was startled by the desperation of Miralee's grip.

CHAPTER 34

The small hand of the old clock moved through the eleven and started the crawl toward the twelve. Coach passed in and out of consciousness, though Estrella and Geoff had staunched the blood flowing from his torn feet. Geoff held the man's hand and prayed silently. Ed recognized the focused expression that others interpreted as mere thoughtfulness.

In a moment of wakefulness, Coach saw the cat and began to tremble. Leslie apologized and explained why she couldn't put the cat out. "He took a bullet to his paw, see?"

He saw. He frowned. He stopped shaking. And then he started chuckling. Ed watched, amazed, as the ailurophobe gestured for Leslie to bring the cat to him. Now it curled up in the warmth of Coach's armpit, man and beast sleeping off their pain together.

Estrella talked Jack into letting her bring

baguettes in for everyone to eat. They dried out untouched in a basket on one of the pantry shelves.

The cordless phone rang once, and Estrella reached for it. Jack snatched it first and hurled it out of the storage room and into the narrow mouth of the brick oven on the other side of the kitchen with startling precision. Ed heard it come to pieces against the inside wall before the residual heat of the morning fire began to melt its parts, crackling and popping like rice cereal.

Everyone but the coach looked toward their lost contact with the outside world, and Ed suspected they were all thinking what he was: now how would they know if Mrs. Mansfield was on her way back?

The detective's loss of composure was all the evidence Ed needed to say that Jack believed his wife was already dead. Ed felt sick. How could his mother find a body that the entire police force couldn't?

Jack was pacing, sweating. He stormed out of the pantry into the kitchen. Ed jumped up and went to the doorway.

It was not the first time Ed had wished he were a defensive tackle rather than a point guard. He knew how to steal a basketball, which was of course larger than a gun and less deadly, but the skill sets were transfer-

404

able. He had long arms, speed, decisiveness, and in this case, youth on his side. The main problem was that Jack wouldn't be doing any passing or dribbling with that firearm. In principle, though, any ball could be stolen if the ball handler was overconfident and distracted, and Ed thought Jack was, finally, both.

He watched Jack pace between the storeroom and the wood-fired oven. When the detective caught sight of Ed, he motioned with his gun for Ed to stay behind the doorframe, then continued pacing. Ed didn't move. Jack didn't notice.

When the time was right he couldn't hesitate.

His game plan: act alone, use surprise. His dad wouldn't support such a plan, and trying to explain a strategy to Leslie or Estrella would only catch Jack's attention. It was his mistake to make, right? Ed prayed it wouldn't get anyone killed.

Jack was walking directly toward him.

Ed would foul the detective with a body slam, force him to drop the gun, kick it away, and beat Jack to it. He wouldn't kick it too far, because he needed to get control of the pistol before Jack had time to reach the backup revolver on his ankle. Train the gun on Jack, get Dad and the others to take the revolver.

If he had time he'd blow a window out to alert the SWAT units outside.

Ed hesitated about that. He'd shot a gun once or twice in his life, but what if he hit someone on the other side of the glass? And did Cornucopia even have access to SWAT?

No window shooting. He'd get Jack to disarm one of the doors.

Jack reached the pantry, eyes on Ed, and turned around. The timing wasn't right. Ed couldn't move until he was invisible to Jack, until Jack's mind was overtaken by its own thoughts of disappointment and injustice.

The stainless-steel workbench in the middle of the kitchen stood to the height of Jack's wrist, hanging at his side. He held the gun loosely in his right hand and came within a few inches of the table's corner as he passed it. All Ed had to do was lunge and force the back of Jack's hand into that sharp metal point. Jack's fingers around the gun would open even if he willed them to stay closed.

The moment passed. Ed chewed himself out. Jack's pacing could stop at any time.

Ed's core muscles were vibrating by the time Jack turned around in front of the woodstove again. Ed crossed his arms and leaned against the doorframe to hide his anxiety.

When the detective looked up, his eyes did pass right through Ed to some spot behind him, which Ed later realized was the spot where Coach lay, faceup on the ground with his broken feet propped up on blood-stained flour sacks, and a wounded cat tucked under his arm. But in that exact second his only thought was the fear that Jack was going to march straight back into the pantry without making another round through the kitchen.

Which is what Jack did. He stepped over Ed's large feet and just out of Ed's reach, pointed his gun toward Geoff's chest, and cocked the hammer of his pistol. Geoff's prayerful eyes stayed closed.

And so Ed reacted without thinking, without deconstructing or reassembling the plan he had waited one beat too long to set in motion. He jumped at Jack's arm, slapped at the gun as if it were an orange ball and the game clock were ticking off the final seconds.

The force of Ed's hit pushed Jack's aim sideways and downward as the gun went off. Jack kept his grip on his weapon. The silencer understated the gun's damage and was upstaged by Ed and Jack falling into one of the freestanding metal shelf units. Jack grabbed hold of the frame with his free hand but Ed, carried forward by his own momentum, found his feet entangled with Jack's, preventing the detective from recovering his center of balance. They collapsed to the left, Ed on top, the pistol pointing without aiming at the others in the small room.

When Ed landed, his face hammered Jack's forearm and smashed the man's elbow into the concrete floor. Jack's fingers opened on the gun and Ed rolled off his body, reaching for it with his right hand.

Jack was fast. He locked his legs around Ed's knees and used Ed's body as leverage to haul himself up and over Ed's back. They rotated as a single unit toward the gun, which Ed grasped first only because his arms were longer than Jack's by fractions of an inch. He pulled the weapon to his chest and tucked into the roll, pushing off the ground with his left hand and hefting Jack into the wall. But Jack was an anaconda around Ed's upper arms; he'd regain the upper hand quickly. Ed kicked out of the man's leg hold and flicked his wrist to push the gun away, straight out the pantry door into the center of the kitchen. It glided like an ice skater across the smooth concrete much, much farther than he had intended it to go. He watched it slip under the wheeled wood bin that stood next to the brick oven.

"Get it!" he shouted to anyone who would know what he meant.

Leslie was hyperventilating in the corner. His father was bent over Coach, and Ed saw his hands slick with blood coming from the man's thigh. Unbelievable. The cat was gone. Estrella darted out into the kitchen but hadn't seen where the gun went.

If Ed were Leslie, he might have been able to calculate how much time it would take to give Estrella directions to the gun, and how much time it would take him to break loose and get it himself, or whether he should stay and battle the much stronger Jack for the revolver on his ankle, or how swiftly Jack, free of Ed, would shoot his father through the head. If he were his father, he might have been able to pray and get an immediate answer about the wise course of action. If he were Estrella, he would have known whether she knew how to fire the pistol if she found it, or whether Jack would be able to disarm her with a scowl.

But Ed was a man who saw his plays through. Nine times out of ten, changing course after a plan had been set in motion worked out badly for the team, and of the five hostages in the room, he'd just appointed himself the team leader.

Ed slammed his head backward into Jack's nose, and Jack's hold on his arms broke. Ed was on his feet and shooting out of the pantry while the detective was still howling. He pushed Estrella out of the way and crossed the kitchen in three strides, sliding into the wood bin and kicking it aside to reveal the gun. And then it was in his hands and he was back on his feet, having never stalled, flying into the pantry to find Jack crouching and fumbling with the holster straps. The detective's nose was bloody and dripping on his shoes.

"Leave it!" Ed shouted.

Jack raised his hands away from his backup in time with the very slow breath he drew in through his mouth.

"Leslie, help Dad get Coach out! Do it! Do it! Estrella! Break a window!" Shouting wasn't necessary, and yet he couldn't speak at any other volume. He worried that he wasn't holding the pistol correctly, that he would forget to shoot with both eyes open and his elbow locked. He believed Jack was even now evaluating all Ed's inexperience and deciding how to best him.

Hurry, hurry.

Leslie and his father dragged Coach out by the armpits, not daring to spend precious seconds trying to stop that pumping artery.

That murderous emotion Ed had felt earlier had been washed away by real opportunity. Ed wasn't at all confident, now standing with the barrel of a gun pointed at a man, with a finger on the trigger, that he could pull it. Surely cowardice was spelled out in neon all over his face, in each nervous inflection of his tone, in his very need to shout.

He heard someone rolling away the bread rack that had blockaded the kitchen and dining room. Seconds later there was a heavy thunking of an object pounding on glass, then the gradual cracking, followed by shouting, the voices of outsiders and authority coming to aid.

Jack lunged for him and Ed jumped away, fired. A box of yeast exploded behind the place where Jack had been standing in a harmless yellow poof.

Whether Jack had meant to merely test Ed, throw him off balance, or escape, he did succeed in somersaulting into the kitchen. Ed spun, leading with the gun, panicked. Without a freshly smashed nose to stun him, Jack probably had all the time he needed to retrieve his revolver.

"Ed!" His father was calling from the dining room.

"Get them out!" Ed called back. He looked at the line he'd have to run through the kitchen. He doubted Jack would go out into that open space himself but feared he had the escape route covered. Did he dare risk it? Risk getting shot from both directions, by Jack and by a sharpshooter who might mistake him for Jack? His skin was clammy and the gun slick in his palms. He thought he might throw up.

It was a one-second-remaining, half-court-shot-to-win-it risk. Ed sprinted for the kitchen-to-café entry. He made it through, saw his father looking toward him from the shattered window while someone in a tactical helmet and bulletproof vest hauled Estrella safely past the daggers of glass. He adjusted his stride to make the necessary leap over the pastry display cases and tossed the gun over to free his hands. The gun hit the floor at the same time that his palms met the cases like they were a gymnast's vault.

Ed felt the flaming pain in his left tricep before he heard the pop of the gunshot, and his joints gave way before he could push off the glass and swing his body over the top.

He stumbled and smashed into the sliding door on the back of the case, his jaw taking the hardest hit.

Jack had him by the ankle before he hit the ground it seemed, and Ed smacked his head on the floor as he came down. His T-shirt rode up on his back as Jack dragged him back into the kitchen, exposing his skin while Geoff protested loudly, sounding much farther away than he really was. Jack pulled him all the way to the pantry along the sticky trail left behind by the coach's wound, and it coated Ed's back and hair with morbid warmth.

"I'll say when it's time to go," Jack said. "It isn't even twelve o'clock yet." Then he kicked Ed in the face and brought a merciful end to the excruciating pain in his arm.

CHAPTER 35

Ed's T-shirt was sticky with his own blood, still dripping off the ledge of his lips. His nose was broken, which he knew because he'd taken more than one basketball to the face in his lifetime. He felt warm bricks at his back and found his bearings in the kitchen against the foot of the wood-fired stove.

"You will be punished at the hand of God for rape and the death of an unborn child," Jack said. "A life for a life."

The pronouncement sent a chill through Ed's skull that shocked his consciousness. He was going to die today, like this, sitting rag-doll-like on the floor of a bakery. His left arm, useless, wilted on the concrete and sent waves of nausea through his belly when he breathed. He focused on the light pouring from the empty storeroom. It took the edge off the unbelievable hurt.

Opposite him, Jack sat with his back

against the wall between the sink and the prep table, legs spread out before him in a V, the revolver ready at his thigh. Ed couldn't look directly at it without being overcome by tremors. The kitchen was dusky like twilight, like the premature end of a life.

A foxhole prayer with a flaming torch tied to its tail ran through the trenches of his mind, wordless and frantic.

Jack's dried blood from Ed's head-butt coated his own upper lip, and Ed's scalp recalled the sensation of taking a hit to the man's teeth. The bruise prompted strange associations in Ed's mind about their blood mixing with Coach Henderson's on the slick bakery floor the way Julie Mansfield's had mixed with his mother's when she slipped on the street.

"Your nose is broken too," Ed said, frightened by the silence. He shifted his aching neck and felt the corners of his eyes like a knife to his sinuses. "We have that in common."

"It's not much," Jack said.

Faint noises reached him from outside. A dull hum of human conversation. Radios crackling. Car doors closing. The sounds of Jack's impending punishment.

Jack, Ed thought, heard the sounds of

backup and support.

"God forgives sins," Ed said.

"Not yours."

"Why not?"

"You think God has some obligation to you?"

Ed started to shake his head, but the stabbing behind his eyes stopped him. "No obligation. Just a promise. Is God going to forgive you?"

Jack shifted the revolver an inch or two. "For what?"

"Anything you want forgiveness for."

"Don't have anything."

A few heavy seconds passed. Jack shifted from the V-sit to a crouch. "You're sorry about that, aren't you? You're sorry that my soul isn't black like yours." Jack moved toward Ed. He stayed out of sight of anyone in the dining room, or of any sharpshooter positioned at the shattered window, and dropped to his knees between Ed's spread-eagled feet. Jack's finger stayed inside the revolver's trigger ring while he talked with hand motions. "You're sorry, because if God had any cause to condemn me, you might think you could claim to be my equal, chosen by the Lord to administer his justice."

Ed's heartbeat knocked harder against the

bullet wound in his arm. There was no reasoning with a lunatic, but silence felt like agreement. "No. I meant —"

"You're not anything like me, boy."

"We are alike, but not in the way you think!"

"Now you know how I think."

"I know you want to kill me," Ed said.

"Yes! Oh, yes! Since the day I learned what you did. But I'm a patient man. I wait for the divinely appointed time. Twelve thirty!"

"So why did you start shooting Coach so early?"

"Nolan Henderson isn't relevant to any discussion about you and me. Are we cut from the same cloth or not?"

"We are!" Ed shouted. "Because I want to kill you too! God help me, I do. It's what's here." He thumped his heart with his good hand. "And it's no different from the way you feel about me. I know it. But I'm not going to act on it, am I? I'm not going to sit here and make up some story about God wanting you dead so that I can do what I want."

Jack looked at the gun and smiled with only half of his mouth. "I doubt you have my self-control, Ed, my spiritual discipline."

"I have more. I have so much more."

"Let's see about that, why don't we?" Jack pressed the barrel against Ed's forehead. Ed closed his eyes. He took shallow breaths and had no sense of how long Jack stayed this way, the metal mouth imprinting a cold round O in Ed's skin. "No, no," Jack murmured. "It's just not time, saith the Lord. Your turn!"

Jack lifted Ed's right arm from its supportive position and spun the revolver on his finger, then clapped the weapon into Ed's hand. "Do you know how to hold one of these?" Jack asked. "Not so different from the Glock, and you were good enough with that. Good enough for this purpose anyway."

The tremors from Ed's fingers moved up his arm and into his neck and into his jaw, which seemed to vibrate as Jack sandwiched Ed's grip with both of his own hands and then leaned into the gun, resting his own brow on the barrel.

"Hold it steady now, or you'll miss."

"I'm not going to shoot you."

"Then God will be disappointed in you. Ready? It's all you, boy." And Jack took his hands away from Ed's and raised his arms out to the sides.

"Why?" Ed whispered.

"Because I have faith that God favors me,

and he'll spare my life. But not yours."

Audrey's head was pounding from the noise of the rotors and from the realization that Julie wouldn't be speaking with Jack. She'd become so hysterical when the medics arrived to transport her that she'd had to be sedated. The other women, wedged in tightly on a bench designed for only two people, didn't speak on the anxious flight back to the hospital.

The cabin was bright with sharp high-noon sunlight. It was 12:15, and within minutes the helicopter left the snow behind. Audrey stared down at the carpet of fog that was breaking up in smoky patches. She began to weep, and the crying was her own this time. The grief belonged to no one else.

Diane took Audrey's hand.

Her tears fell onto the cell phone in her lap. The police had made all the calls, but Audrey hoped for one more chance to reach her men. It was impossible to know what Jack would do now, if he'd believe his own colleagues' word that Julie lived.

Diane picked up the phone and wiped it dry with the cuff of her sleeve. The pressure of her swiping woke the screen and revealed all Audrey's applications. She studied the little icons for a moment. Then she touched one. The screen became a monitor.

"It's a camera?" she mouthed to Audrey.

Audrey nodded. Diane gave her the phone and pointed to Julie. "Show Jack!" she said loudly.

It wouldn't satisfy Jack's demands — at this point, nothing would. A photo of Julie sleeping might be worth little more than a photo of Julie dead. But Audrey snapped a grainy, slightly blurry picture of Julie on her gurney and sent it to Captain Wilson.

The act planted a seed of hope in her mind. She tried to water it for the remaining minutes of the flight.

A police cruiser was waiting at the hospital helipad. Julie was first off, and taken directly indoors. Miralee trailed behind her, head down, without saying good-bye. Diane helped Audrey down and then shielded her from the whipping air as they crouched and met the officers who'd come for them.

They ducked into the backseat and slammed the doors.

"Your husband's out," the one driving said right away.

Audrey's heart split in two. *Thank God!* "And Ed?"

His hesitation brought a wave of fear over Audrey's head. "Don't lose faith yet," he told her.

It was going to take much more than a photograph to convince Jack to spare her son's life. Audrey pulled the Hall family's pendant out of her pocket and turned it over in her fingers.

"We'll show him that," Diane said, looking at the diamond.

Audrey let the chain pool in her lap, and she set the stone on top. "This necklace hasn't saved anyone yet." She scooped it up and held it out to Diane. "In fact, it's yours. I didn't even ask."

Diane folded Audrey's fingers closed over the jewelry and pushed her hand back. "It's my mother's, and Julie's, and mine, and yours. With a legacy like that, who knows what it might speak to Jack?"

"It's just a stone on a chain."

"That's like you saying you're just a baker's wife. Look at what you did today."

"I didn't do it."

"Is that your way of saying God did it? Through you?"

Audrey offered a tiny smile.

"I'd like to see what else he can do," Diane said.

The ride to the bakery lasted only five minutes. The streets were blockaded as they were the morning of Audrey's accident, but this time sunshine illuminated the scene, and a crowd of bystanders had collected in the park and at the storefronts near the intersection. People were taking pictures. And drinking coffee. The female officer who'd taken Audrey's bloody clothes moved a barricade to let the cruiser through.

Audrey saw Geoff with Captain Wilson and jumped out of the sedan before it came to a complete stop. Geoff saw her at the same time, and they reached each other in seconds.

His arms around her waist filled her with hope; his breath in her hair was peace. She squeezed his neck and whispered, "Where's our son?"

"Playing hero," Geoff said, and when he drew back from Audrey his eyes were wet. He pointed toward the crowd gathered at the mouth of the park behind them. "He got all of us out."

Audrey saw Diane moving toward Estrella, who was surrounded by her husband and grandsons. Estrella lifted her hand, waving Diane to join them. Julie's student Leslie sat on the curb hugging the bedraggled alley cat. Someone was applying a bandage to the cat's rear foot.

"Coach is at the hospital," Geoff said. "Wilson's getting ready to send a team in."

"What's Jack saying?"

"Nothing. I'm going to go talk to him, Audrey."

Audrey looked at her feet. "What can you say that Wilson and his guys can't?"

"Lots of things. I'm a pastor."

"What are you *going* to say?"

"I'm going to beg him to save Ed's life."

Audrey shook her head in frustration and felt tears rising again. "I couldn't bring Jack what he wants."

"No one can, Audrey. No one."

She groped at straws. "There's a picture of Julie —"

"Wilson showed me."

"And there's this." She cupped Geoff's hand and set the pendant in his palm. "It's something Julie took with her. Maybe Jack will . . ." She didn't know what she was trying to say.

Geoff wrapped his arms around her again. She rested her ear over his heart and he prayed, "Lord, bring me and my son back to this woman you gave us." He kissed her on the top of her head.

Audrey stood alone in the center of Sunflower and Main while someone took Geoff to don a bulletproof vest. She didn't understand why Geoff's going in was necessary, why Wilson would allow it. Not even God was getting through to Jack.

"Your husband ees *loco.*" Estrella stood at Audrey's elbow.

"Just the right amount of crazy for God to work with," Diane said behind them both.

Audrey hoped so. She prayed so. Hearing her friends say it aloud made it seem possible.

CHAPTER 36

Jack leaned into the barrel of his own gun, feeling more holy than ever in his life. He was prepared to lay down his life for his enemy, for the sake of rightness and righteousness. But God would step between him and this unholy child and spare his life, and the boy would be humbled. Humiliated.

God's will be done.

The gun was quivering in Ed's hands. It would be impossible for the boy to shoot it, because he knew Jack was right.

Jack withdrew his forehead from the gun and straightened his body. He sat back on his heels. A pleasant shower of satisfaction came over him, and also warmth radiating from the open mouth of the oven, which retained its heat forever like the glory of God. Ed lowered the gun to rest on his thigh and exhaled noisily, obviously disappointed in God's decision not to bless him.

"Thank God that's over," Ed said.

"Interesting choice of words."

They evaluated each other for a few moments.

"I could have killed you."

"But God intervened," Jack said.

"He did."

"He won't intervene when your time comes."

"When's that?"

Jack glanced at the clock.

"I think I have more time," Ed said.

"I didn't say how much you have."

"That's okay, though. Because I still have this."

Ed raised the weapon toward Jack's chest once more, but Jack felt no fear. The kid was careless. His finger wasn't even wrapped around the trigger.

Jack reached to take the gun back. Ed jerked it just out of his grasp.

"Do you know what God told me when I was thinking about blowing a hole through your head?"

"I doubt it was God speaking to you."

"He told me how we're going to get out of this mess."

"Yes, he's told me that too."

"I don't think you and I are hearing quite the same thing," Ed said.

Only a cocky Harlem Globetrotter could

have done it, Jack thought as he watched the gun arc upward out of Ed's flicked wrist and toward the mouth of the five-hundred-plus-degree oven directly over his head. Or a son of the devil.

He felt true fear then, while the revolver was still rotating in the air, while his frantic grab for it missed, while he listened to the metal hit the oven floor and slide, grinding across the heat until it hit the back wall, where he could not reach without his flesh melting.

The clock marked seconds — in Jack's mind, hours — and then the bullets started cooking off. They were tiny bombs, mere puffs of smoke and brass, aimless bursts too small to cause any real damage. But they decimated Jack's theology.

The weak sounds of the bursting bullets, which went off like six pieces of popcorn, had barely died out when Jack let out a primal yell and overturned the metal prep table in the center of the room. The corner gouged the wall before the table edge slipped on the smooth cement and thundered onto its top. Metal bowls and cups and utensils rattled across the floor in a terrible noise. Jack continued to scream as he cleared the counters of their pans and flours. An empty bread basket hit Ed in the chest. Uncooked muffin batter thickened by six hours of exposure oozed out of its bowl where it fell. Glass shattered as it hit the basin of the sink.

Jack grabbed the arm of the industrial mixer with both hands and started shaking it, screeching. His fury and his weight weren't enough to budge the machine, so he started kicking the bowl. It snapped off of its base but was caught by the dough hook. Jack kept kicking, his screams morphing to grunts. Dents formed in the bowl's sides.

Ed pulled his feet up, rolled to his knees, and began to crawl toward the door with his left arm tucked up by his rib cage. Jack's drumming on the mixing bowl ceased, and he took up insane, unintelligible muttering. Ed didn't look.

He nearly reached the passage into the dining room when Jack grabbed hold of Ed's limp left arm and yanked him onto his side, then started dragging him. The agony caused Ed to yell, the noise of his own lungs preventing him from losing consciousness. He gritted his teeth and wished for his father to bear down on the scene in full-combat gear. A real fantasy.

Jack pulled Ed to the back door and began

to peel off the plastic explosive he had applied there after sending Diane Hall away. He needed two hands and dropped Ed onto his face, still babbling.

Sweat dripping off Jack hit the back of Ed's neck.

Ed rolled off his gunshot wound, nauseated. Another window in the dining room broke then, giving way to the butt of a rifle and the shouts on the street. Jack seemed not to notice it. Ed jerked his head sideways to look but couldn't see anything except the bottom of kitchen appliances. He rolled away from Jack and pushed himself up again with his good arm. His limping crawl was frantic this time.

"Jack! Ed!" someone shouted. Ed didn't answer, afraid of becoming an adrenaline-boosted gunman's target.

Once more he reached the doorway between the kitchen and rear of the counter, and this time he passed through without Jack's intervention. He concentrated on getting out of Jack's sight. His arm was sticky with blood but he didn't think he'd lost that much, and his bones seemed to be as straight and strong as they ought to be. But that hole through his muscle was a searing fire.

The invasion seemed too understated, too

orderly. No Hollywood commotion or frantic shouting from all, just a single voice rising above the rest with clear direction.

"Jack, let the kid come out now. Your wife is alive."

The voice seemed to bring Jack back down to earth. His ranting and crazed fumbling stopped. Ed froze in the new silence.

"You're not playing by the rules, Rutgers," Jack said to the speaker. His breathing was still heavy. Ed glanced back over his shoulder and saw Jack facing the entryway, hefting a small and misshapen gray lump of a bomb in his palm. A detonating wire protruded from the side. "Stay where you are, Ed. It isn't twelve thirty yet."

Ed obeyed. The detonator, which had been rigged to the jamb in such a way to be triggered if the door opened, was in Jack's other hand. This was a confusing sight.

Clicking radio static from the next room filled the silence.

"Stand up," Jack said to Ed. "And stay with me."

Ed had sickening thoughts of that detonator going off and creating a terrible chain reaction of electric *kabooms*. The plastics wouldn't explode if Jack dropped them or even if a sharpshooter blasted them out of Jack's hands — Ed's grandfather had told stories of burning the stuff for cooking fires in Vietnam — but that other device had all the catalyst needed to kill them all, standing up or lying down. Ed opted to stay put, even if it didn't improve his chances much.

"Jack," said Rutgers, "we have Julie."

His hands dropped half an inch as his attention passed to the dining room.

"Back door's disarmed," Ed yelled, "but he's got a detonator!"

Displeasure messed up Jack's expression, but he had no means to punish Ed for that. He reached back and turned the dead bolt on the exit.

His dad would have the key, Ed thought.

"Where's my wife?" Jack shouted.

After a short silence Rutgers said, "She's on her way." Ed shared Jack's evident doubt.

"I want her *here.* Now. Where she belongs."

"We should be seeing her any second, okay? She's been sick, so we're all going to be patient. Why don't you let Ed go while we wait. How you doing, Ed?"

He put a lot of effort into sounding fearless. "Doing okay."

"You hurt?"

"Not re—"

"I've been patient!" Jack yelled. "I don't think you've got her! I know your tricks —

431

have you forgotten who I am?"

"No, Jack. We all respect your record. Let's keep it as clean as we can. Julie's counting on you. What might happen to her if you lose it now? Do you catch my meaning?"

"I need justice."

"That's exactly what she's going to get, Jack. It's the justice system you serve. It's never failed you yet, has it?"

Ed saw Rutgers's error in the disgust that smeared Jack's expression. The man had made the mistake of assuming Jack's insanity, of jumping to the conclusion that because Jack was having some kind of breakdown, he could no longer reason like a man.

The wrong conclusion, Ed thought.

Jack was reasoning like any man who had lost his life's playbook. It was the way Ed had reasoned after losing Miralee and their baby and his college acceptance and, for all he could figure, the smile of God — a frantic mental search for any explanation that made a smidgen of sense. Ed suddenly felt lucky his desperation hadn't hurt many bystanders.

"That's the first true thing you've said yet," Jack said loudly. "The system will do what it does best. It'll punish me, but not the person who stole my wife. Maybe I should save the taxpayers a few dollars." The anger was gone, replaced by bitterness. His eyes went to the device he held.

There was a scrambling in the front room. "Jack, don't," Rutgers said. "Think twice. Your wife's alive. I'm not lying to you."

The bell on the door jangled. They must have got the explosives off it. Air was moving through the closed-up bakery again, through a cross breeze allowed by broken windows and the open door, and the oxygen felt clear to Ed. Weightless and free of the heavy fog. From the floor where he lay, the natural light seemed more yellow than gray.

"Well, you're not telling me the truth about *something*," Jack said. "Have you seen her yet? Have you seen my wife?"

A brief silence was followed by, "Not with my own eyes." A new voice. Ed's father.

Jack cursed. Relief killed Ed's every pain; his muscles relaxed. His heart thanked God.

"I wasn't asking you," Jack said. "Why did they let you in?"

"Because I'm not going to tell you what you want to hear."

"Is that so? What do I want to hear?"

"That your wife loves you and was taken from you against her will. That you have someone besides yourself to blame."

Jack's lips became a pinched wad of muscle, then he smoothed them out again and set the ball of explosive down by the upended stainless table in the center of the kitchen.

"That kind of talk isn't going to get your son out of here alive," Jack said, fiddling with the detonator. Ed couldn't guess whether the plastics would take out the entire bakery, including the apartment upstairs, or only the little table in front of Jack, or something in between. Like him.

As discreetly as possible, Ed used his legs and good arm to drag himself inches farther out of the kitchen.

"I think we'll all get out fine," Geoff said. "We know you, Jack. You're a good man who just wants to get it right. And you know that killing yourself, or my son, or me, or any other person within your reach isn't right. That's something both God and the world can agree on."

Jack licked his lips. "God let me down."

"Julie refused to come," Geoff said. "She's getting medical attention right now. But she's going to pull through this. Either she cares for the life of my boy as little as she cares for her own, or she doesn't believe you're capable of killing anyone. What do you think?"

"I think I'm capable of killing whoever I want."

"I was wondering what Julie's thinking."

"Ask her."

All of Ed but his feet were out of the kitchen.

"You've never killed anyone," Geoff said.

"I don't believe anymore that God cares one way or the other."

"There's a million reasons why he asks us to do the right thing," Geoff said. "I know maybe ten of those reasons. The rest is a mystery, but I have faith."

Jack wandered a few paces away from the little bomb. "I never had an exit strategy," Jack said. "I was so sure this scenario would end exactly the way I wanted it to."

"Most of us think that too."

"It can't end like this," Jack said.

Like what? Ed wondered. He pulled his knees up under his belly and hoped his blood wouldn't rush out of his head when he jumped up to run.

Jack continued, "Julie's not coming because your wife killed her."

"I brought something to prove she didn't. Julie's necklace."

"You took it off her dead body."

"I'm giving you truth, Jack. That's all I've ever given you. Here it comes."

Geoff tossed the necklace over the counter and Ed heard the pendant hit the floor first, followed by a silky pouring of the chain. The piece slid to rest near his feet.

And from his crouch he saw Jack behind the wall, staring at the silver, alone in the world with it. He bent to scoop it up with his free hand.

Ed burst out of his position then, not knowing how Jack would react to anything. He didn't attempt to jump the pastry cases this time, being too close to them to get the momentum he needed. His head came up over the top of the glass and he saw two of the three officers in the room swing their guns toward him.

Geoff shouted, "No! That's Ed," at the same time that a bullet hit the chalkboard menu on the wall. Ed heard the initial shot after all this and thought it might have been Jack's detonator. A second shot chased it.

The grip of his dad's strong arms caught Ed at the end of the counter and swung him around, channeling his momentum toward the open front door. Geoff's body was a shield across Ed's back. Someone shouted, "Secure!" He sensed the slipperiness of his own blood smearing all over his dad's shirt. He anticipated an explosion before they reached the exit.

None came except father and son bursting through the front door of the bakery, their bodies knocking against each other out onto the sidewalk, where they propelled themselves across the evacuated intersection and into the outstretched arms of the woman who loved them both.

When Geoff and Ed stumbled out of her childhood home bloody but very alive, Diane stepped away from Audrey. She didn't need Diane or Estrella to hold her up just then, the way she had during the waiting — through those ominous gunshots. When Audrey let go of her hand, Diane felt the pleasure of having done something good for another human being. Its warmth soaked into her like sunshine.

The crowd burst into cheers and applause at the sight of the family reunion. Diane laughed and joined them, her eyes sweeping the moment, taking everything in. Her sight snagged on a pair of familiar eyes focused on her.

Harlan Hall stepped out of the gathering of spectators and crossed Sunflower without letting go of her gaze. She couldn't decide whether to go meet him or run away, and so she did neither. By the time he reached her, the warmth on her head had reached

her toes and rooted her feet to the ground.
Nerves quivered just under her skin.

"You were on the radio," he said. It took a
few seconds for Diane to understand what
he meant. "Dimwit," he explained. "Though
I usually go by a different handle."

"Oh." Diane nodded. She was flushed and
off balance, the way she'd been once when
Donna coaxed her into drinking a few
bottles of beer. "That was Miralee. With the
name-calling."

"I wanted to contact you, to tell you all
was forgiven."

"But Mom . . ."

"She had trouble letting go." Harlan
cleared his throat. "I should have done it
anyway."

"I'm so sorry, Dad."

Her father clasped his hands behind his
back and said, "I thought I'd lost you all.
Donna, you, your mother, little Juliet. That
last bit was my fault, you know. I don't think
I ever said real clear how much I liked her
coming around. How much we needed her
all those years. And when Cora Jean left me,
I . . . But then there you were, like an angel
out of heaven, your voice bringing two of
you back to me at once. Usually it's only
bad news on the airwaves anymore. The
stuff I hear . . ." He stopped himself, shook

his head. Harlan let one of his hands loose, palm up, to gesture in her direction. "There's no medicine like this to heal a man who's sick at heart."

Diane caught hold of his hand with hers and squeezed.

"Forgive me?" he whispered.

"You forgave me first," she said. "I wish I'd known."

Relief and gratitude played together in a bright field of his green eyes. "Am I as old as you look?" he asked. "The years go by."

She smiled at him. "We still have time."

CHAPTER 37

Audrey and Geoff gave Estrella the week off and started working again the next day, the moment the crime scene was cleared. None of the damage made baking bread impossible. Even more simply, making bread and feeding it to hungry people was what they did — what they would continue to do as a couple.

With one bandaged arm in a sling, Ed helped his parents nail sheets of plywood into the frames that awaited new picture windows. He cleaned up the bloodstains in the storage room left behind by Coach Henderson's wounds, and Geoff scrubbed up the small pool that had gathered under Jack's shoulder after his own man's gunshot caught him on the collarbone, inches away from a deadly hit. Jack dropped the detonator, which didn't go off, but he kept his wife's silver necklace locked in his closed fist, even while they carried him out to the ambulance.

Audrey pulled Geoff away from the pastry case that bore the evidence of Ed's injuries after Geoff stood staring at it for several minutes, unable to shake off how close his son had come to dying. She cleaned up that horror and sent the guys for a carryout dinner.

At five the next morning, Geoff turned on the lights in the dining room as it began to fill with the scents of rising grains and toasted herbs. Diane rose early from the guest room at her father's house and drove the cruise ship to the bakery to help take over some of Estrella's tasks. Her father followed at six, unannounced, and sat himself down at the same table where Geoff had once pulled out her chair. After a moment's surprise, Diane took him a hot carrot muffin and told him it was on the house. When she rang it up at the register and tried to slip her own cash into the drawer, Geoff shut it and said it was time for her break.

Audrey watched all this from the worktable in the center of the kitchen, where she could see into the dining room while she shaped round loaves of rosemary-potato bread with flour-coated hands and then slashed the tops with a razor to form a slightly lopsided cross.

"You're better at this than I am," she said when Geoff came back in. "Mine always look like I used a chain saw."

"It's your special flair. They're perfect." He kissed her temple and she patted the side of his face, placing a clownish flour print there on purpose. He grinned and pretended not to know what she'd done, then began scooping up the loaves and sliding them onto the oven's hot platform.

They worked in a comfortable cycle through the morning while Ed and Diane took care of people. Audrey and Geoff kneaded, proofed, and shaped, loaded and unloaded the ovens, scraped down the tables and spread them with fresh flour, and filled the dented industrial mixer with the same four basic ingredients of bread many times over.

While Audrey worked, a tiny pressure like a dull drill pressed down on her sternum. She tried to ignore this sensation, insisting to herself that it was only in her mind even when Geoff saw her place her palm over her heart and asked her if she needed to go home and rest. Of course she refused. She wanted today to look and feel and operate just like any other day before Jack's and Julie's breakdowns. She wanted it to be this way, as normal as normal could be — in spite of the plywood boards in the window gaps and the uncharacteristic sunshine on the other side of them.

The sunshine should be enough, she thought. Why wasn't it enough to restore her sense of peace?

The drill probed the bony protection around her heart, and she kept thinking of Julie, inconsolable Julie who had rejected her sympathy twice. What more was there for Audrey to do?

She worked pensively through the day. Two o'clock, and the delivery of the last French and Italian loaves from the ovens, seemed to come hours early. By three, the baskets, shelves, and cases were nearly empty, and Ed loaded the few leftovers into bags for the soup kitchen down the street.

Audrey set aside a loaf of rosemary-potato bread without thinking too hard about why she did it. Rosemary for remembrance, the saying went. What was she trying to remember? She wasn't planning to cook supper that night.

People lingered in the afternoon light that warmed the front room as the aromas waned and the ovens were shut down. Harlan and Diane left together to visit Cora Jean's grave, then to take supper to Juliet. Leslie, still clearly shell-shocked, courageously came into the bakery with her parents, who brought fresh steaks and profuse thanks for Geoff and Ed's care of their daughter during the crisis. They shared gratitude that their families were still intact.

Leslie asked for permission to put a cheerful paper-covered box on the counter that bore snapshots of Jack, Julie, and Coach. A sign on the slotted top said *Please offer your prayers and support for our friends' recovery.*

Geoff placed it squarely in front of the cash register.

"Eat well tonight," Mrs. Wood said. "Together."

The Woods' plans to visit Coach Henderson at the hospital next prompted Ed and Geoff to hang up their aprons and follow suit.

Audrey didn't rush anyone away. She made kind small talk with the stragglers and sidestepped invasive questions about Jack and Julie with the practiced grace of a pastor's wife. Perhaps there wasn't any difference in this new role after all.

When the last customer left, she swept up the dusty floor. She wiped down tables without seeing them, thinking of the people who had gathered around the round tops, and the men who would, God willing, sit down with her at the dinner table tonight.

Eat well, together. They would, as they always did.

Gratitude overwhelmed her.

But there was another family in town who might not ever eat together again, who perhaps had not truly shared the blessings of a joint meal in months. Years. The sadness of this bore down on Audrey until she finally gave into it, as she should have from the beginning.

She locked up the front, drew the curtains, and turned on the security lights. She shouldered her purse and hugged the rosemary bread and let herself out the back, where her car was parked.

Audrey's heart was thumping as never before, fearing another rejection. She didn't understand the peculiarities of this situation, the ridiculous fear. She'd been rejected on other occasions. Good grief. Her gift of Geoff's bread had been mocked now and then. There was nothing at stake today, nothing for her to lose.

Until she realized that the fear was not for her own well-being, but for the one who might not know what she really needed until it was far too late.

She drove past the city courthouse and wondered where Jack was being treated. The consequences he faced were out of their hands, overtaken by the district attorney and anyone who threatened to file a civil suit against the detective. The Woods had suggested that was something Coach Henderson ought to do. Audrey and Geoff already knew they wouldn't. Geoff had lightheartedly claimed that punishing Jack with daily visits would be revenge enough, then looked appropriately embarrassed when he was the only one who laughed. His jokes were like her bread-dough slashes, and she *did* smile at his effort.

Audrey steered the car around the public hospital and saw Geoff's truck in the lot near the main entrance. She wondered if he might think to drop in on Julie, if the Halls weren't already there. Julie would have her own legal price to pay eventually. Apparently the city frowned on people who left their vehicles unmanned in dark intersections and poured their blood out on the street and monopolized the taxpayers' resources.

For that matter, Audrey was expecting a citation and fine from the National Park Service for destroying the road barrier. At least she hoped that would be her only punishment.

Six more tree-lined blocks brought her to an old residential area of modest homes.

She drove to the one that belonged to Jack and Julie, who might never return to the house even if free to do so. Audrey parked in the driveway and leaned over to scoop the bagged rosemary loaf off the passenger seat.

She walked to the front door and wondered what she might have done differently the first time she was here if she'd been able to foresee all that came after. The question that was powerless to change the past, though the answer would forever inform her future.

The drilling in Audrey's heart had brought her here, confident that Miralee wasn't keeping vigil at her mother's side or running away to complete her college term. The survivor's guilt that accompanied this particular kind of regret was the emotion that Audrey recognized as being different from Julie's grief, an impenetrable, victimized sadness that degraded into selfishness.

She had a sneaking maternal suspicion, in fact, that Miralee had never actually enrolled at Davis but had merely escaped her home, which was decimated in her absence. And now, like Julie, where was Miri to go?

Audrey knocked, and no one answered.

The ache in her chest deepened.

She pounded again.

Through the closed door she heard Miralee say, "Now's not a good time."

Audrey sighed. Now, of course, was the only time. She knocked more gently but spoke loudly enough to penetrate the door. "You shouldn't be alone right now, hon."

Miralee refused to answer and seemed to be waiting for Audrey to give up.

"Okay, girl, I'm ready for history to stop repeating itself!" Audrey said, and a flock of birds wintering in the oak tree scattered. She strode back down the walkway and past her cooling car, entered the side yard through the gate, and marched around to the rear of the house. Just like the last time she'd entered uninvited, she walked straight through the garage and into the kitchen through the unlocked door.

Miralee was standing at the kitchen sink with her back to Audrey, looking out through the window across the faded winter lawn. Her lack of surprise tipped off Audrey right away. The girl had hoped that Audrey would kick in the door of her tough exterior.

Why oh why weren't people free to just say what they needed? Life would be so much simpler. Less interesting, perhaps, but simpler.

Audrey closed the door. The pressure clamping down on her heart eased up enough for her to take a deep breath.

"I see you didn't pay much attention in your Security for Single Women seminar," Audrey said.

"I was never as good a student as Ed," Miralee said. "He should never have lost his acceptance. I'm sorry about that. Really."

The plastic of the bread bag was slick in Audrey's palms. She placed it on the counter at Miralee's elbow, and the crinkling sound caused the girl to turn and look. She placed both hands on top of the loaf, feeling its roundness through the protective covering.

"I didn't think you'd come in this time. You know, without the high stakes — without having to save anyone's life."

"How about your life?"

"That's overstating it a bit, isn't it?"

"You tell me."

Miralee sighed. "I think they're going to keep Mom in the hospital for a while. Wait for the infection to clear up. She has a suicide watch note posted outside her door, but no one would talk to me about that." She untwisted the tie and opened the bag, then held the bread up to her nose.

"It would be a terrible thing to lose your mother that way. I can't imagine."

"It would be worse to turn out like she

has." Miralee hugged the bread to her chest then, and faced Audrey. "Did I actually say that? I didn't mean it. I love my mom."

"I know. Of course you do."

"It's just, I never thought I'd see her the way she was up in that cabin, like a sick little baby, like a nutcase. I was supposed to leave home, and she was supposed to stay here, to be here whenever I need to come back. She's . . . she's supposed to be *my mom*."

Audrey took a step toward her and cupped her palm protectively around Miri's elbow. Her fingers tingled. "I don't think Julie expected you to see her like that. If she'd known you'd come . . . well, it's impossible to say."

"I hate hospitals." Miralee tore off a chunk of the bread and placed it in her mouth.

Pungent rosemary scents filled Audrey's nose.

"I hate the way they smell," Miri said around the food. "The way you have to beg and wait for some shred of good news. They expect you to be patient *and* optimistic. That's unreasonable, if you ask me."

Audrey nodded. Miralee chewed and stared at the tile floor. She tugged another piece free of the loaf and held it up to her lips.

"Mom told me to leave," she said without biting the food. "She didn't want me . . . with her."

"Oh, Miralee. I'm so sorry." Audrey leaned against the counter and placed her arm around Miralee's shoulders. "We hardly know how much we hurt the ones we love when our own hearts are split wide open."

"She had so many other options besides leaving like that. She didn't have to do to my dad what he did to her! It's unending misery! For *me*."

"I doubt your mom realized what would happen when she made those choices."

"Why not? She should have."

"Did you — when you set up Ed and then ruined my husband's career? Did you ever think it would go this far?"

Miralee sagged against the counter, shaking her head. "I don't know what to do."

"You don't have to figure that out to-night."

"I don't even know whether to go to sleep or stay awake."

Standing at Miralee's side, Audrey squeezed her in a gentle hug and felt the muscles of the girl's back tense. She shifted, reading the flinching as a request for space, but then Miralee started to cry and turned in toward Audrey's arms, squashing the

451

bread between them.

"Please tell me what to do."

It was easy for Audrey to be a mother, the most natural role in the world for her to step into. This time she didn't try to avoid the pain and wasn't afraid of what it might do to her. She surrounded Miralee with her arms and invited the girl's heartache to become her own, all the confusion and fear and anger and doubt, so that it would be easier to bear.

"Come home with me," Audrey said.

"Then what?"

"We'll decide that later. For now, don't be alone. That's all you have to figure out."

"I . . . I can't. Ed . . . Geoff . . ."

"Will be the first to forgive you. Though an apology would be good for everyone."

Miralee pulled away, snuffling. She noticed the damage she had done to the bread. "I wish I had more answers."

"Me too."

"More chances to get things right the first time."

Audrey knew exactly what she meant.

"This is really good bread," Miralee said, finally eating her second piece.

"Let's go, then." Audrey opened the garage door. "I've got more of it at home."

ACKNOWLEDGMENTS

To the experts who helped to knead and shape *The Baker's Wife* so it could rise to its potential, thank you:

Dan Raines, agent, and Allen Arnold, publisher, have stood by me patiently during a verrrrrrry slooooooow rise. To everyone at Creative Trust and Thomas Nelson: I will not forget.

Ami McConnell, acquisitions editor and story lover, punched down this lump of dough when it threatened to expand to proportions worthy of a Woody Allen hyperbole. Everyone sighed with relief, no one louder than I.

L. B. Norton, whip-smart professional and bosom friend, traveled alongside me on this particular road with a perfectly timed raspberry cordial, and

453

that made all the difference.

Leah Apineru, BLS and mastermind
of Impact Author Services, continues
to machete a path for me to follow
through the social media jungle.
Without her, I might long ago
have succumbed to the fate of the
enthusiastic but unlucky explorer
Percy Fawcett.

Chuck Eklund, physicist, brought the
specifics of Audrey's collision down to
earth. He also exposed me to horrific, real
videos of cars versus motorized bikes. Note
to self: don't ride a two-wheeler in Asia.

William Alexander, author of *52 Loaves:
One Man's Relentless Pursuit of Truth,
Meaning, and a Perfect Crust,* inspired
me with his stories of wood-fired brick
ovens, leaden peasant bread, and the
unpleasant fate of certain Kwik Lok tabs.
Surely the man who can get a bag of
sourdough starter through airport security
can do anything.

Peter Reinhart, award-winning baker,
writes cookbooks that read like poetry.
Reading *The Bread Baker's Apprentice* was

almost as good as eating a fresh, still-warm loaf. Almost.

READING GROUP GUIDE

1. What are some of the ways in which Geoff and Audrey's bakery is like a church?
2. When God directs Audrey to comfort others, she's assured of his guidance and protection, but sometimes she resists his prompting. Why is it sometimes hard to be compassionate? What obstacles hinder Audrey from entering the suffering of people like Julie?
3. What are the risks of ignoring God's call to compassion?
4. What is in Jack's philosophy that causes him to judge everyone in his life so harshly? Is he wrong to expect God to reward righteousness and punish sin?
5. How do Audrey and Jack represent a human understanding of mercy and justice? Can the two coexist? How might God's mercy and justice be different from our human versions?
6. Jack responds to crisis by trying to seize

more control over it. Geoff responds by submitting to the crisis and trusting God. Describe the strengths and drawbacks of each approach. How is Ed's reaction a combination of these?

7. How do the characters in the bakery show support for each other? What advantage does this give them over Jack as the hostage situation progresses?

8. Julie had the capacity for empathy at some point in her life — she showed long-suffering kindness to Diane, the Halls, Coach, Leslie, and others. How was this good quality stripped away from her and replaced with such a strong desire to inflict pain on her family? Was there any way she could have averted the disaster? Why wasn't her rescue by Audrey, Diane, and Miralee enough?

9. Compare the Bofingers' marriage to the Mansfields' marriage. How are Ed and Miralee directly impacted by their parents' values?

10. What did Diane learn from Audrey about redemption and forgiveness?

11. Have you ever failed to express compassion to someone who seemed to need it? What stopped you? Would you do it differently next time? On the flip side, have you ever had a memorable experience sup-

porting someone emotionally? What difference did your empathy make?